THE SOULMATE

RONA HALSALL

Boldwood

First published in Great Britain in 2025 by Boldwood Books Ltd.

Cover Design by Head Design Ltd.

Cover Images: Shutterstock

A CIP catalogue record for this book is available from the British Library.

Paperback ISBN 978-1-83603-117-8

Large Print ISBN 978-1-83603-118-5

Hardback ISBN 978-1-83603-116-1

Ebook ISBN 978-1-83603-119-2

Kindle ISBN 978-1-83603-120-8

Audio CD ISBN 978-1-83603-111-6

MP3 CD ISBN 978-1-83603-112-3

Digital audio download ISBN 978-1-83603-114-7

This book is printed on certified sustainable paper. Boldwood Books is dedicated to putting sustainability at the heart of our business. For more information please visit https://www.boldwoodbooks.com/about-us/sustainability/

Boldwood Books Ltd, 23 Bowerdean Street, London, SW6 3TN

www.boldwoodbooks.com

For all the widows, missing their other half. It's not easy, is it? Let's have a group hug x

1

Holly wandered through the shopping mall, killing time until her train from Glasgow to Dumfries was due. The sound of live music caught her attention, drawing her to a small crowd. They were gathered around a piano at the side of the Plaza, watching a man play and she stopped to listen. He was probably a few years older than her. His face was a bit too long, his mouth a little on the wide side, his nose larger than might be classed as attractive. But put all that together with his floppy blonde fringe and the whole effect was quite beautiful. The way he played was bewitching, his fingers caressing the keys, putting so much care and meaning into each note. His dress code reminded her of Ed Sheeran – in his well-worn jeans and hoodie, but in a way that said he didn't really care about clothes or hair styles, he was all about the music.

He sang as he played, his eyes closing as he reached the high notes of the Coldplay anthem, 'Fix You'. When it got to the line about tears streaming, her eyes stung, making her blink, a flush of emotion filling her chest. It never ceased to amaze her how music had the power to release emotions you didn't realise were close to the surface. But she recognised this sadness within, recognised that she, herself, and her life come to that, could do with a bit of fixing. God knows, she'd never taken the easy road.

She edged closer, humming along, and then she found herself singing, unable to resist joining in. He looked up, surprised, and caught her eye. Oh my word, she thought, how can anyone have eyes that colour? They were the blue of a summer sky, giving his appearance a whole new dimension. When his face split into a grin, his eyes sparkled and she grinned back, captivated, her heart racing like a horse galloping along a beach, tasting freedom and not wanting to stop.

He had long, elegant fingers, she noticed. And as he played the introduction to his next song, he gave her a questioning look, silently asking if she knew it. She smiled and stepped closer, her hand on top of the piano now. Of course she knew it. This was her favourite song, the soundtrack to her life. 'Fly Away' by Lenny Kravitz.

'You have a lovely tone,' he said. 'I heard you harmonising on that last song. You want to join me on this one?' His voice was smooth and gentle, mellow as a fine wine. 'You take the lead, if you like, and I'll do the harmonies this time.'

Take the lead? Could she, did she have the nerve? It was a while since she'd sung in public and she glanced around, wondering if anyone would be filming, because that would mean her answer would be no. But there were only a few people watching now and no phones to be seen. *It'll be fine,* she reassured herself, the desire to sing and enjoy this unexpected moment overriding her need to hide her whereabouts. *He'll never know,* she whispered to the doubting voice in her head.

Her palms were sweaty, but she was excited to have this

opportunity. She'd loved performing when she was younger, before her life took a sudden turn.

'Okay,' she nodded. 'I'll give it a go.' What did it matter if she messed up? She didn't know any of these people and singing was her release, a way to deal with everything that was going on in her life. Anyway, she was confident this guy had her back if she was struggling at any point. He had an aura of kindness about him.

Her vocals soared, her eyes closing as she sang like she was feeling every single word. Because she was. The lyrics echoed her feelings precisely. She wanted to get away. She needed to escape her life. She longed to have freedom.

Her body felt like it was melting, as their voices melded together in perfect harmony. So perfect it brought tears to her eyes. When they sang the last words and the final notes hung in the air between them, their eyes locked and something weird happened. Something she'd never felt before, like her heart had been jump-started. *Did he feel it too?* That connection, just the two of them, lost in their music.

The sound of applause from passers-by broke the spell and she blushed, covering her mouth with her hands, delighted by the enthusiastic reception and the shouts of 'more'. She'd been so engrossed in her vocals, she hadn't noticed how many people had stopped to listen. Her cheeks burned. Was it the applause, or something to do with the way his eyes were fixed on her, never leaving her face as he played the introduction to another song for them to sing together?

She wasn't ready for this moment to end and sang the next song with him too, letting him take the lead while she did the harmonies. After he'd played the final note, he stood and moved round the piano to stand next to her. He grabbed her hand, raising it up above her head, going for a theatrical bow. She laughed and joined in, his fingers entwined with hers in a way that felt natural and right.

But it couldn't be right. She had Finn, didn't she? And God knows what he'd do if he found out she'd been singing with this man, let alone holding his hand.

2

'Oh, that was fun,' he said, looking a little flustered as he released her hand from his grasp. 'You've an amazing voice.'

She laughed, embarrassed and delighted and more than a little bewildered. Nobody had said that about her voice before, but in another life, she would have loved to have developed a professional singing career. Unfortunately, she'd burnt that bridge many years ago and this was as close to public singing as she was ever likely to get.

'So do you. And you play so well.' The buzz from the applause was incredible, making her glow from head to toe. She hitched her bag on her shoulder and broke eye contact. 'You just played my three favourite songs, which is kinda weird.'

It was probably time for her to go, to leave this encounter as something lovely to remember, but she couldn't get her feet to move. She wanted a little bit more.

'Can I get you a coffee or something?' he said, glancing around. 'There's a great coffee shop by the entrance over there.'

She flicked a glance at her watch and frowned, making a calculation, then flashed him a smile. 'Okay, that would be nice.

I've got a while until my train.' *It's just a coffee,* she told herself. *What harm can it do?*

'Brilliant. I'm Mark, by the way.' He grinned at her and she felt herself melting inside, which was the loveliest sensation she'd ever experienced.

'Oh, um... Holly.'

He leant to pick up his phone, which had been propped on the piano, and she realised with a jolt of nerves that he must have been recording himself playing. *Oh God, what if he posts it online? What if Finn sees?* She watched him pick up his bag and tuck his phone inside, trying to shake the negative thoughts from her mind. *He'll never know,* she reassured herself, thankful that Finn hated social media and thought Instagram was stupid.

She was unwilling to let anything tarnish this encounter or spoil the moment. Who knew when she'd ever feel this way again? It was like she'd been sprinkled with stardust and for once in her life something truly magical was happening. Of course, it was just a moment, she knew that, but she'd been feeling so down recently, this encounter had lit a spark of hope in her heart. Nice things did happen to people and for once they were happening to her.

'So, where's home to you?' he asked as they walked towards the coffee shop, a sudden awkwardness wedged between them.

'I live near Dumfries.' She paused. 'For the time being.'

'Where's that?' He laughed. 'I haven't a clue about the geography of Scotland. I'm just passing through.'

'Oh, it's a couple of hours south of here on the train.' She shrugged. 'I've no idea what the actual distance is though.' She flashed him a smile, unnerved to find his eyes meeting hers. 'I don't really know the geography of the area either. I haven't lived up here for long.'

'Ah, I didn't think you had a Scottish accent.'

'No, I come from... further south.' That was suitably vague, and she reminded herself to be more careful. One unguarded comment could get her into trouble. In fact, being with this man at all was a mistake. *Walk away,* instructed the voice of reason in her head. But she'd no intention of being that sensible. Not when she had the chance to enjoy the company of this lovely man for a little while longer.

He opened the door of the coffee shop and held it for her, letting her enter first. *Isn't that a nice, gentlemanly thing to do?* Finn never opened doors for her, leaving her trailing behind him like a forgotten pet, something that always rankled.

'Shall we sit by the window?' She pointed to an empty table and he followed her, letting her choose which seat she wanted before putting his bag on the chair opposite. 'I'll get this,' he said. 'As a thank you for your amazing performance.'

She laughed and blushed. *Definitely a gentleman.* 'Okay, thank you. I'll have a hot chocolate please. I think I've had enough coffee for one day.'

He went to the counter to get their drinks and came back with a couple of slices of cake to go with it. A sign, she hoped, that he was as keen to linger as she was. They chatted about music and he told her he worked with music producers, making promotional videos for tours and new releases. But his hobby was going round the country, playing on public pianos. Apparently, there was a national directory, and he was gradually ticking them all off.

'Is that like trainspotting?' she said, getting a sudden attack of the giggles. Because it was a bit of a nerdy thing to do in your spare time. Nerdy was okay, though. In fact, she liked nerdy. It was endearing and way better than arrogant and self-assured. As hobbies went, it seemed so wholesome, it made her like him even more.

He laughed with her. A nice laugh, soft, not jarring. 'Yeah, I suppose it is. And yeah, you guessed it, I'm a bit of a piano geek. They're all different, you see. They all have their own personalities, their own different sounds.' He pulled his phone out of his bag. 'I make recordings and put them up on my Insta page.' He tapped and swiped at his screen. 'Do you want to have a look at us singing?'

Her heart started to race, her brain in a panic. 'Would you mind not...' She grimaced. 'The thing is... I'd rather you didn't post it on your page. I like to keep things private on social media.'

He gave her a curious look. 'Okay. No worries, I understand not everyone wants me to share things. But I can send you a clip if you give me your Insta details.' His eyes met hers, his finger poised over his phone, waiting. 'I'm happy to keep this just between me and you if that's what you'd prefer.'

She sagged with relief. Nobody else would ever see, but a part of her wanted something concrete, a reminder of this lovely encounter. 'Okay. Here, give me your phone and I'll type it in for you.'

He shuffled round to sit in the seat next to her, watching as she put her details into his phone before handing it back. He sent her the clip, then played it, their heads bent together, his shoulder touching hers as they listened. She was mesmerised, not just by seeing and hearing herself, but also noticing the way he was looking at her as she was singing. She leant into him a little, revelling in the contact, the scent of him. No aftershave, just a natural male muskiness that made her want to grab him and give him a kiss.

It was almost unbearable being this close, all her nerve ends tingling, but it was delicious at the same time. Surely he could feel what she was feeling? Like that sensation on the fairground ride when you're at the top of the track, just before the big drop. His hand brushed hers and she didn't move away. Instead, her fingers curled round his.

Think about Finn.

She swallowed and pulled her hand away, thoughts of her boyfriend making her check the time. 'Oh my God,' she gasped, glancing at the door. 'I'm so sorry but I've got to go. I'll be in so much trouble if I miss this train.'

She reached for her bag, slipping it over her shoulder as she started to stand. The cuff of her sleeve dropped a little, showing the bluish tinge of a bruise. The place where someone had held on to her wrist too tightly. She saw him notice, watched his jaw tighten, and she hurriedly pulled her cuff down, a wave of heat coursing through her body.

'Can I have your number?' He looked hopeful but she shook her head, eyes flicking towards the door again.

'Sorry, no. That's...' She sighed. 'It's not a good idea. Finn would go ballistic. He doesn't like me chatting to other men.' She gave him a weak smile, silent for a moment, her hands holding the back of her chair, reluctant to let go. 'It's been lovely meeting you. Really lovely.' There was such an echo of regret in her voice, she was sure he must have heard it.

He stood and grabbed his backpack. 'The least I can do is walk you to the station.'

She smiled. 'Okay. But it'll have to be more of a jog than a walk. I'm going to be late.'

He grabbed her hand as soon as they were out of the café and pulled her along, doing a running commentary as if they were in some sort of televised sporting event. It was so funny she thought she might choke on her laughter, and they arrived at the station with five minutes to spare. Her cheeks were glowing, his too, and when their eyes met, she couldn't stop herself from reaching up and giving him a kiss.

It was stupid and wrong and ever so right. His hand squeezed hers. He felt it too, she knew he did.

'Keep in touch,' he called as she backed away from him, her eyes fixed on his, her heart thundering in her chest. How could she not keep in touch when they had a connection she couldn't explain and didn't want to end?

She sighed, her mind filled with one question and one question alone. *What am I going to do about Finn?*

3

Holly settled in her seat by the window, the train doors closing seconds after she'd got on board. *Phew, that was close.* Her heart was racing, not just because she'd had to run. Her spirits were soaring in a way they hadn't done since... She frowned, thinking for a moment before deciding she'd *never* felt like this before. It was better than being tipsy on drink, better than the excitement of a surprise or a holiday or an unexpected win. She smiled at her reflection in the glass. It was the best feeling ever and she was going to hold it to herself and enjoy it for as long as possible. She had two hours on the train and she would spend them reliving the last wonderful hour and a half of her life.

It had been so nice to have a conversation with somebody other than Finn. Someone who loved music and singing and knew all her favourite tracks. Someone who knew nothing about her, or the horrors she'd left in the past.

I bet Mark doesn't come home covered with blood.

Finn was a gamekeeper at a large estate in Scotland. It had sounded romantic and unusual when he first told her, although she'd admittedly just polished off three double gins at the time. Had she known exactly what his job entailed, she might have thought twice about starting a relationship with him. But here she was, stuck with a man who took delight in killing animals and was so possessive and jealous, he hardly let her out of his sight.

She gazed out of the window, the glass blurred by the splatter of rain. A bank of grey clouds filled the horizon, hiding the mountains from view, making the evening prematurely gloomy. Yet another rainy day. There had been so many recently, but it was autumn and to be expected, although it felt like the weather was in tune with her general mood.

Her thoughts shifted back to Mark, and she smiled to herself, knowing she would feed off their meeting for quite some time. It was her secret and she'd hold it close, like a precious gift, taking it out in quiet moments to unwrap and experience all over again. She pulled her phone out of her bag and opened the clip he'd sent her, slipping on her headphones so she could turn up the sound.

Her mind filled with the words of the song. And the man she'd just met. Mark. A good, solid name for a surprising person. All unassuming on the outside but a musical genius underneath. The tone of his voice was caramel smooth, his piano playing gentle and evocative, and as she listened to their voices harmonising, it brought goosebumps to her skin.

She used to sing all the time growing up, being in a band at school with a bunch of her mates. They were pretty rubbish but it had been a lot of fun and she'd been infatuated with the lead guitarist. He'd been a couple of years older and her parents didn't approve, but she was fifteen and rebellious and nobody could tell her they shouldn't be together.

Until the incident that had ruined her life.

Looking back, she supposed it was inevitable that her behaviour would lead to trouble. But she hadn't quite anticipated how *much* trouble and how it would hound her like a tracker dog, constantly driving her on, making her into a nomad. She huffed, aware she only had herself to blame, but at the time, she'd been a foolish teenager who didn't know anything. And it seemed grossly unfair that one slip up had tainted her entire life from that moment forwards.

A tear rolled down her cheek, quickly followed by another. Why couldn't she have met Mark earlier? Why had she chosen to be with someone like Finn? But the answer to that was simple. Finn had been in the bar that night, not Mark, and he'd been her only choice.

She felt the weight of her bag on her lap and remembered her secret mission, the reason she'd been in Glasgow. She pulled out the envelope and reached inside for the brand-new passport, turning to the back page. It was a horrible photo but definitely her, unlike the name next to it, which wasn't hers at all. She closed it and stroked the cover, like it was precious, and it was, its value beyond money. Because this gave her options that she didn't have before. This gave her the chance of freedom.

Her jaw hardened as the image of her boyfriend loomed large in her mind, pushing Mark out of the way. *Finn.* Her feelings for him were a muddle of conflicting emotions, her mind a jumble of images and words that she found impossible to untangle. In recent weeks, they'd been going through a bad patch, always arguing, and she'd felt increasingly trapped. He got so frustrated with her, his body language left her in no doubt that he wanted to strike out. Fortunately, he never had, but he did grab her by the wrist and pin her against the wall to make her listen, shouting into her face. That had driven her desire to get a passport. All she had to do now was get enough money together and then, for once, she'd actually have a choice.

4

Mark stopped at a service station on the long drive back home to North Wales. He bought himself a sandwich and a coffee and found a table where he could sit undisturbed for a little while. From the moment he'd left her at the station, wistfully watching her disappear into the crowd, his head had been buzzing with thoughts of Holly.

Oh my God, she was perfect. Everything about her. She had the sweetest singing voice, a cute smile, a grace when she moved. She was long-limbed and lithe, only a little shorter than him, with matching blonde hair and blue eyes. Except her eyes were paler, like ice crystals that twinkled when she smiled. And that laugh, it was almost musical.

She was 'the one', he was sure of it. The woman he was destined to be with. He'd felt it in her kiss, that fleeting, beautiful touch of her lips. How magical that had been, and so unexpected. His lips still tingled at the thought.

He chuckled at himself, aware that some would consider it a fanciful, romantic notion, but he believed in love at first sight. Hadn't that been the story of his own parents' relationship?

Well, at least that's what his mum had told him. Unfortunately, he had very few memories of his dad, who died in a farming accident when he'd been helping a neighbour. His mother had never told him the exact details but the expression on her face whenever he'd brought up the subject was pure horror, which made him assume it was a gory end.

For most of his life, it had just been him and his mum, and he'd felt comforted by the stories she told him about his dad and what a wonderful, warm human being he'd been. How he'd swept her off her feet from the moment they'd first met in a baker's shop in Bala. She was behind the counter, serving, and he'd come in to buy a pasty for lunch. Then he'd waited all afternoon for her to finish work and had taken her out for dinner and they hadn't spent a day apart after that. Married within three months and Mark on the way just a few months later.

His dad was ten years older than his mum and had his own cottage, the place where Mark had grown up and lived for most of his life. He liked to think he was following in his dad's foot-steps, a chip off the old block, and now he too had fallen in love at first sight. Or should that be first sound, because it was Holly's voice that had touched his heart initially.

He finished his sandwich and pulled his phone out of his bag, watching the video of them singing together one more time. When he got home, he'd tweak the sound a bit and do some editing and then he could send her a better version. It was a shame he couldn't put it on his Insta page, but a promise was a promise. She was clearly a private person and he felt there was a story behind that.

Looking at her Instagram profile, he could see she'd posted regularly until seven months ago and then nothing new since, which was odd. The last picture she'd posted was a selfie with a

group of women, all eating something. The caption said 'My
first brandysnaps worked a treat – got to test them, haven't you?'
with a winking emoji. So, she could cook as well, how fabulous
was that?

He settled back in his seat and played the video once again
before he plucked up courage and sent her a direct message.

> So lovely to meet you today. You made a nerdy
> pianist very happy. Hope the train home isn't
> too slow. Keep in touch. Xxx

Were three kisses too much? He wasn't sure, his finger
hovering over the send button. One kiss was friend-zone terri-
tory and he wanted to show her she meant more to him than
that. He shook his head and pressed send. Sod it. Who dares
wins. No point being too reticent... or did three kisses come over
as presumptuous or arrogant? He was starting to feel a bit hot,
worried that he'd got this wrong, but it was done now, he'd just
have to wait and see what she said.

He sipped at his coffee, still unsure. Why was it so hard to
know what to do in these situations? Other people didn't seem
to have the same problems as him, but reading women's body
language, or picking up the subtext of conversations, did not
appear to be in his skillset. He played their whole encounter
back in his mind, feeling it all in the core of his being. Their
eyes meeting, their skin touching, the way she laughed at his
jokes, listened to what he was saying, her reluctance to leave.
Her hand holding his, the kiss. However bad he was at reading
the signs, surely to God all that suggested she was interested
in him?

She has a boyfriend, the voice in his head reminded him,
always ready to damp down the flames when his heart caught
fire. *They always have bloody boyfriends.* That was the trouble

when you got to your thirties. Everyone was already taken. But he wondered if she was happy.

In his mind's eye, he could see the bruise on her wrist. A nasty bruise, dark blue. It would have taken some force to create a bruise like that. A level of force that wasn't normal in a healthy relationship. And from what she'd said, her boyfriend was the jealous type, which couldn't be an easy thing to live with.

He let his mind wander off, creating a scenario where she told him she wanted to leave but couldn't and he was the one who saved her. Call him a romantic, but these things did happen. If he kept in touch and continued chatting to her, who knew where it could lead? He played them singing the Lenny Kravitz song one final time before he got on his way again. That would always be their song now. And he was determined to make her wish come true. He'd help her get away, if that's what she wanted, and then they could fly away together.

5

Holly must have dozed off because she woke with a start, the passport in her hand. The train had stopped and she jumped to her feet, thinking for one awful moment that she should get off, until she heard the announcement and realised it wasn't her stop. Flopping back in her seat, she stuffed the passport into the envelope and tucked it at the bottom of her bag. It would open a whole new world to her, and she had to think of a safe place to stow it until she'd made up her mind about leaving and had a plan in place.

For the first time in her life, she had formal identification. She could travel. And that gave her the option to escape from the latest hole she'd dug for herself. In fact, she could draw a line under her life to this point, move abroad and start again. Properly this time. It was an exciting prospect, but it also felt quite daunting and maybe it was a step too far just now.

It would be easier to get a job now she had ID. One that paid a decent wage, instead of the cash in hand work she'd tended to take, where you were open to exploitation because people knew there was something a bit dodgy about you.

Her previous lack of ID had forced her to travel up and down the country, chasing seasonal work. Until four years ago, when she'd landed a job at a hotel in Buxton, in the Peak District, and life had started to look up. The manager, Sofia, was very maternal, originally from Spain, and had taken a liking to Holly. She'd been desperate for staff and had given her work in the kitchens, provided her with living accommodation and trained her as a sous chef.

'If you know your way around a kitchen, you'll always have a job,' she'd said as she showed Holly how to chop vegetables without slicing her fingers. She'd pointed the knife at her, a serious glint in her eye. 'When I first came to the UK, I had nothing except my cooking, and look at me now. I have a whole hotel.'

She never asked Holly for details about her past and with her guidance, Holly blossomed. At last, she felt safe. And because she'd been in one place for years, instead of the usual months, she'd been able to get her passport photos signed by her GP to say they were a true likeness. Unfortunately, she'd had to leave before she could send her application in and it was only recently that she'd been able to complete the paperwork and attend an interview at the passport office.

Things had been going great at the hotel until Greg joined as head chef. She huffed at the very thought of him, her body giving an involuntary shudder. It was his fault she'd had to leave. His fault she'd found herself trapped in a gamekeeper's lodge in the grounds of the castle in Dumfries.

A frustrated growl stuck in her throat and she shook the image of Greg from her mind, not wanting to give him the opportunity to poison the glow of optimism the day had given her. He was in the past. Hopefully.

Nobody at the hotel knew where she'd gone, not even Sofia,

because she'd just taken off in the middle of the night and ended up in Scotland. At the time, Dumfries had seemed like a random enough destination and there was sufficient distance between her and Greg to feel comfortable. But instead of having Greg's wandering hands to worry about, she now had Finn's temper.

She'd wondered about picking up her passport and not going back to Finn, but decided against it, because she didn't want a repeat of the mess she'd found herself in before. It was hard being in a new place with little or no money, forced to make significant compromises just to keep a roof over her head and food in her belly. This time, if she was going to leave, she wanted to go on her own terms, in her own time, when she had sufficient funds to make the transition.

Just a couple more months.

She could manage that, couldn't she? Her eyes dropped to her wrist, the edge of the bruise poking out from her cuff. She shuffled in her seat, shifting her gaze to the window, tracking the raindrops that snaked down the glass. Last week was the first time he'd ever hurt her. Yes, there'd been arguments, sharp words, attempts to kick dents in her self-confidence, but nothing physical.

It was confusing, because the guy was so lovely most of the time, and then she just had to say the wrong thing or not keep up with the housework, and it was instant combustion. It came out of nowhere and it seemed to disappear just as fast, like a tornado twisting through town, leaving a trail of wreckage in its wake and sunny skies overhead. *It's not right,* she told herself, massaging her bruised wrist, feeling a jab of pain. He'd done that to her for burning the edges of a lasagne she'd made.

'I can't eat that,' he'd snapped, his lip curling as he stared at the dish she'd pulled out of the oven and set on the hob. She frowned, annoyed he was making such a fuss. He was behaving as if she was asking him to eat a tin of dog food, not a painstakingly created lasagne. And it was only a bit singed round the edges, nothing major. 'How hard is it to keep an eye on the meal when it's cooking? It's not like you've anything else to be doing, is it?'

That was a dig at the fact she wasn't working, the irony being it was how he *wanted* things to be. There were cash in hand jobs available locally, but he'd kept telling her she didn't need to go out to work. He was going to look after her, and in return, he expected her to look after him. The fact that it wasn't an arrangement she wanted didn't seem to matter, but they'd argued about it a few times now and she'd learnt it was an argument she would never win.

Looking at the singed lasagne, her mouth twisted to the side. 'It's just the edges that have caught. You can have this middle bit. Look, it's fine.' She dug the serving spoon in, putting a generous portion onto his plate, giving herself the burnt edges.

He was sitting at the table, expectantly, a napkin already spread out on his lap. He had surprisingly old-fashioned views for a thirty-year-old man and liked the table to be set properly, like his mum had always done. She'd been a housewife as well and it seemed Holly was judged against her standards and found lacking. She put their plates on the table and sat down opposite him, biting back her urge to tell him not to be so picky.

He still looked angry and her stomach roiled, the muscles in her neck tensing as she watched him take a first mouthful, then screw up his face and spit the food back out onto his plate. 'It tastes burnt. The whole thing is tainted.' He pushed his plate away in disgust. 'That's inedible.'

'No, it's not. There's nothing wrong with it. It took me ages to make and it's only a little bit over-cooked. I can't believe it tastes —' She yelped as he reached across the table and grabbed her wrist with his shovel-sized hand.

'Stop it, Finn. You're hurting me.' She squirmed, wincing as his grip tightened, tears springing to her eyes.

'Don't you tell me what's edible and what's not.'

He flung her arm back at her, making her tip back in her chair. She reached out to grasp the table, but only managed to grab the cloth, pulling the plates and drinks and cutlery with her onto the floor.

He stormed out of the kitchen, slamming the door behind him, her lovingly crafted meal splattered across the tiles.

Thinking about it now, she knew things had changed after that. No matter how many times he apologised, no matter how many bunches of flowers he brought her, something in her heart had hardened. But more than that, she realised she was scared. His mood swings frightened her.

6

She gazed out of the window as the train sped along the tracks, daydreaming about a new future and what it might look like. Sunshine would be nice. She could almost feel the heat on her face as she imagined sunlit plazas and golden beaches, turquoise seas and the smell of suntan lotion. Flights to Spain were dirt cheap and she'd learnt a lot from Sofia about the best places to live, how things worked over there. She'd even learnt some common phrases. Yes, Spain, she decided as she watched the rain-soaked landscape slip by.

Music permeated her brain, memories from the afternoon butting into her daydream. *Mark.* It was impossible to explain her feelings, but her heart raced every time she thought about him, a glow suffusing her body. Their connection was undeniable, but it was more than that. It felt significant.

The way he'd looked at her had given her goosebumps. When had anyone ever been that attentive? When was the last time anyone had properly listened to what she was saying? He'd really heard her and when they'd been chatting, even though they'd only just met, it felt like they'd known each other for years. And then, that kiss... She sighed, reliving it all over again. If she'd been Sleeping Beauty, that kiss would definitely have woken her up. It was hard to say what made it so special, but her lips were still tingling. How often would something like that happen in her lifetime? It had been magical. Yes, that was the word, magical.

Her phone pinged with a notification and she took a look, smiling when she saw it was a message from Mark. *How sweet of him.* And there were three kisses. Three. She hugged her phone to her chest, knowing now that Mark had felt it too, that connection between them, she hadn't been imagining it.

Another ping, another message from Mark.

> I hope you don't mind me saying this but I couldn't help seeing that bruise on your wrist and I just wanted to say that I have a car and if you ever need to get away for real, I will come and get you. I can't bear to think of anyone hurting you. Xxx

Her heart melted; he really did seem the kindest guy. She was a bit ashamed that he'd noticed the bruise and jumped to a conclusion, but the fact that he would help her made her feel stronger somehow. Perhaps she wasn't stuck in this situation on her own any more. Perhaps she had an ally.

She typed a message back:

> That's so kind, but I think it was a misunderstanding. The bruise, I mean. I dunno, but thanks for the offer.

She hesitated, before adding three kisses.

Almost instantly, another message pinged onto her phone. A picture of two people hugging.

No worries. I just want you to know you've got
a friend in me. Xxx

If only she was with a guy like Mark. He'd sensed there was a problem. He was a man with emotional intelligence. How rare was that?

What if he was the guy she'd been waiting to meet her whole life? Her destiny. Could that be true? Had fate stepped in to help her?

There was an ache in her heart, a longing for a normal life. A life where she could stop running and put down roots. A life where she could make proper friends, and go back to being Erin Stamper, rather than pretending to be Holly Rhodes.

7

Holly was thirty-two now, and had been calling herself Holly for exactly the same amount of time as she'd previously been Erin, her birth name. Sixteen years. Now, it felt natural to be called Holly, and her passport said she was Holly, so that's who she was and nobody in this world, apart from her, and a youth worker in Birmingham, knew any different at this point in time. Erin was the past she wanted to forget. Holly was the future.

The train pulled to a halt and she realised with a start that this was Dumfries, her stop. The journey was still unfamiliar, this only being the third time in her life she'd arrived at the station. She jumped up and hurried down the carriageway to the nearest door, taking a deep breath as she mentally prepared her story.

Finn was waiting in the car park, his vehicle unmistakable with the Castle Drumlanrig logo. It was a pick-up truck, the back fitted out with dog crates for the Labradors and spaniels that went along to the shoots with the gamekeepers. When the dogs weren't working, they lived in kennels at the back of the cottage, never allowed inside or treated like pets in any way.

Something Holly was glad about because she was a bit scared of dogs, much preferring cats.

He was leaning against the cab, smoke curling from a roll-up pinched between his finger and thumb. He was a big man, a typical brawny Scot with Viking genes in his make-up somewhere. He was wearing a baseball cap, his ginger hair curling from under it at the back, a thick beard covering half his face. Despite it being autumn, and really quite chilly, he was dressed in jeans and T-shirt, his tattooed arms bare. He looked like the sort of man you wouldn't want to pick a fight with and she supposed that's what had attracted her to him. She'd seen him as her protector, thought he was a hard man with a soft centre. That's how he'd come across when they'd first got together. A big softie, and she'd been proud to be his girlfriend. For a short while anyway, until she'd started to understand exactly what she'd got herself into.

'At last,' he said in his Scottish drawl when he spotted her. 'I've been waiting for ages.' His eyes met hers and her shoulders tensed. That steely glint, a tic by his right eye, usually heralded trouble. She ran her tongue round dry lips, flashed him a smile, trying to behave as if she hadn't noticed, as if everything was fine.

'There was a delay on the line. Something to do with signals,' she said, hearing the tremor in her voice, her hands holding her bag a little tighter.

'How was your *mother*?' He emphasised the last word.

She didn't dare break eye contact. But she could feel a blush warming her face and hoped he wouldn't notice in the dim light. *Keep calm, just keep it together,* she cautioned herself. 'She's a lot better thanks, but they're keeping her in hospital for more tests.'

'And what exactly is wrong with her? I'm not sure you said.'

His eyes were boring in to hers and she hesitated a beat too long, her mind unable to pick a specific illness from a myriad of options. 'A stroke,' she gabbled. 'It was a stroke.'

'Right.' He nodded and took a last drag on his roll-up before flicking the stub across the car park.

The slap caught her unawares, sending her head snapping to the side, a burning pain pulsing in her cheek as she staggered against the truck.

'You lying bitch,' he snarled.

She edged backwards, but he grabbed her jacket in his fist, pulling her so close she could feel his spittle on her face when he spoke. 'I know you've been to the passport office. Do you think I'm stupid? I've got a tracker on your phone. I knew I couldn't trust you.' He opened the truck door and hurled her inside like she was a sack of dog feed, before grabbing her bag and throwing it on the back seat.

There was a second or two, while he was walking round the truck to get in the driver's seat, when she could have run. A moment of opportunity that she missed because she was in shock, lying across the front seat, completely disorientated and paralysed by fear.

He's got a tracker on my phone?

Her heart did a double beat, her pulse pounding in her ears. That's what he'd just said. It had never occurred to her that he'd stoop so low. Never for one minute had she imagined she no longer had freedom of movement. There'd be more questions, she was sure of it, when they were in the privacy of his home. Now that he'd hurt her once, it seemed he'd broken through a mental barrier and there was nothing to stop it happening again.

She was shaking, so scared, she couldn't move.

The slap was just for starters. But it signalled an ending for her as well. If she'd had doubts about leaving before, she had none now. It was just a question of when and how. She closed her eyes, imagining she was holding Mark's hand. He'd come, he said he would. *But does he mean it, or is it just words?*

It was a big ask and they'd only just met, and was any man reliable in this sort of situation? She pushed herself into a sitting position, her face still throbbing, tears stinging her eyes. She was going to have to be more careful about everything. Delete Mark's messages. The video of them singing.

'Get your seatbelt on,' Finn said pleasantly, like nothing had happened. 'We don't want you getting hurt now, do we?'

8

The next morning, Mark gasped when he saw the picture of the handprint on Holly's cheek. His jaw dropped as he read her message, appalled that things had escalated so quickly.

> Look what he did to me last night. He slapped me when he picked me up from the station because I went to the passport office and didn't tell him that's where I'd been going. He put an app on my phone to track me!!!

If blood could actually boil, his would be bubbling away right now. He studied the picture. That was a massive handprint, covering most of Holly's cheek. It made him wonder how big this Finn guy actually was, but from the scale of the picture he would say he must be at least 30 per cent bigger than Mark. Without doubt he would be stronger, because Mark was a musician, and more of a Greyhound than a Rottweiler. He puffed out his cheeks, his mind in turmoil, but at least he knew what he was up against now and could plan accordingly. No direct confrontations with Finn, that was a given.

He tried to remember what Holly had said about her partner, but he couldn't recall very much. She'd said he was a gamekeeper and they lived on an estate near Dumfries, but she'd been a little cagey about precise details. He wondered how many estates there might be in that area and did a quick Google search. Well, that was a surprise; apparently there were quite a few.

He made himself a coffee and sat down to respond to Holly's message. He'd had time to think about things now and he knew he needed to get some essential jobs done at home before he could go and rescue her, if that's what she wanted. But why else would she send him that picture? Domestic abuse was not a subject you'd casually chat about to a virtual stranger. It wasn't something that didn't matter, that he could ignore. No, this was clearly a cry for help.

It took him a little while to get his wording right, typing and deleting several times, tutting at his ineptitude. *Keep it simple.* He deleted most of what he'd written and pressed send:

> Can I come and get you? Take you somewhere safe? I'm worried about you. xxx

He chewed at a nail as he waited for her response, but nothing pinged back and he decided to get on with some research while he waited, see if he could pin down where she was living. He knew her boyfriend was called Finn, so he went through the 'Meet Our Team' section of the websites for all the estates close to Dumfries. After almost half an hour of searching, he found him. Drumlanrig Castle.

The estate was impressive. It stretched over thousands of acres of moorland, boasting a variety of accommodation options, and at its heart was a very regal-looking castle. Apparently, there was a mix of detached cottages available to rent in the grounds, along with apartments in the outbuildings of the castle. But the main draw was the premium accommodation for shooting parties in the castle itself, and the lodges out on the moors where parties could relax after a day shooting the local wildlife. As far as he could tell, grouse and pheasant season was underway, which meant Finn would presumably be busy.

Already, Mark was picturing himself screeching to a halt outside her house, Holly dashing out with a couple of suitcases and them making a quick getaway before Finn knew anything was amiss. That was the perfect scenario. No confrontation, just a quick, covert operation.

He checked his Insta notifications but still she hadn't answered. His heart was beating a little faster, nerves twisting in his belly. *What if it's already too late? What if Finn has really hurt her?* The thought was too much to bear and he sent another message:

> Are you okay? Do you need me to come now? I'm really worried about you! xxx

Whatever she answered, he was going back up to Scotland. He had to see for himself that she was safe and well. What if he got a message back saying she was fine, but it wasn't actually her who'd sent it? People did that. He corrected himself. *Abusers* did that and if Finn had put a tracker on her phone, then he obviously didn't trust her. Would he be checking her messages as well?

His heart was full-on racing now, terrible images flashing through his mind of her broken, injured body. That bloke hitting her, kicking her. It was like a horror movie in his head. His jaw hardened and he grabbed his car keys. Things to do. He would get all his jobs sorted double-quick and he'd go and make sure she was okay.

And if she's not okay?

His body tensed. No, he couldn't think about that.

9

The next morning, Mark arrived in Dumfries feeling utterly spent. It had taken him longer than he would have liked to get all the essentials organised at home and then, once he'd finally set off, he had a puncture on the motorway. He couldn't get the bloody wheel nuts loose, so he'd been stuck there for a while, feeling like a useless idiot. Thankfully, a patrol car had finally come to help and got him going again, but at that point, he was so exhausted, he knew he wasn't safe to be driving, and he needed to sleep. Now he had a crick in his neck from sleeping in the car and his teeth felt furry, his breath stale. He was desperate for a shower and a freshen up but that would have to wait.

Holly still hadn't answered his messages, and that ramped up his anxiety another notch, but there was no point reporting it to anyone, because for all he knew she could have blocked him or something. Or lost her phone. Or broken it. The fact that she hadn't answered didn't mean she was dead or dying, as his overactive imagination wanted him to believe. It just meant was she was not currently communicating with him on Instagram.

The only way to put his mind at rest was to physically go and see her.

Mark wasn't a religious man, but there were times when he thanked God for making things possible. In the skills he'd been blessed with and the way he lived his life and earned his money. It was all totally flexible, creating space for a mercy dash like this. Was God smiling on his mission? It was a comforting thought.

His eyes weren't really focusing properly as he pulled into a car park in the centre of town and he knew if he carried on driving, he was going to end up having an accident. As strong as his urge was to find Holly, he needed a break and to refuel with breakfast first.

He also needed to find somewhere to stay. Fortunately, there was an abundance of handsome-looking hotels and guest houses in the town, all built in the local red sandstone, and plenty of vacancies as it was out of season. In the end, he picked one that was in the middle of the price range and made his booking based on the fact that the woman who answered his call had a lovely accent and was a delight to deal with. Poor customer service was one of his bugbears, and he was very happy to patronise an establishment that clearly prioritised pleasantness. He had to wait until 3 p.m. to check in though, so he went in search of coffee and something to eat.

There were plenty of cafés dotted round the town centre and he found somewhere that was serving breakfast. Goodness, did the Scots know how to cook a hearty meal. It was astonishing it all fitted on the plate, but he tucked in like he hadn't eaten for a week, thinking this would keep him going for the rest of the day.

The place was quiet and he chatted to the waitress about Drumlanrig Castle and what he might find there.

'Going up to the castle is a lovely day out,' the waitress said, looking wistful. 'Miles of walking trails and a great adventure playground. We often take the kids up there with a picnic. It only costs a couple of quid to park and they wear themselves out running around.'

'Does it get busy, then?'

'Och no, not really. Only at the weekends. I think you have to book if you want a tour round the castle and they only do those a handful of times a year. Other than that, there's plenty of space if you're wanting to just get out and enjoy nature. Sometimes you don't see another soul, even when there are plenty of cars parked up.'

'Sounds perfect,' he said, smiling, thinking it really did. Nobody would be challenging him for walking around the place, and if he strayed into an area where he shouldn't be, he could just say he was lost. They must get that all the time. His main problem, though, was finding out where Holly and her boyfriend might be living, but perhaps the waitress could help with that too? 'A friend of my dad's worked there at one time, so I thought I'd come and have a look while I was in the area. He told us so many stories about the place.'

'Oh, there's lots of staff houses and apartments on the estate. Did he say which one? I know a few people who work up there.'

Mark pretended to consider. 'I can't quite remember. But I do know he was a gamekeeper.'

'Ah, well, I know exactly where he'd be living.' She beamed at him. 'It's the cottage on the right, next to the woodlands, not far from the entrance. Backs on to the river and if you take the footpath round the side of the house, you'll find a lovely waterfall and picnic benches. Then you can walk over the wooden bridge, through the woods and up onto the moors on the other side. We often walk round that way. It tends to be a bit quieter.

When the dogs are in the kennels, they can make a bit of a racket when you go past, but they soon calm down. Nothing to be worried about.'

He smiled as she chattered on, watching her wiping the tables, tidying up the condiments, his mind busy now he'd had a caffeine boost. Today was shaping up to be a good day, he thought as he filed the information away for later. He knew exactly where he was going now. And this was why it paid to be nice to people. They helped you in ways they couldn't possibly imagine.

He'd been in a bit of a panic before he left home, trying to get all his jobs finished, and he'd neglected to bring clothes suitable for walking and being out in the Scottish elements. The waitress directed him to the nearest outdoors shop, which was in the middle of town, and with the help of a delightful young man, he kitted himself out with a full set of walking gear so he'd look the part. And stay warm.

He had no idea how his mission would pan out, but he envisaged time standing in bushes, observing, waiting for the right moment to intervene and let Holly know he was here to help. At least he had to be prepared for that, given she still wasn't answering his Insta messages.

The clothes added up to an eye-watering amount, but what price could you put on saving a damsel in distress? Not just any damsel, though. Holly was the woman he was destined to be with. He could tell by the way everything had fallen into place so quickly and easily. He was being guided towards her by powers greater than himself, he was convinced of it.

From everything the waitress had told him, he also had to be prepared for barking dogs. Thinking about it, his best bet was to turn up mid-morning, then surely the gamekeeper would be out doing whatever gamekeepers did. And the dogs would be with him and that would make everything much simpler. That was his theory anyway. But he'd found, from experience, that it was best to be ready for all eventualities, so he found a pet shop and bought some dog treats just in case.

Once he'd changed into his new gear and packed his rucksack with essentials, he had another coffee to sharpen his brain. By that time, it was eleven o'clock and time to go and find Holly.

10

The gamekeeper's house was easy to locate. It was a red sandstone cottage, of a design that seemed so prevalent in this part of the country, with grey slates on the roof and ornate ridge tiles. There was something about the architecture that suggested a gingerbread house to him, like a place you'd find in a fairy-tale. It had a low wall and neat lawn at the front, with roses growing up the side of the porch. The wooden door was painted white with black metal studs, a huge metal ring of a door knocker in the middle. A tall privet hedge separated the front garden from a gravel driveway, which appeared to lead round to the back of the property. Best of all, it was surrounded by woodland, providing plenty of places for him to hide while he was doing his recce.

He couldn't stop outside, because he'd be blocking the road, so he just slowed to look on his way past, to get an idea of the lie of the land. The cottage was in such a secluded spot, nobody would see what happened in there. The thought made his heart clench, his concerns for Holly multiplying by the minute.

The castle itself was at least half a mile further up the

curving entrance drive, which was bordered on each side by an avenue of mature trees, standing tall and regimented like a line of soldiers. He pulled into the car park, stopping in a corner, shaded by overhanging branches. Somewhere he wouldn't be noticed. Thankfully, there were only a handful of other cars and nobody else in sight.

He changed into his walking boots, put on his baseball cap and hefted his backpack over his shoulder. This felt good, like he was doing something positive to help Holly, and it spurred him on.

He'd always been a sucker for a romantic storyline, desperate to believe that happy ever afters could exist. He just hadn't been lucky enough to find his yet. As he'd got older, he was aware of time ticking away and his chance to build the family of his dreams inched further from his grasp. He was thirty-six now and he did have moments when he felt desolate, like life was slipping away from him. But when he'd met Holly he'd just... known. This was the chance he'd been waiting for and if he didn't follow his heart now, the opportunity could be gone. It had happened to him in the past, wasting a chance by being too hesitant, and he was determined it wouldn't happen again.

'Nothing in life is easy,' his mum had always told him. 'You don't get what you want without a bit of effort. And anything good is worth fighting for.' Over the years, those words had been burned into his mind, becoming his motto for life. He would be that caped crusader, that knight in shining armour. He would put in the effort, whatever it took, to win the heart of his woman.

A large illustrated map stood on wooden stilts at the edge of the car park, and after studying it for a few minutes, he was clear about the geography of the place. There was a footpath

marked, just as the waitress had said, which would take him
from the car park, through a bit of woodland, crossing over the
entrance drive he'd just come down, right past the cottage. He
could see a river marked, a bridge over it at the back of the
cottage, then the path went on into another stretch of woodland
before popping out onto the moors. It was part of a circular
walk so there would be nothing untoward about him taking that
path. Perfect.

It was a glorious autumn day, the sun sending mottled
shadows dancing on the ground as light filtered through the
branches of the trees. Golden leaves fluttered around him in the
breeze. The air was full of birdsong and he smiled to himself as
he marched along, eager to see Holly again, hoping she was
okay.

After walking for ten minutes or so, he could hear the sound
of fast flowing water and he crossed the road, following the path
round the edge of the house. He was delighted to find the waterfall and the bridge practically at the bottom of the garden.

The property stood on its own, no neighbours within half a
mile. The thought made his stomach churn, the whole situation
having an essence of danger. Especially when he thought of the
size of Finn's handprint on Holly's cheek. But he knew one thing
for certain. There was a reason why he and Holly had met. It
was fate. And the universe had given him the job of getting her
away from what was clearly an abusive relationship. Forces
larger than Mark were at work here, and he had to let his
instincts guide him.

He puffed up his chest and put his shoulders back,
immensely proud of the role he'd been chosen for. He might
not be the beefiest guy, and he'd be no match in a physical
battle, but he had the brains to match any adversary.

The house stood quiet and still, no signs of life. *Is Holly at home?* She hadn't said if she worked and he hadn't thought to ask. Their conversation had been all about music and the songs they loved, artists they followed, events they'd been to. He knew she wasn't a professional singer, that it was just a hobby for her. From her Insta page, he'd seen pictures of her working in a kitchen but he'd no idea if that's what she did now.

He stood in the trees, close to the bridge at the back of the house, watching the cottage through his binoculars for a little while. A shadow moved behind the glass of what he thought must be the kitchen window.

Is it her? He took a deep breath. There was only one way to find out.

He pushed himself off the tree trunk he was leaning against and walked back over the bridge and along the path next to the house, taking the opportunity to peer over the hedge into the back garden. He could see the kennels and the runs for the dogs, but all was quiet. No sign of a vehicle in the drive either, which was a relief because no way did he want to come face to face with her boyfriend. But then, he reasoned, Finn didn't know him. He had no idea Mark had fallen in love with Holly.

Nothing to worry about, nothing at all.

Having convinced himself she was alone, he made his way to the front gate, hesitating as he lifted the latch, his heart racing as he made his way up the path. He banged the door knocker, startled at the sound. It was louder than he'd expected, his three quick taps reverberating through his hand and up his arm. He stepped back, his fingers fidgeting behind his back, his body tensed and ready to run away.

Out of the corner of his eye, he saw the net curtain twitch in the bay window to his left. A few seconds later the door opened a crack and there she was – well, one eye and a sliver of her face – peeping out at him.

He beamed at her, relieved and delighted that she'd opened the door and not Finn. 'Hello, stranger,' he said, keeping his tone light while his heart fluttered in his chest. She was even lovelier than the image in his mind. And his imagination was already two steps ahead, picturing taking her in his arms, telling her he'd always keep her safe. She would cling to him, gratitude shining in her beautiful eyes.

'What the hell are you doing here?' she snapped.

11

Mark recoiled like he'd just been attacked. But as their eyes locked, he understood he shouldn't take her words at face value. He knew fear when he saw it and it was there in her eyes, plain as day.

'I thought...' His hands clenched and unclenched, his mouth no longer working properly, unable to articulate exactly what he *had* thought. He started again, trying to work out if he'd misunderstood, if he'd got it all wrong. 'When we were talking, I sensed things weren't right with you at home. Then your last message, and that picture you sent, got me really worried. Especially when you didn't reply.' He stepped closer, his hand resting on the wall of the porch, desperate to touch her, to repeat that wonderful kiss they'd shared. But she didn't move, just stared at him. 'I thought... you might need a friend.'

She shook her head, her eyes looking even bigger now. He noticed how pale she was, a bead of blood appearing on her lip where she must have nipped too hard. 'You've got to go. Right now, you've got to get the hell away from me.'

The door slammed in his face.

He stood staring at it for a moment, not sure what to do. It was clear things weren't right but why was she sending him away? He knocked again. She didn't answer this time. Nor the next. *Persistence is key,* he told himself as he kept trying. He was about to knock for the sixth time when he heard the purr of an engine followed by the crunch of tyres on the gravel driveway, which was hidden from view on the other side of the hedge. His hand let go of the door knocker, his mind going into overdrive.

Finn's home.

He turned on his heel and hurried away.

12

Holly stood in the hallway, leaning against the wall, her eyes tracing the pattern of the black and white floor tiles. Her pulse was racing, her mind racing even faster. She was willing Mark to go away, but a part of her wanted him to stay because she'd feel a whole lot safer if he was close by. However, if Finn knew she had a visitor, a male visitor, then she would have a lot of explaining to do. It wouldn't end well, she knew that for a fact. Look what had happened last night. No way was she going to pour oil on that particular fire.

The fact that Mark had been worried enough to drive all the way back to Scotland to check on her was quite a surprise, even if it had been the very thing she'd subconsciously been wishing for. How sweet was he for doing that? But how on earth had he found out where she lived? She frowned, going back over their conversation, unable to remember any mentioning of Drumlanrig Castle. She'd intentionally kept it vague, but she must have let something slip. Enough of a clue to enable him to find her.

He cares about me.

She closed her eyes and held that thought to her heart, feeling a delicious warmth spreading through her body. She could hear the Lenny Kravitz song in her head, could see them singing together in her mind. It had been an undeniably magical encounter. The sort of thing you dreamed about as a teenager. If she believed in fate, she might have a different take on things, but she'd decided long ago that her future was in nobody's hands except her own.

There was no denying the attraction she'd felt between them. In fact – and this was the weird thing – if she'd described her perfect partner, it would be Mark. Okay, maybe not to look at, but with regard to the more important things, the stuff she'd got so wrong up to now. She'd gone for men with muscular physiques and brooding good looks, your archetypal hero figures like Finn. But what Mark could offer was more appealing. His musical talent, the way their voices had blended so beautifully, his self-deprecating sense of humour and apparent lack of ego. His kind and caring nature. All of it was what she wanted but had never found.

He was such a lovely guy, and she thought it was wonderful that he'd put his career to one side while he cared for his mother until she'd passed away. He'd explained that he'd given himself time off to grieve but had just started working again. She couldn't even remember what type of job he did because she'd been drowning in his gaze, those big blue eyes swallowing her up. She wished things were different, that she'd made other decisions. But then, she never would have met him.

Her toe scraped at a bit of mud on the floor. Could she talk to him, explain the mess she'd got herself into? Oh, it was so tempting to give the solving of her problems to somebody else, but she knew in her heart that it wasn't the answer. It would only create more complications and it was better to keep things simple. She could only deal with the here and now, not think about the what ifs and maybes. Finn had a fiery temper and if he became aware of Mark's presence, it would only cause her harm.

She felt stronger knowing she wasn't completely alone, but Mark had to be her secret weapon, her hidden strength, and she hoped he'd taken the hint and disappeared for now. He'd stopped knocking on the door, so that was a good sign.

The bang of the back door closing made her head snap up, her breath catching in her throat. *Christ, that's all I need.* Finn was home.

He wasn't supposed to be home. He was supposed to be out on a shoot all day. It was never good when he came home unexpectedly. It usually meant something had gone wrong and that always put him in a foul mood. He really wasn't good at dealing with the unexpected, taking his frustration out on everything around him.

Stay nice and calm, she told herself, feeling anything but. *Deep breaths, pretend nothing's going on.* She dashed into the lounge and flicked the net curtain aside, relieved to see Mark had gone. She sank into a chair, her hand rubbing her forehead, wondering how much more stress she could take.

It's not for much longer, she told herself, thinking of her passport safely tucked away at the back of her underwear drawer. Finn wouldn't look in there.

On their way back from the station, after he'd picked her up two days ago, she'd been worried that he'd take it off her, especially when the questions started.

'So, tell me...' Finn's voice had broken into the uneasy

silence. 'What were you doing at the passport office?' His question had caught her unawares, her mind already two steps ahead, wondering how things might escalate after the slap, what he might do next.

'Oh, I, er... I had to go for an interview.'

'Why would you need an interview?' His voice was calm, no sign of anger.

'Because it's my first passport and they had some questions and wanted to see me in person. It's what they do now, to stop fraud.'

He'd nodded, his lips pursed. 'Right. Okay. But why do you need a passport in the first place?' He'd glanced across at her. 'And why tell me a lie about visiting your mother?'

Her eyes had dropped to her lap, while her mind got busy, threading a story together. It was a moment before she'd responded. She pulled back her sleeve and held up her arm, the bruise he'd caused clearly visible. 'This is why I didn't tell you the truth. Because I'm frightened of what you're going to do to me.' She turned her head, pointed at her face, the skin still smarting where he'd slapped her. 'And this.' She glared at him, anger rising in her chest, giving an edge to her voice. 'And I need a passport for ID. And I need ID to be able to live a normal life nowadays, like everybody else.'

She'd turned back and stared through the windscreen, her chest heaving, wondering if she'd played it right. He'd been mortified about bruising her wrist, apologising to her for days afterwards. Presumably, he'd feel the same about the slap to her face, although there was no guarantee. But for her to keep her passport safe, for him to not want to look for it, she'd had to take a risk.

He was quiet for a moment.

'So, it was just an interview?'

She'd nodded, tight lipped. 'That's right. It'll be a few weeks until my passport is ready.' He didn't need to know that she'd been for the interview eight weeks ago, when he was staying at one of the estate lodges with a group of celebrity clients. She hadn't been able to risk having it sent to her, so she'd had to make this trip to pick it up.

He was silent for quite a while after that. Finally, as they turned into the castle grounds, he'd said, 'I'm sorry. If it was just an interview, I may have... overreacted.'

She didn't reply, because if he'd hit her for going to pick up her passport, the implication was that he wouldn't have been sorry. At all costs, she had to keep that a secret, had to try and keep her position on top of the moral high ground.

Finn's behaviour had cemented a plan in Holly's mind. If they could draw a line under this latest episode, and she could behave as he wanted her to for a little longer, it would allow her to get enough money together. Then she'd be on her way. For the last few weeks, she'd been stealing the odd note from Finn's wallet when he'd been spark out after drinking with his mates. It was a regular occurrence, and she figured he hadn't a clue how much he spent on a night out, so he wouldn't notice as long as she didn't get greedy.

Patience was key. Her intention was wait until 1 December, which was seven weeks away. That was the date of a big meet for their top tier clients, and he'd be staying out for a couple of nights. If she made her move then, she could be well away before he even noticed she'd gone.

Seven weeks felt like a very long time though. Especially now he'd started being rough with her.

It was disorientating how things had flipped a full one-eighty in her mind. Increasingly, he scared her and since she'd come back from Glasgow, she'd felt him watching her all the time. The balance had shifted and she understood that she'd got it wrong. She'd never been *someone* he wanted to protect. She was *something* he wanted to keep. All to himself. No sharing.

She massaged her temples, trying to keep a tension headache at bay. Heavy footsteps stopped in the doorway.

13

Holly glanced up. To her relief, Finn looked contrite. So, he hadn't come home because something had gone wrong. He must have come home to check up on her, which was a first.

'There you are. I've put the kettle on.' Her eyebrows twitched. That was a first too. 'I thought we could have a brew before I get out with the shoot. We're just waiting for one of the guests to arrive. Hold-up on the M6 or something.' He came and sat beside her, took her hand, his eyes scanning her face. He traced the back of his fingers down her cheek where he'd slapped her. 'I'm so sorry about... I honestly don't know what got into me. But I promise it won't ever happen again.'

She didn't answer. What could she say? She definitely wasn't going to forgive him. But she was glad that he knew a line had been crossed. Hopefully a slap was as bad as it was going to get.

His eyes dropped to her lap, where his hand held hers. 'I know you're still mad at me and I can't say I blame you, but I got myself all worked up while you were gone, thinking you were getting a passport so you could take off.' He was silent for a beat. 'You wouldn't do that, would you?'

She couldn't look at him and tell a barefaced lie, so she kept her eyes on the floor, swallowed. 'I told you I need a passport for ID so I can get some work. That's all it is. It's not like I've got any money to go anywhere, is it? But our lives would be much better and there would be less pressure on you if you let me get a job.'

He sighed. 'I've told you there's no need to get a job. We're managing okay, aren't we?'

'But I don't like being totally dependent on you for money. I need some of my own to buy new clothes. I need a waterproof jacket. My trainers are falling apart. And I hate having to ask every time I need something.'

He reached into his pocket and passed her his bank card. 'You can buy online, can't you? Put them on that.'

She took the card, aware that he would know exactly what she was spending money on. 'Thank you, but it's not quite the same. Having my own money would give me a bit of independence.'

He cleared his throat, the atmosphere in the room shifting, along with the tone of his voice, which now held a note of suspicion. 'What do you mean independence? You make it sound like you're a prisoner.'

She was at a loss, for a moment, to know what to say, but decided the truth was the best option. If she could get a bit more freedom, then her escape could happen sooner.

'Sometimes it feels like that. I don't have any transport. I don't have a job. I haven't been able to make friends with people because you don't want anyone to know I'm here full-time. I understand it's against the rules, but still... I'm just stuck here all day on my own and there's only so much housework needs doing in a place this size.' She gave an exasperated sigh. 'I'm bored.'

She risked a glance at him and saw the hurt in his eyes, felt his hand tighten round hers. Unease trickled down her spine. *Was that too honest?*

'I... I didn't know you felt like that. You know, my dad was very traditional and my mum was a homemaker. It's how I was brought up, what I've always known, and they were so happy. It's what I've aspired to.' He gave a frustrated huff. 'I don't want my wife to have to work.'

'It's not about *having* to work, it's about *wanting* to. And I'm not your wife,' she murmured.

'But you could be.'

Oh my God, was that a proposal? Her breath caught in her throat, the very thought of being married to this man repugnant. 'Not now you slapped me.' She glared at him, relieved to have that ammunition in her armoury. It seemed every cloud did have a silver lining after all.

He frowned, his hand holding hers so tightly now, it was on the edge of being painful. 'You won't accept my apology?'

This conversation could go horribly wrong, she was well aware of that, but she'd started down a road and there was nowhere to reverse.

Anger burned in her chest and with right on her side she couldn't hold back her true feelings. 'I can never be with a man who hurts me. And this isn't the first time, is it? This is the second time. Not to mention the rough sex, which I told you I don't like, but you won't listen.'

Something clicked in her brain. A little voice telling her that now was the time. Sod getting more money together. She didn't have to live like this a moment longer. Mark had said he'd take her wherever she wanted to go if she didn't feel safe. She took a deep breath, looked Finn straight in the eye. 'I'm leaving.'

He blinked. She tensed. *Oh my God, I said it. I actually said it.*

In an instant, he'd dropped her hand and jumped to his feet, his body blocking the doorway as if she intended to race out of the house at that very moment. She could see the panic in his eyes. 'Just... don't be rash.' His chest was heaving. 'Let's allow things to settle down. You've got to give me another chance.' He sounded on the edge of tears. 'Please, I promise I'll never hurt you again.'

She shook her head, her voice firm. 'No, Finn. There's no going back from this. I can't trust you now. You've given me no choice. I'm going.'

His eyes narrowed, his voice hard. 'Going where?'

She hesitated, because she couldn't have him following her. 'Margate,' she lied. 'I've got an aunt who lives there.'

'I don't believe you.'

Her jaw tightened as she told herself to stay strong. 'You don't have to believe me.'

He was silent for a moment, his head bowed so she couldn't see his face. 'Look, I've got to go to work now.' His voice was slow and heavy, he sounded defeated. 'But if you really want to leave, I'm not going to stop you. If you want to get your stuff packed, I'll give you a lift to the station when I get back this evening.'

Bloody hell, that was easier than I thought it was going to be. She let out a sigh of relief, so glad that she'd fought the fear and stood up to him.

His gaze met hers and her heart stuttered when she saw the mean glint in his eye, heard the snarl in his voice. 'Or maybe I won't do that. Maybe I'll get straight on to the police in Buxton and tell them where you are, shall I?'

14

Mark leant on the bridge at the back of the cottage, watching the water surge beneath his feet, cascading over the jagged rocks before falling into the deep pool thirty feet below. There was something primal about the constant roar of it, the flow of the water hypnotic and soothing. He wasn't sure what to do now. It was obvious that Holly was frightened; she hadn't told him to go away because *she* didn't want to see him, but because she was scared of *Finn* seeing him. The answer was either to wait until Finn went out again or go away and come back later. He decided to wait. There was nothing else he had to do, nowhere else he needed to be. Not for a few days anyway.

Reconnaissance was never wasted, as he'd learnt from the survival programmes he loved to watch on TV, so he decided to walk on through the woods for a bit and explore the area surrounding the cottage. Walking helped him to think and as his mum liked to say, a watched kettle never boils. If he went away, the chances were high that Finn would have gone back to work by the time he returned.

The weather had changed, a brisk breeze blowing up,

causing the branches of the trees to sway and dance above him. He carried on through the woods, the path taking him up the hill towards the open moors. When he finally reached the boundary of the woodland, he stood on top of the stile, ready to carry on, but he was facing into the wind now, and he could see a dark band of rain in the distance, heading in his direction. He changed his plans and scurried back the way he'd come, having no desire to get a soaking. He'd have to try again tomorrow.

Hurrying back towards Holly's cottage, the path twisted and turned through the woods and he found himself looking down on the property. The back garden was a long lawn, bisected by a stone path with flower borders on either side. It was very neat and tidy, the soil clear of weeds, the path cleared of leaves. A recently trimmed privet hedge ran round the perimeter. To the side, he could see a stone outbuilding with kennels attached at the rear, but there was no sign of dogs, which could only be a good thing.

He carried on across the bridge, noticing a narrow path that went round the back of the hedge along the side of the river. He followed this, his heart in his mouth as he found himself slipping and sliding in the mud. It felt quite precarious because the bank of the river had been eroded here and it was a ten-foot drop onto the rocks below. If he fell, he'd be lucky to get away with a minor injury. In fact, given the force of the water, he'd probably end up going over the waterfall. He crouched down so the top of his head wouldn't be seen from inside the house, inching his way along the path, one hand grabbing hold of the hedge to try and keep his balance.

Where the hedge ended, there was a wooden fence enclosing the back of the kennels and the path broadened out a bit, making progress much easier. He crept on until he was peering down the side of the outbuilding towards the driveway, hoping he hadn't been seen. The path wasn't an official one, more like something the owners of the house used to maintain their boundary. He shouldn't be here, and the thought of Finn spotting him was making him hot and sweaty, his heart thumping in his chest.

He let out a relieved breath when he noticed Finn's truck had gone. Emboldened by his absence, he went through the gate and onto the path that led along the side of the outbuilding to the driveway. It was an odd little building and he cupped his hands against the window, peering inside. His curiosity had got him into trouble many times in his life, and this was another impulsive action that he instantly regretted. What he saw made him rear back, and he stumbled away from the window, his hands over his mouth in case the contents of his stomach decided to empty themselves over the gravel.

That is disgusting.

He blinked a few times, trying to remove the image from his mind. The dead birds, pheasants, grouse and ducks, hanging upside down in a long row. Unfortunately, it was one of those shocking visions that was reluctant to move from his brain. *You should have known what would be in there,* he scolded. *What did you think a gamekeeper would have in his outbuilding?*

Mark had always been an animal lover and had become vegetarian when he was a teenager, much to his mum's dismay. She wasn't fond of cooking as it was and had refused to cook two meals every evening. That's when he'd learnt to cook for himself, and in an interesting twist, it was now one of his passions. It just went to show that good things came out of adversity. A timely reminder because he was definitely facing adversity now.

He waited a few moments for the nausea to pass and made his way down the drive to the front of the house, knocking on the door once again and hoping that this time Holly would open it. The curtain twitched. The door opened a crack, and there was Holly, her face red and puffy, her cheeks wet with tears.

His heart went out to her, anger firing through his veins. 'Oh Holly, what has he done to you?'

'We had a row,' she mumbled, eyes on the floor.

'That picture you sent me...' Mark couldn't remember ever being this angry and it filtered into his voice, making his words snappy and harsh. 'You don't have to put up with it, you know.' He thought she was going to close the door and realised he'd come on too strong. He sighed and softened his tone. 'Please, let me help you.' He studied her body language, the drooping shoulders, her head bent so he couldn't see her face. Noted her silence. 'That *is* what you want, isn't it? That's why the song we sang together meant so much to you?'

'I can't,' she murmured, so quietly he could hardly hear.

He took a step closer, fighting the urge to reach out and wipe her tears away. 'I know it's hard to walk out of a relationship, but I promise I can help.'

She glanced up at him and he saw the utter defeat in her eyes. 'If you could help me, Mark, I would jump at the chance. But nobody can help. Not now.' Her chin wobbled. 'And it's my own stupid fault. You've got to go, Mark. There's nothing you can do.'

Once again, she shut the door in his face.

15

Mark stared at the closed door, completely and utterly baffled. He hadn't considered the possibility she might not let him help her. What was he supposed to do now?

The patter of rain on the leaves alerted him to the changing weather and within seconds, the heavens opened, a squall of hail splattering against the windows, stinging his skin. Finding the gap between his jacket and the back of his neck. Icy rivulets took his breath away, and he fumbled his jacket hood up, his trousers already wet. It would take him ten minutes to get to the car and by that time he'd be drenched.

He needed to find shelter and the only obvious place he could think of was the outbuilding at the back of the house. He expected it to be locked, but when he tried the door, to his surprise it opened. He didn't relish the idea of being in there with the dead birds, but it was better than getting pelted by a hailstorm. *I can close my eyes,* he told himself. *Stand with my back to them.*

He burst inside, closing the door behind him. There was a light switch on the wall and he flicked it on, the space not so creepy under the glare of the fluorescent tube. In front of him was a large, stainless-steel bench, which was so clean it gleamed in the light. In fact, the whole place was incredibly tidy, everything organised and stored in its own space. Including the birds, trussed up by their feet, their limp bodies hung on hooks from a horizontal metal bar attached to the ceiling.

He tore his eyes away and scanned the rest of the room. It was probably ten feet by eight. There was a metal cabinet at the far end, fastened with a padlock. Possibly where Finn kept his guns. Next to that, a huge chest freezer hummed; no prizes for guessing what that was for. Tools were hung on the end wall: a shovel, spade, fork, rake, hedge-trimmer, chainsaw, log splitter, axe, all in their allotted spaces, going down in size. A metal bin. A sweeping brush. Finn was clearly a neat freak, even more so than Mark.

The bench had a couple of drawers, and he opened the first one to find it full of freezer bags and string, presumably for tying up the joints of meat. The second drawer was full of knives and a deadly looking meat cleaver, like he'd seen butchers using for chopping through bones. He pushed it shut and turned around. Next to the door, against the wall, was an industrial-sized stainless-steel sink.

A butchery. That's what this place was.

He didn't like it, not one bit, and he was glad to have turned his back on the limp bodies that not so long ago had been enjoying their innocent lives. The hail hammered on the tin roof, so loud he could hardly hear himself think, and he was glad he'd decided to take shelter rather than make a run for his car. Funny that he should end up in a place like this, though, full of potential weapons. *Should I need them.* Not that he was thinking about violence as a solution but, you know, if push came to shove he'd learnt from experience it was good to be prepared.

He smiled to himself and opened the drawer with the knives again, studying the selection more carefully. The noise of the hail on the roof told him he wasn't going anywhere just yet, so there was time to have a nosy. He picked up a boning knife, noting how thin the blade was, how sharp.

'What the fuck are you doing?'

The man's voice made Mark spin round, horror gripping his throat like he was being choked. A hulk of a man, who could only be Finn, stood in the doorway.

16

Mark held the knife behind his back, gently closing the drawer and leaning against it. His mouth was dry and he had to wet his lips before he could think about speaking.

'I'm so sorry. I know I'm trespassing.' His voice was squeaky and ridiculous and he coughed, tried again, hoping to sound like a normal human being. 'I got caught out in the hailstorm and I needed somewhere to shelter until it passed.'

The rattling of the hail on the roof intensified and he could see balls of ice bouncing off the concrete path outside. Surely that was a decent excuse? What reasonable human being would turf someone out of the dry into this sort of weather?

Finn took a step forward and closed the door behind him, standing with his legs apart, his arms hung by his sides like a gun slinger in a Western movie. He had huge hands, Mark noticed. Long arms. He'd definitely be able to reach Mark before he could touch Finn, even with the blade in his hand. His heart raced faster. Oh, how he hated confrontations like this. He got tongue-tied and stupid and he was frightened of saying the wrong thing in case the guy decided to hit him.

Finn just stared at him while Mark's heart raced so fast he thought he might pass out.

'I'll go,' he gabbled. 'It's okay. I mean, it's only water, isn't it?' He gave a nervous laugh. 'I'll dry out.'

Finn's eyes narrowed. 'What have you got behind your back?'

Mark's heart stuttered. *Oh my God, what do I do?* If he dropped the knife there would be a clatter and Finn would hear it. If he put it onto the workbench, it would be noticed as being out of place. The last thing he wanted was to draw attention to the thing and for Finn to decide he wanted to use it. On Mark. The very idea made him think he might pee himself.

He slipped the blade up his sleeve, wincing as it scraped his arm. It was all he could do to stop himself from crying out, but he managed to keep his eyes on Finn the whole time, hoping his face hadn't given him away.

He held out his hands, noticed they were shaking. 'Nothing. I've got nothing behind my back. I was just leaning against the bench.'

He took a step towards Finn, sensing a bead of blood trickling down his arm, making its way towards his wrist. Nerves twisted in his gut and he could honestly say he'd never been so scared in all his life. He'd never been hit by another man, but knew that being hit by Finn, who had hands the size of shovels and arms as big as Mark's legs, would not end well. The trickle of blood was tracking towards his hand now and his pulse rate shot up to another level.

I've got to get out of here before I start dripping blood all over the place.

He cleared his throat and pointed at the door, his finger shaking. 'I'll get off now. And I'm so sorry for intruding. Really, I can't apologise enough.'

'Bloody tourists,' Finn grumbled, a fierce frown on his face. 'Think you own the place, don't you?'

'No, no, not at all. I didn't think there was anyone at home. Didn't think there was anyone to mind.' Finn glared at Mark, and Mark stared at the door, thinking he might be sick any time now. It didn't look like Finn was going to let him out.

His words were having no impact whatsoever on Finn's stony demeanour and the terrible uneasy feeling in the pit of his stomach grew stronger. No wonder Holly wanted to get away. How on earth had she ended up with this neanderthal in the first place? His mind scrabbled for something to appease this roadblock of a man. Something that would allow him to get out of this godforsaken hellhole. 'I can pay you for your trouble. More than happy to do that.' He pulled his wallet from his jacket pocket, which was awkward with his left hand but he couldn't use the other one without slicing his arm to pieces.

'Och, I don't need your money.' Finn sneered and waved a dismissive hand. 'Get away with you, and don't come onto my property again.' He opened the door and stood to one side to let Mark through. The hail was starting to ease now and Mark dashed out of the building and across the road as if Satan himself was after him.

Mark had been in no fit state to drive by the time he'd arrived back at the car park, panting hard after running the whole way and shaking like a leaf. He sat in his car for a bit until he regained some semblance of calm, but then he started thinking about Holly, more worried for her safety now that he'd actually come face to face with her boyfriend.

If he was asked to explain what he'd been doing all afternoon and evening he wouldn't be able to give a precise answer. Worrying, dithering, second-guessing himself, getting out of the car, walking round in circles. Going back to the house to check on Holly, only to find Finn was still there and immediately running away again. Telling himself not to be such a wimp, he'd gone back, prowling round the perimeter of the house, wondering what was happening inside. Listening, hoping and generally feeling completely helpless.

His pathetic response to Holly's dire situation was so far removed from his fantasy of how things would play out it was laughable. Talk about deluded. He was more like Mr Bean than a fearless saviour, rushing in to save his love.

In the end he had to give up. And somewhere along the way, he'd dropped the knife. Which was good in one way, but bad in another. It would be fair to say the day had not gone to plan and it was almost dark by the time Mark got to the hotel. At which point, he was tired and starving hungry and more than a little confused.

He'd gone over his two brief conversations with Holly in his head, and knew something had happened to make her believe she had no choice but to stay with that awful man. But without her being a bit more forthcoming as to what was keeping her there, how could he possibly convince her to leave?

He pondered on that question while he had a hearty supper and drank a few too many drams of whisky. Amazingly, it did the trick, and by the time he staggered up to his room, he knew exactly what he was going to do.

17

Finn had left Holly reeling when he said he was going to tell Buxton police where she was. He'd given a satisfied nod when she hadn't had an answer to his threat, confident that he'd won that particular battle.

When Mark had turned up at the door again, she'd believed all her options had been taken away from her, and she sent him away. But once he'd gone, her despair turned to anger. Why couldn't she be with someone lovely like Mark? Why didn't she deserve anything better than this prison she was currently living in, and a man who scared her more every day? But if she wanted things to change, she knew she had to do something different. In that moment, her resolve hardened and she decided she would fight back.

Domestic violence was something she'd never experienced herself before, but she'd met several women who'd been through terrible ordeals. There was a common thread violence escalated and she reminded herself of that now. It started off small, and when that became the norm, the violence got worse until... *No.* She pressed her lips into a tight line. Her mind was not going to go there, to the terrible conclusion and what her fate might be if nothing changed.

The truth was... something *had* changed. She now had Mark on her side and he'd been so persistent, so genuine in his desire to help, she knew she had a proper ally. He wouldn't just go away because she'd told him to. Nobody who really cared would do that when they were aware that domestic violence was happening. She was confident he'd still be around, ready to help.

Mark's presence made her naively courageous, and when Finn came home a little while later, she called his bluff, because she could smell freedom. She was in the kitchen, pulling the laundry out of the washing machine and decided now was as good a time as any to have her say.

'I've been thinking about your threat. What you said before.' He closed the back door behind him, raised a curious eyebrow, a wary look in his eyes. 'You won't get the police involved.' She straightened up to face him, hands on her hips. 'Not when you're selling off the castle's game meat illegally. You won't want anyone looking into your business, will you? And if you tell on me, then I'll tell on you.'

The shock on his face gave her a buzz of satisfaction. *There, how's he going to get out of that one?*

Of course, she had no intention of doing any such thing, it not being in her interests to have anything to do with the police, given her background, but she sounded convincing.

If she'd been looking to get a reaction out of him, she hit the jackpot with that little taunt. It was as if he'd been jump-started, and she wasn't expecting any of what happened next. While she was focused on winning an argument, she'd forgotten a very important principle that every child learnt in the playground.

Some people don't play fair and you have to expect the unexpected.

For a big man, Finn was pretty agile, and before she knew what was happening, he had an arm wrapped round her neck, securing her in a headlock. His bicep was pressing against her windpipe, her body bent at an uncomfortable angle. She gasped and spluttered, slapped and scratched, but nothing made him loosen his grip. Her vision was blurring, and she started to feel light-headed, unable to get enough oxygen into her lungs. In desperation, she kicked at his shins, but she was wearing slippers and it probably hurt her more than it hurt him.

'Stop being stupid,' he snarled, tightening his grip and slamming her against the wall for good measure. She gasped, the force of the blow such a shock, her body went limp as a rag doll. It was getting harder and harder to breathe, but there was nothing she could do. *He's going to kill me,* she thought, as dots started to encroach on her vision. *I'm dying.*

18

Keeping her in a headlock, Finn dragged Holly across the kitchen, opened the cellar door and threw her in. The door closed with a bang, the bolt slamming into place. She stumbled on the stone steps, her feet losing their grip in her fluffy slippers as she gasped for air. Gravity took hold of her body, the momentum sending her hurtling forwards, tipping headfirst, down, down towards the cellar floor. Until her hand snatched at the wooden handrail, grasping it tighter than she'd ever held on to anything in her life.

Her body jerked to a halt for a second, but her hand was too slick with sweat to hold on. Thankfully, there weren't many stairs left to fall down, and she bumped down the last couple of steps on her bottom until she landed in a heap on the cellar floor.

The mustiness was overpowering, filling her nose, her mouth, her lungs. Making her cough so hard she thought she was going to be sick. She knelt on the floor, dry heaving until her body decided it could cope without vomiting after all. She slumped on the bottom step, shocked and shaking. That was quite a tumble she'd taken and with not much meat on her bones, she'd felt every bang and bump. She was so stunned she couldn't move, and stayed there for quite a while, trying to gather her senses.

It wasn't completely dark. There was a dusty, oblong slit of a window just below ceiling height, which was above ground level outside. It was hung with a veil of cobwebs but allowed enough light in to lessen the gloom. She could see a bike propped against the far wall. Old fashioned, with one of those baskets on the front for shopping. There were boxes and bin bags full of stuff, piles of old curtains, a rolled-up carpet, all of it covered in a layer of dust. It was clear nobody had been down there for quite some time. She hadn't even known there *was* a cellar; she'd thought the funny little door in the corner of the kitchen was a cupboard, but had never bothered to investigate.

Since she was a child, she'd been scared of the dark and cellars gave her the creeps. This one was no exception. Given the number of cobwebs on the window, there was an army of spiders down here. Along with a whole range of other insects, and that thought was the motivation she needed to get herself up off the floor, brushing her clothes down, imagining creepy crawlies making their way up her trouser legs, dropping off the ceiling into her shirt.

Now she was standing, she tested out her limbs and joints and decided nothing was broken, everything was working, but she'd feel sore in the morning. At least she could be thankful she hadn't been hurt. But she could have been killed if she hadn't managed to catch hold of the handrail, because stone was very unforgiving and skulls were more fragile than you'd think.

She sat on the second step and waited. He'd let her out at some point, wouldn't he? Her body gave an involuntary shiver as she thought about spending the night in the dark cellar with the spiders. She pushed the idea out of her mind, unwilling to consider how terrifying that would be and concentrated on listening instead.

His footsteps clumped across the kitchen floor above her head, thumped up the stairs, down the stairs. The back door banged. It was quiet for a while, but she didn't hear the engine of his truck starting so she knew he was probably in the outbuilding, sorting out the dead birds.

He loved it. The plucking, the gutting, the butchery. He also loved the extra money he earned by selling off meat from the birds on the sly. He'd told her that he never kept an honest count of what had been shot and collected, always holding back a few extra birds for himself. Nobody noticed, they didn't really care. It was all about the experience for the guests on the shoots. They weren't too bothered about accounting for the spoils, and because Finn was in charge, they trusted him to be honest.

Ha! Honest. Mind you, she'd thought the same when she first met him. That was the persona he presented. Generous, kind and trustworthy. A good sort. She thought she'd landed on her feet when he brought her back to this picture-perfect cottage. In the grounds of a genuine castle, for God's sake. What could be more trustworthy than that? Seems she still hadn't learnt the lesson that you could never judge a book by its cover.

Now she was locked in a damp, smelly cellar. She sighed, wishing she'd taken up Mark's offer immediately and just run out of the house with him. She could have been far away from this terrible place by now. She could have been free. But he'd caught her by surprise turning up like that, and she hadn't been mentally prepared.

He said he'd messaged her, but she could no longer access her Insta account, so she hadn't seen what he'd written.

Yesterday, just before she'd sent the picture to Mark, Finn had caught her tapping out her message in the kitchen, while she'd said she was making a cup of tea. He was immediately suspicious.

'What are you doing? Who are you messaging?' He strode across the kitchen.

She quickly pressed send before putting the phone on the worktop and returning to the task of making tea, her cheeks burning. How could she be so careless? More to the point, what the hell was she going to do? She handed him a mug of tea. 'I was just scrolling through Insta while I waited for the tea to brew.' She tried to keep her voice nonchalant, forced herself to smile. 'I wasn't messaging anyone.'

'Liar. I saw you.' He slammed his mug of tea onto the work-top, the drink spilling over the sides, then reached for her phone. But she snatched it up and moved it away from him. 'I told you, I wasn't messaging anyone, just scrolling.'

He reached again, holding her arm now. 'I just watched you type something.'

'No, you didn't.' She was skating on thin ice arguing with him like this, but if he did manage to get her phone and open it now, he'd see her messages to Mark, which she hadn't had a chance to delete. It wouldn't take him long to find the video of them singing together, and she couldn't imagine how he'd react to that.

Fear made her head spin, adrenaline spiking in her veins. His face was inches away from hers, his voice menacing as he pulled at her arm. She was no match for his strength, her teeth gritted as she fought against him, hoping he'd give in.

'I was in the hallway. You couldn't see me, but I saw you.' He grabbed a handful of her hair and she screamed. 'Give it to me.'

'Okay, okay,' she gasped, pretending to comply, but instead managed to drop the phone, hearing it clatter onto the tiled floor, bits of phone casing and shattered screen skidding all over the place.

'Look what you've done now,' he snarled, giving her hair a last tug before letting go. He picked up his mug and glowered at her. 'Well at least you won't be messaging anyone now, will you?'

She swallowed, trying to keep her tears at bay. 'I told you, I wasn't messaging.'

He gave a dismissive huff before walking back into the hallway towards the lounge, turning his head to throw a parting comment over his shoulder. 'You must think I'm stupid.'

She tidied up the mess, her heart sinking when she realised her phone was now useless. However, she did have an old phone tucked in a bag upstairs and she could use this same SIM card. The only problem was, she didn't have a charger for it. She'd only kept it because it had all her old photos and she couldn't move them over to her new phone because it was a different operating system. There was a remote chance that Finn's charger might fit. She'd just have to wait for him to go out.

Now, she sat on the cellar steps thinking that her phone being broken had actually turned out to be a good thing, because the lack of communication had got Mark so worried, he'd come to find her. And then she'd sent him away, for God's sake, because of Finn's threat to tell the police about Buxton.

She'd rather face that and be alive than dead and rotting with the spiders in this godawful place.

Dead. Saying the word in her head brought a shiver to her bones. Finn's behaviour had become increasingly violent and she wrapped her arms around her chest, dread creeping up the back of her neck. *What's he going to do to me?*

19

Hours later, she heard the bolt slide back and the steps were flooded with light as the door to the kitchen opened. She stayed where she was, sitting on the second to bottom step, her body stiff and sore after her fall. Her muscles tensed, her thoughts freezing, fearful of what might happen next.

Her mind had been on overdrive while she'd been locked away. Finn couldn't stand the thought of her leaving him, but he knew that's what she'd been planning. She'd told him, hadn't she? He knew, at the first opportunity, she'd be gone. Unless he kept her prisoner down here, which of course was an option. But the thing her brain had fixed on was much worse than that. If he didn't want anyone else to have her, would he decide to end her life? He had the means to do it and definitely wasn't squeamish about killing. The thought made her feel sick.

His footsteps came closer and she hugged herself tight, eyes closed, preparing for the final blow. Or a gunshot. Or a quick flick with a knife across her throat. She whimpered, so frightened she thought she might wet herself.

He sat next to her, his arm brushing hers. She held her breath, eye squeezed shut.

'I'm so sorry,' he said, turning her head towards him. His lips brushed hers. A kiss so gentle it was hard to believe he'd had her in a headlock a matter of hours ago. 'I'm so ashamed. I shouldn't have done that. I know I shouldn't. I promise, I'll do better. Honestly, I will.'

She burst into tears. The shock of the whole incident – being locked up with her morbid thoughts and then this kindness – was all too much. Too contradictory. She had no idea what to make of it, but the relief that he wasn't about to kill her made her wilt. She surrendered to the sobs that wracked her body, covering her face with her hands.

'Hey, it's okay, love.' He gently lifted her hands from her face and brushed away her tears. 'I'm sorry. I'm so very sorry.' There was a tremor in his voice, as if he might start crying too.

How could she tell him it was okay, when it was as far from okay as you could get. But then she was frightened of what might happen if she didn't forgive him. When her sobs shuddered to a halt, she wiped her face on her sleeve, still unable to find any words. She couldn't let her anger out of its cage because that would make things worse, but she would struggle to behave like nothing had happened either.

Just pretend, she told herself. *What does it matter if it buys you time?*

'Let's get you out of here,' he said, clambering to his feet and helping her up the stairs. She had to lean on him for support. Her hip was so sore after her fall, each step was a challenge, but she was repulsed by the proximity of him. Didn't want to touch his skin, breathe the same air, or smell his musky odour. It was amazing how lust could turn into loathing in such a short space of time. But his behaviour had done that. If he'd carried on being nice to her, like when they'd first met, they could have had a proper relationship.

When would she ever learn? It was time to change her type when it came to men and, from now on, she would prioritise personality over looks. Which made her think about Mark. Thank God he was close by. Or at least she hoped he was.

She clenched her teeth against the pain as she made her way up the final steps and emerged into the bright lights of the kitchen. The table was laid for a meal, flowers in a little vase, candles flickering. The smell of cooking made her mouth water and she saw what looked like a lasagne sitting on the worktop. Perfectly cooked, not a burnt edge to be seen. Garlic bread next to it.

'I made us supper,' he said, pulling out a chair and gesturing for her to sit. 'It's the least I could do after my... after I...' He shut up, struggling to articulate exactly what he'd done.

She sat and played with her food, taking tiny mouthfuls, too nauseous to eat much. And still, she couldn't say anything. Nothing he'd want to hear anyway.

'You're very quiet.' He stopped eating and glanced at her. 'Is the meal okay?'

She nodded and took a bite of her garlic bread, making sure not to catch his eye. Because if she did, he'd know she was furious. Would work out that her compliant behaviour didn't match the thoughts fizzing round her head.

'Why don't you make yourself comfy in the sitting room while I load the dishwasher? Then we can watch something, if you like. Your choice.'

It was never her choice, but she let it pass and did what he suggested. She shivered, chilled to the bone from sitting so long in the freezing cellar. The fire was nearly out in the stove and she bent to pick up a log to keep it going. But when she opened the stove door, she couldn't stop the strangled scream that burst from her lips. There, lying in the grate, was a little scrap of cardboard with an embossed gold emblem. All that was left of her passport.

He must have heard her cry and came rushing in. 'Are you okay?' He took the log from her. 'Hey, let me do that. You sit down.'

'It's my hip,' she said, pointedly. 'Where I landed on the steps. I'm wondering if I've broken something.'

Oh yes. That's what I need to do. Get him to take me to hospital. Then I can claim domestic abuse and they won't let him near me.

Hope filled her heart, her mind already working on what she would tell the doctors when Finn said, 'I doubt it. Here, let me have a look.'

In an instant, the possibility of an escape route evaporated. No way was she pulling her trousers down to let him inspect her hip. Who knew what that might lead to. No, her clothes were staying on, which meant her idea wasn't going to work.

She shook her head and mumbled, 'It's okay. You're probably right.' She caught his eye and forced a small smile. 'I don't suppose there's any wine left, is there?'

They watched a movie, Holly huddled in a corner of the sofa, while he insisted on massaging her feet. It was his way of saying sorry, she supposed, and although she just wanted him to leave her alone, she couldn't say that. Couldn't risk firing him up again when she was feeling so fragile.

It was a relief when he said he had to go out for a little while. She heard him locking her in and her heart turned to ice. So, this was her fate if she stayed; she was going to be his actual prisoner. Her jaw tightened. She was done with his nonsense.

20

Holly wandered around the house like a caged animal, rattling the doors to confirm her suspicion was correct. And it was. She let out a growl of despair, until she remembered Mark. If she could contact him, then he'd come, she was sure he would. Her fingers found the SIM card in her pocket, rescued from the remains of her phone on the kitchen tiles, and she held on to it like it was the key to the door. Her way out.

She heaved herself up the stairs and had a good rummage in her holdall at the back of the wardrobe, the one she'd brought with her only a few short months ago. Her heart leapt when her hand closed round her old phone and she pulled it out of her bag, hugging it to her chest for a moment before slipping the SIM card in. Now she just needed to charge it up.

Her pulse raced as she allowed herself to hope that she might be able to escape before Finn came back. But her phone charger didn't fit and neither did Finn's because it was a different make. Why hadn't she thought of that? Her brain wasn't working properly, panic scrambling her logic, and she sat in the lounge, her old phone in her hand, wondering what to do. In the end, she took it back upstairs and tucked it in her pillowcase while she started to pack. Not everything, just the essentials, so Finn wouldn't guess. But it seemed prudent to have an escape bag ready.

She stuffed the bag back in the wardrobe and stood there, in the middle of the room, hands on hips as she tried to think what else she could do. *Windows. I can get out of a window.* The thought sent her round the house, checking. It was amazing what you didn't notice, she thought as she came to the end of her fruitless mission in the kitchen. Every window in the house was the same design, only having an opening at the top, hardly big enough for a small child to get out of. But she supposed that was the point, although she wondered how it squared with fire safety regulations.

Her eyes scanned the kitchen and a new idea popped into her head. *People keep old chargers stuffed in drawers.* The thought set her off on another circuit of the house, rifling through every drawer and cupboard. She finished back up in the bedroom and slumped onto the bed, completely spent. In her heart, she'd known it was a thankless task, that she wouldn't find what she was looking for. Finn liked order and went mad if things weren't kept in exactly the right place. He was one of those people who didn't have an obsolete electrical leads drawer like everyone else she knew. She heaved a sigh. Contacting Mark, it seemed, wasn't an option. She'd just have to hope he came back, and if he did, she'd be ready.

Her fingers rubbed at her forehead, annoyed with her thinking. *I don't want to be reliant on another man.* Wasn't it time to do something different?

But it didn't need to be for long, she reasoned, just long enough to get her out of this place and on her way. A means to an end, that was all.

It was after 10 p.m. now, and Holly had been expecting Finn to return a while ago, but there was still no sign of him. She sat still and listened, waiting for the sound of an engine, the crunch of tyres on gravel, the bang of the back door, the clump of footsteps up the stairs. But there was nothing, only silence.

Oh, she was tired. So very, very tired, but she knew she was too anxious to sleep. She lay on top of the covers, her hand finding her old phone in the pillowcase. *Maybe I should put that in the holdall?* She was terrified she might forget it if she had to make a quick getaway, then she would have lost all her contacts, people she might need to rely on at some point. It was hard to summon the energy to move but she forced herself to roll onto her side, then pushed herself into a sitting position on the edge of the bed. Taking a moment before stumbling over to the wardrobe and hiding the phone at the bottom of her bag. Okay, now she was ready.

Relax, relax, relax, she told herself as she lay back down, her eyes closing. But her mind was too busy for sleep, going over the events that had led her to this place, this predicament. If only she could turn back the clock and do things differently.

Before she'd gone to Glasgow to collect her passport, things had been on an even keel with Finn. More or less. She kept the place clean and tidy, just how he liked it. Did the laundry and the cooking. Really, what else was she going to do? She had no job and at least the cleaning, and everything else she did to look after Finn, filled the day. They got along well enough, as long as she played by his rules. Yes, she'd planned to leave, but there was no urgency, and the desire to build up an escape fund had been greater than her urge to get away.

Unfortunately, things had gone distinctly pear-shaped since she'd got back from Glasgow, lurching from bad to worse in a way she could never have predicted. There certainly *was* an urgency to leave now. It was all she could think about. If she stayed, she was going to end up dead, of that she was sure. In fact, she could be dead now if she'd landed badly at the bottom of the steps. And he didn't even come and check she was okay for hours. Her resolve hardened. There was only going to be one winner here and it had to be her. She just needed to calm down, engage her brain and think.

Should I break a window?

She frowned, thinking it through. Double glazing was pretty hard to break, and realistically, she was in no fit state to climb out. If Finn caught her in the act, well, the consequences didn't bear thinking about, and he could turn up at any minute. Now was not the time and she didn't dare risk it.

Wait until tomorrow. Yes, that was the best thing. Get some rest and once Finn had gone to work, she'd have all the time she needed to make her escape.

21

For a long time, she lay there, expecting to feel the weight of him crawling in bed next to her, the smell of drink on his breath.

He often disappeared in the evenings, taking himself up to the castle to socialise with some of the other staff. They were a close-knit team, like a family, he'd said, although she wouldn't know because she hadn't been introduced to any of them.

Nobody here knows I exist.

That thought made her eyes spring open. Because if nobody knew she was living with Finn, then nobody would notice if she disappeared. Finn could kill her, dispose of her body and carry on with his life. No wonder he felt he could use violence to control her. And if she refused to be controlled... She sat up and swung her legs out of bed, covering her face with her hands.

I've been so stupid. Understatement of the century. Why on earth had she thought it was a good idea to come home with Finn in the first place?

Her mind travelled back to the night she'd met him, and she remembered what a sorry state she'd been in after running away from Buxton. She didn't have enough money for a hotel room and was getting herself nicely drunk so she wouldn't mind quite so much when she had to sleep rough for the night. In her inebriated state, the idea of sharing a nice warm bed with a handsome stranger had seemed more appealing than being out in the rain. To be fair, though, at the start of their relationship, things had been great in their loved-up bubble. It was only when she started wanting to go out on her own that things turned sour, and she saw a side of him she'd never imagined existed.

The sound of a car engine, then a door banging, made her sit up straight. Listening. Was that one car or two? Yes, there, another car door shutting. Voices. He'd brought someone back with him. She went over to the window and peeked through the curtains. The back end of a black car was visible in the driveway.

Finn had always told her to stay quiet and keep out of the way if he brought someone back to the house. He wasn't supposed to have anyone living with him in castle property unless they were his spouse or they worked there as well. Everyone had to be formally vetted, due to the likelihood they would come into contact with the paying guests. And most of the paying guests were people with money. Affluent and influential people, who wanted to be assured that whatever they did at the castle would remain private. Holly's background meant she was not in a position to be vetted, she was not married to Finn, and therefore her presence had to remain a secret.

The voices didn't come inside, although she thought she heard the back door open, then close, and the dogs barking, which probably meant Finn and his visitor had gone into the outbuilding. It was likely his visitor was one of the guys who bought the meat off him. Those deals seemed to happen in the middle of the night. That's how she'd guessed it was illegal. Stealing. But it was none of her business so she'd never said anything, just let him get on with whatever he was doing. It was his life and she was happy to keep her distance.

She sat on the edge of the bed, waiting for him to come in. Why did time seem to pass so slowly at night? After a while, she moved out of the bedroom and inched her way down the stairs to make herself a hot drink, thinking it might calm her nerves. *Did I really hear the back door open?* She was second-guessing herself now and went to try the handle, surprised when the door offered no resistance to her pull.

Oh my God. I could go now.

A burst of adrenaline fired round her body as she pictured it in her mind, grabbing her holdall, sneaking out of the back door. *But what if he sees me?* Chances were he'd only be a few minutes doing his transaction. She didn't have time. The risks were too great. She nodded to herself. *Better to wait.* It would be easier to hitch a lift in the morning. Safer. The truth was, she wasn't in immediate danger, not right now.

The cold night air brought goosebumps to her skin, the moon hanging low in the sky, lighting up the path. She frowned. What was that she could see by the flowerbed? Something shining, out of place, and Finn hated anything out of place. She stepped outside and bent to look, picking up the knife with her shirt sleeve over her hand because that thing was not going anywhere near her fingers.

She hurried back inside, closing the door slowly so it didn't make a sound, then she took her drink and inched her way back up the stairs. Much later, weary beyond words, her body feeling like she'd been hauling sacks of coal, she lay down and went to sleep.

22

The sun was streaming through the thin bedroom curtains when she woke up, the alarm clock telling her it was after 9 a.m., much later than her normal routine. Something felt different and as her mind started to properly wake up, she knew what it was. Finn wasn't in bed. His side hadn't been slept in. The house was quiet.

Where is he?

She clambered out of bed, her muscles objecting to every move as she hobbled downstairs. No sign of him.

His boots weren't by the back door. His coat wasn't on the coat rack where it would normally hang. She peered outside and could see his truck still in the driveway. The dogs were barking, which was unusual at this time of day. He would normally have taken them for a walk and fed them by now. That kept them quiet for a while, but their barking was frantic. She shoved her feet into a pair of wellies and went outside to check if he was there.

The outbuilding was open, the door ajar, and she gingerly peered inside, nerves twisting in her stomach. It was gloomy and she flicked on the light. Her hands flew to her mouth, her breath catching in her throat. *That isn't supposed to be there.*

Lying on top of the stainless-steel worktop was a knife. That in itself would be unusual, because Finn was meticulous about cleaning everything and putting it away. What was bothering her were the drips of blood on the edge of the worktop and on the floor. Her eyes tracked the trail and settled on a big red stain.

Oh God. Is that... Finn's blood?

It might not be, of course. Because this was where he butchered the animals. There was always blood in here. But not on the floor. Never on the floor. She backed out of the building, closing the door behind her, and hurried to the house, panic fluttering in her chest, not sure what to think.

Finn was not at home but his truck was. The dogs hadn't been fed. There was blood on the outbuilding floor. None of those things were normal and all of those things suggested something might have happened to him. Something terrible.

She sat at the table, chewing a fingernail as she tried to work out what to do. Had Finn told anyone she was here? Had he shared his secret after a few drams had loosened his mouth? Perhaps the best thing was for her to take her bag and leave. Even if Finn was fine, this was surely her best chance to go.

23

Mark had an early breakfast and set off for the castle again, with a certain amount of trepidation. Holly had been a bit cryptic the previous day when she'd sent him away for the second time. And although he'd been replaying the conversation in his head for half the night, he still couldn't work out what she might have meant. If he could cajole her into explaining, he'd have something to work with, a means of persuading her that life could be different. Better.

He parked up and walked to the cottage, hesitating when he saw Finn's truck in the drive. He decided to watch for a little while, hidden in the shade of the trees.

After a few minutes, when he'd detected no signs of movement, he put his head down and hurried across the road, onto the public footpath that ran past the house, speeding up when he heard the dogs barking. He jogged over the bridge and up into the woodland, stopping at the point where he had a view across to the back of the property.

He let his backpack drop from his shoulders, wincing as the strap scraped over the gash on his arm. It could probably have done with a couple of stitches but he'd made do with plasters, sticking the edges of the cut together as best he could. It would have to do for now, although he could see the bloom of blood on his shirt, seeping from the cut where he'd just caught it.

God, it hurts. He gritted his teeth and did a little jig on the spot while he waited for the burn of pain to ease. He wasn't good with pain. If he'd been a woman, he would never have been able to consider having a baby. Just the idea of that whole process made him feel physically ill. Women were warriors in his eyes. He was a mere man. One who was more squeamish than he'd like to admit.

He told himself to give over being a baby and pulled his binoculars out of the bag, training them on the back of the house. His gaze moved from room to room, starting with the bedrooms at the top and working his way down to the kitchen and living room. A flicker of movement made his breath catch in his throat, and there she was in the kitchen, standing by the window.

It looked like she was doing the washing up. Or something at the sink, her head bowed. He willed her to look up, desperate to see her lovely face, but she was intent on whatever it was she was doing. He was disappointed when she disappeared, but a few minutes later, he could see her through the bedroom window. Or the shadow of her. Not her face.

He scanned the garden, then the kennels and outbuildings. No sign of Finn, but he hadn't expected to see him because it was a work day. He waited, just in case, but nothing happened except Holly going to the kennels and feeding the dogs. He didn't dare call to her, in case Finn was actually there, so he just watched, his eyes glued to his binoculars, willing the stupid man to get in his truck and go to work.

Finally, he decided to make a move. It was cold sitting in one place for so long and he needed to get some heat in his body. Could he risk trying to knock at the door? Maybe give her some sort of coded message? She still wasn't responding on Insta and although he'd sent her his phone number, he wasn't sure she'd got it. He'd written it on a piece of paper so he could give it to her in person. At least then he'd know she had it if there was an emergency.

He stopped on the bridge and gazed at the water rushing over the rocks for a little while, mesmerised by the constant movement. As he turned to go, his attention was drawn to the pool at the bottom of the waterfall, something catching his eye, making him stop and stare.

There, in the water, pulled in a lazy circle by the currents, was the body of a man. And Mark knew for certain, from the face staring up at him, that man was Finn.

24

Mark's breakfast threatened to make a rapid reappearance and he turned his back on the gruesome sight, shaken to the core. Death could be hard to accept when you'd seen a person alive and kicking less than a day ago. And as he knew all too well, it could take a while for the truth of the matter to sink in.

He leant on the bridge while he waited for his legs to stop shaking.

Thankfully, his brain was working at hyper speed. With Finn dead, Holly was now free and maybe he could entice her away before anyone else noticed Finn's body in the water. His heart leapt as the idea took hold. They could just go and nobody would have a clue Mark had ever been there.

A woman's scream shattered his thoughts and he looked up to see a middle-aged couple standing on the other end of the bridge, all kitted out in walking gear, binoculars round their necks. They too were staring at the pool beneath the waterfall.

Mark would swear his heart actually stopped for a second before he leapt into action. 'Oh my God,' he shouted, hurrying across the bridge to where the couple were standing. He pointed to the pool. 'There's a man in the water.' Hopefully they wouldn't realise Mark had known this for a little while.

The woman was sobbing into her husband's shoulder while the man tried to work his phone. He put it to his ear. 'Police,' he said, his voice firm and deliberate. 'There's a man in the water at the back of the gamekeeper's cottage, Castle Drumlanrig, near Dumfries.' He stared at the body in the pool as he listened. 'He's clearly dead. And it looks like' – he swallowed – 'it might be murder.'

'Murder?' Mark gasped, wondering how the man could have come to that conclusion. Surely it was possible Finn had been drunk and fallen in. The man's eyes met Mark's while he listened to something on the phone, his gaze seeming to hold him in place. He had an authority about him, something that said he was used to being listened to.

'Hmm... Yes... Well, from where I'm standing, I can see blood on his torso. It looks like he might have been stabbed. And he's floating face up, eyes wide open. I'd say he was dead before he went into the water.' He listened again, nodding his head, eyes still pinning Mark to the spot. 'Yes, yes, I'll do that. I'm Doctor Alan MacPherson. I have a practice in Dumfries, just happened to be out for a spot of birdwatching with my wife.' He was silent again, more nodding. 'Yes, I'll stay. There's another chap here as well.' He nodded again. 'Okay. Will do.'

The call finished and the doctor tucked his phone back in his pocket, before escorting his wife to the picnic tables on the flat area beside the bridge. She was still sobbing and he handed her a packet of tissues from his pocket, murmuring soothing words while he leant over, rubbing her back. Mark watched, his eyes flicking towards the cottage, wondering at what point he could reasonably walk away. The doctor was dealing with the police so he wasn't obliged to stay, was he?

The woman appeared to be a little calmer now, and the doctor gave her shoulder a pat before walking back onto the bridge, coming to a halt next to Mark. He pulled out his phone, taking pictures of the body. Mark couldn't bear to look at it, keeping his eyes on the doctor instead. 'The police asked me to get some snaps,' the doctor explained. 'Just in case the body breaks out of that eddy and gets washed further downstream.' There was a note of excitement in his voice and Mark had the distinct impression the guy was enjoying himself.

Mark closed his eyes and gave an involuntary shudder. 'I was not expecting to see...' He cleared his throat. 'The thing is... I bumped into that man yesterday, when I was sheltering from the hailstorm.' He turned and pointed to the house. 'He lives right there.' As soon as he'd said it, he wondered if he'd made a mistake, biting his lower lip to stop himself from saying more.

'Good to know,' the doctor said, still taking pictures. 'You can tell the police when they come. They asked you to stay and give a statement.'

'Oh, but I can't,' Mark blustered, appalled at the idea of talking to the police. More than appalled. The idea horrified him. 'I've got to go. I've got commitments at home... I need to get back. Anyway, I haven't seen any more than you have.'

The doctor stopped taking pictures and slipped his phone back in his pocket, giving Mark his full attention now. 'You've got to stay. They won't be long.' He gave him a hard stare. 'And what could be more important than helping to find a man's killer?'

Mark glanced around, desperate for an excuse to leave, but he couldn't think of a single thing that would make leaving sound like something an innocent person would do. An innocent person would want to help the police with their enquiries, wouldn't they?

He gritted his teeth in frustration. If only he'd got here earlier, he could have avoided being involved in this whole rigmarole with the police. Obviously, it was awful that Finn was dead, but he'd be a hypocrite if he said he cared. Not after the way he'd treated Holly.

He turned away from the doctor while he gave himself a little pep talk. *It's not the end of the world. Just a delay.* And giving a statement shouldn't take long. No, there was no reasonable excuse to leave; he was going to have to man up and get through it.

He glanced at the house, wondering how Holly would react to the news, still desperate to go and see her. But that was out of the question now with this doctor watching his every move. He could see suspicion in his eyes and he realised, with a jolt, that he thought Mark may have done this. And it was feasible he could have, when he thought about it, if the murder had happened just before the doctor and his wife had arrived.

He buried his head in his hands. *Oh God, can this day get any worse?*

25

Mark stood at the end of the bridge, his back to the water and the dead body. He didn't need to keep looking at that, thank you very much. But he couldn't sit with the doctor and his wife either, because she was still crying and that would feel beyond awkward. He'd never been able to deal with crying women.

Finally, after what felt like years, but was probably twenty minutes, the police arrived. Three cars and six officers. Clearly, there was little else going on in the Dumfries area, Mark thought, as he watched them gather in a huddle before separating out into three teams of two. The first two went towards the house. Another two delved into the boot of one of the cars and pulled out reels of crime scene tape. The final two headed towards the picnic bench, where the doctor and his wife were sitting.

Mark had to summon all his mental energy to face his fears. Ever since school, when the police had come in to talk about a spate of windows being broken all over the village, he'd had a mortal fear of the police, always imagining he was in trouble for something he must have done. To be fair, he had been part of the problem at the time. But even when he couldn't think of a single misdemeanour, whenever he was faced with a police officer, the guilt was still there, burning through him. They just had to look at him and his stomach convulsed, palms starting to sweat. He couldn't even watch police dramas on TV without feeling stressed. His mum told him he was being stupid, but it was a response he could never shake.

Now, his legs were trembling, threatening to buckle under him, such was the strength of his phobia. He wondered if he could use it as a way to avoid being interviewed, but dismissed the thought as soon as it arrived. He had to be brave and get on with it. Otherwise, they'd think it was proof he had something to hide.

He went over and sat at the second picnic bench, waiting his turn to make a statement, watching the bustle going on around him. It was quite interesting, really, seeing how the real police dealt with a crime scene. He watched a van full of forensics people arrive, saw them get togged up in the white overalls. Then an ambulance pulled up, followed by the police divers who went into the water to recover the body. What a lot of manpower to get the job done, but they all seemed to know what they had to do and it wasn't long before the body was being lifted out of the pool and hidden in a forensics tent.

With nothing left to see for the time being, his mind wandered.

Obviously, it was sad that a man had died, but at the end of the day, Finn being dead could only be a good thing from Mark's perspective. Holly was now a free agent and once he'd got through this interview, and everyone had dispersed, he would come and collect her and whisk her away to safety.

He smiled to himself, a little fantasy playing out in his mind of them driving back to Wales. Just the two of them, getting to know each other. Bonding in the face of adversity. He gave a contented sigh. *Every cloud has a silver lining and the silver lining to this one could be pretty special.* He just had to get through the questions.

After what seemed like an inordinately long period of time, the doctor and his wife stood up and headed back towards the car park. Mark's stomach roiled. It was his turn.

The interviewing officer came and sat opposite him at the picnic bench, the whole thing sagging when he sat down. He was probably early thirties, with a square jaw and a buzz cut and a physique that suggested he might play rugby. He had a serious demeanour, which was exactly what you'd expect in a murder enquiry, but his accent was strong and he spoke so softly, Mark had to really concentrate hard to work out what he was saying.

'Hello, I'm Detective Sergeant Roy Campbell. And your name is...?'

'Mark.' The officer gazed at him. Mark gazed back.

'Surname?' the officer said with a weary sigh.

'Oh, sorry. Davies with an e.'

'Right, thank you. And judging by your accent you're not local, are you?'

'No, no, I'm Welsh. Just visiting the area for a few days.' *So far, so good.* Mark wiped his hands down his trousers, hoping the officer couldn't tell how nervous he was.

'Now... the doctor said you knew the victim.'

Mark wondered how best to explain his presence on the bridge. And the fact he hadn't rung the emergency services straight away. Had the doctor mentioned that? Had he told the police Mark was behaving in a guilty manner? Did he—
He put the brakes on the stream of questions in his head, aware that he was whipping himself up into an unnecessary

panic. *Just answer the questions. Nice and calm. No need to get hysterical.*

He cleared his throat. 'No, I didn't *know* him as such. I just came across him yesterday when I was walking here, in the woods.'

He glanced at the detective, who was taking notes, but when he wasn't writing, he was watching Mark intently. That in itself made his body break out in a cold sweat. He hated being scrutinized at the best of times but it was a hundred times worse when the person doing the scrutinising was a police officer. Someone trained to spot lies. He remembered now, if you looked in a certain direction when you were talking it was a sign you were lying. If only he could remember which direction that might be.

'I see,' the detective said, and it was amazing how those two little words, said in a certain way, could convey mistrust.

Mark was well aware that he needed to maintain eye contact but was finding the effort of it excruciating. He'd swear his eyeballs were sweating along with the rest of him. The silence went on for way too long before the detective asked another question and broke the spell.

'Can you fill me in on your movements, up to the point at which the doctor's wife noticed the body please. I believe she screamed.'

'Yes, yes, that's right.' Mark nodded. 'I was standing on the bridge, watching the water tumbling down over the rapids there and towards the falls, lost in my thoughts. Then she screamed and I nearly jumped out of my skin and I saw them on the other end of the bridge and they were staring into the pool. I hadn't even looked over that side, but when I did, there was a man's body in the water.'

The officer nodded. 'We'll come back to that, but let's start at the beginning. What time did you arrive?'

Mark blinked. 'Oh, well... I'm really not sure. I'm on holiday so I'm not clock-watching, but I do know I had breakfast at about eight because the news was on in the hotel dining room. It was a leisurely affair. My God, they give you a proper plateful. And top-ups of coffee.' Christ, he could do with a coffee now. His brain was not working half as fast as he would have liked and his fingers tapped on the wooden bench as if playing a tune. It was a nervous tic when he was anxious. He shrugged. 'Maybe an hour before I went back up to my room to get ready. Let's say I left at quarter past nine, in which case I'd be here around half past or maybe ten, I can't be sure.'

'We can check the CCTV on the castle gate to get a precise time.'

CCTV? Why had he not thought about that? Of course they'd have security cameras on the gates. Bugger. That was going to make things a bit more difficult but thank goodness he'd found that out before he said something stupid. 'Like I said, I haven't been clock-watching so that's just a rough estimate.' He smiled at the officer. 'I'm sure the security cameras will prove to be very helpful in finding your killer.'

Did he sound unconcerned? That's what he'd been aiming for, but to him, his voice was a little higher than it should be, slightly strangled.

'Can you tell me what your plans were for the day?'

'I was going to have a mooch around, do a spot of birdwatching, just enjoying the peace and tranquillity really. I was here yesterday but my walk was cut short by a hailstorm, so I thought I'd come back now the weather's better.'

The officer's face was blank and Mark wasn't sure he was

convinced, thankful he still had his binoculars hanging round his neck.

'So, tell me, what happened once you'd parked your car?'

'Well, I took the path that goes into the woods and comes out opposite the cottage over the road there.' He swivelled in his seat and pointed. 'I was heading up through the woods to the moors to see if I could see any partridge. I've never seen a partridge. Or grouse.' In truth, although he'd never seen living examples of these birds, he had seen them dead, hanging in Finn's outbuilding. But there was no need to mention that.

'The doctor said you were on the bridge when he and his wife walked along the path. In fact, they'd followed you from the car park. They came in through the main gates immediately after you did, but they stopped to watch some bird or other in the woods.'

Mark shrugged. 'I didn't notice.' He gave a tight smile. 'Lost in my own little world, Detective.'

'Okay... so you walk through the woods, cross the road and then what?'

'I carried on walking, and stopped on the bridge to look at the waterfall. I think I must have been there a while because it sort of hypnotised me and I wasn't in a rush. Then the doctor's wife screamed and when I turned to see what she was screaming at... that's when I noticed the body.'

'And was there anyone else around, either when you came in or walking in front of you?'

Mark shook his head. 'No. There was just me. I think.' He frowned. 'I can't be 100 per cent sure about that. Like I said, I wasn't taking much notice.' Mark sighed. 'Honestly, Officer, I don't think there's anything more I can tell you. The doctor and his wife probably noticed more than I did.'

The officer gave a weary sigh. 'Well, thank you for your help and if you do think of anything else that might be relevant you can give us a call any time.' He handed Mark a card, which he tucked in his pocket. 'And what are your plans now?'

'I'll be going back to the hotel.'

'I meant in the near future. Are you staying in the area?'

'I'm booked for tonight, then I need to head back home.'

'We'd prefer it if you could stay around for the time being, sir. It's very early in the investigation and there's a good chance we'll want to speak to you again. Oh, and I could do with seeing your ID and getting your contact details, please.'

Mark lifted his backpack onto the bench beside him and pulled his wallet from the top pocket. He slid his driving licence across the table to the officer, who took a picture, then he rattled off his address and phone number and that was that. Interview over.

He headed off back to the car park, giddy with relief. That had been intense. Talk about mentally draining, he was completely wrung out and he drove back to the hotel in a daze, collapsing on his bed in the sanctuary of his room.

Finn is dead.

The thought wouldn't leave his head, spinning round and round, like Finn's body in the pool, refusing to go away.

26

Holly had just thrown the last few bits and pieces into her bag, and was almost ready to leave, when there was a loud rap on the front door. She hesitated, then pulled the zipper closed, deciding she would ignore whoever it was. Officially, she wasn't here and if anyone was looking for Finn, then she couldn't help them. Better to lay low until they went, then she could be on her way.

She only needed to grab a couple of things from downstairs then she could get off. It had taken her far longer than she would have liked to get herself organised, her brain scuttling around like a trapped animal, abandoning any attempt at rational thought. *All that blood...* That's what she kept coming back to, unable to shake the terrible image out of her head.

She took her bag to the top of the stairs and was about to head down when the knocking came again, followed by a shout. 'Open up! Police!'

Her heart leapt up her throat, her body paralysed with panic.

The police? Why would they be here?

She was so shocked, she almost lost her balance, but the banister came to her rescue and she clung to it while her brain tried to work out what to do. *Did this mean...? Could it be...?* An image of the large red stain on the concrete floor filled her mind. *All that blood.* She gulped, thinking she might be sick. *Is this about Finn?* It had to be. This wasn't about her past catching up with her because nobody knew she was here. She tried to calm her breathing as she listened.

Silence.

The crunch of feet on gravel. *Are they going?* She hardly dared breathe, straining to hear every sound from outside. The murmur of voices, footsteps retreating. She let out a long breath and was about to make her way downstairs when the banging started up again, almost making her jump out of her skin.

They were at the back door now. The door that wasn't locked. Her heart sank when a voice shouted, 'Police! We're coming in!'

She hung on to the banister, unable to move. Two officers arrived in the hallway below her: an older woman with a very severe haircut and a young man with an acne rash covering his cheeks and chin, who looked like he should still be at school. They peered up at her while she looked down on them, nobody speaking until Holly broke the silence.

'I'm sorry I didn't come down to let you in. I've had a bit of an accident and I'm awfully slow on the stairs at the moment.'

'And you are...?' the woman asked.

Oh God, what the heck should I say? Which identity to choose? Old or new. Which would cause her the least trouble? 'Holly,' she said, eventually, because if they searched her bag, they would find documents with that name on it. 'I'm a friend of Finn's.'

Talk about stating the bleeding obvious. Get a grip. But her brain wasn't listening and she gabbled on, her voice breathy and sounding nothing like a normal person, mindful of the fact that she wasn't supposed to be here on castle property. 'I've been visiting while I got better. I had a fall, you see. Finn said I could recuperate here if I wanted. Just for a few days.'

Her chest was heaving and she knew she sounded panicked. Possibly guilty. Which made her heart race even faster.

The female officer moved to the bottom of the stairs and stared up at her for a moment, her eyes settling on the holdall by Holly's side. 'Going somewhere, are we?'

Holly swallowed. 'Yes, that's right. I'm due to leave today.'

'Hmm, are you now?' The officer cocked her head, her steady gaze unwavering.

'I was waiting for Finn to give me a lift to the station. I'm not sure where he's gone.'

The young man grunted. The woman frowned at him before turning her attention back to Holly. 'I'm afraid that's not happening.' She opened her mouth to carry on, then obviously thought better of it, her voice a little softer. Less confrontational. 'Would you like to come downstairs and then we can talk in the lounge maybe? I'm getting a crick in my neck here and I'm worried you're going to take a tumble. You're looking a bit shaky.' She glanced at the young man, frustration spiking in her voice as she gave him a shove. 'Don't just stand there gawping, go and help her.'

The officer hurried up the stairs and prised Holly's hand off her holdall. 'I'll take that for you,' he said, in a surprisingly gentle tone. He offered her his arm to hold while they slowly made their way down the stairs, her other hand still clamped to the banister. The holdall bumped down the steps behind them.

Even with support, she had to stop a couple of times, her heart beating so fast she was feeling dizzy. And in her head, she could hear that strident voice, sounding very much like her mother, telling her she was stupid. So very, very stupid and now she was going to prison.

The young man led her into the lounge and she sank onto the sofa while the female officer stood in front of the fireplace.

'Can I get you a drink?' the young man asked. 'You're looking awful pale and I could feel you trembling all the way down the stairs.' He didn't wait for her answer, but went into the kitchen and came back carrying a glass of water.

She took it from him, knowing that drinking anything was likely to make her sick, her stomach churning with nerves. Her hands were shaking, making ripples on the surface of the water, and she put the glass on the little table next to her, worried she'd spill it all over herself. *Calm down*, she told herself, annoyed that her body was signalling her anxiety so clearly. *Just calm the heck down.*

'It's a bit of a shock to see you here.' She could hear the tremor in her voice. 'It's got me worried.'

'And why would us being here worry you?' The female officer's stony gaze felt like a challenge.

Holly looked at the floor, her hands wrapping themselves together in her lap. 'Because Finn isn't here. But his truck's in the driveway. And I haven't seen him this morning and I knew he hadn't fed the dogs because they were going mad.' She glanced up at the female officer. 'It's out of character. And I didn't know what to do, so I just got myself ready like we'd planned, hoping he'd be back any minute.' She blinked. 'And then you turned up.'

The young man sat in the chair by the fire and pulled a notebook out of his pocket, flipping to a clean page, before he started scribbling notes.

'I have some bad news for you, I'm afraid,' the female officer said. She paused. 'Finn has been found dead in the pool under the waterfall. Just at the back of the house.'

Holly's hands covered her face and time seemed to stop as reality hit. *Dead. Oh my God. Finn is actually dead.*

It was hard to take in and she sat there for a moment, her breath rasping in and out as the words circled in her mind. *Dead.*

The terrible realisation that she was in very deep trouble sent adrenaline pumping round her body, and her brain finally woke up. She leant forwards, her elbows on her knees, fingers pinching the bridge of her nose as her options spun in her head. *I've got to get this right.* Finally, she sat back and took a sip of water, her hand shaking so much it was hard to keep hold of the glass.

'He was acting a bit weird yesterday,' she said, looking at the female officer over the rim of the glass, glad that it offered her a bit of protection, a barrier between her and them.

'What do you mean by weird?'

'You know, all agitated and a bit distracted. Off in another world in his head.' She took a gulp of water, put the glass down carefully before whispering. 'Did he... Was it... suicide?'

Silence for a beat.

The female officer's gaze didn't waver. 'No, we believe it was murder.'

Her heart leapt as the easy option flew out of window. 'Murder? Oh my God.' Her hands clasped at her chest. She shook her head, momentarily lost for words. If it was murder, they were looking for a suspect and right at that moment, she must be top of their list. How suspicious did it look that she had her bag packed and was ready to go? Her pulse raced faster. The very last thing she needed was the police investigating her and digging into her past. That would really taint their opinion of what might have happened.

'We'll be getting a search warrant, of course, but at this stage we need anything you can tell us about yesterday. Anything unusual or suspicious.'

They didn't appear to be talking to her like she was a suspect, which gave her a smidgen of hope. She took another sip of water, put the glass back on the side table, giving herself time to think. 'Okay, well there were a few things.'

She started to speak, mentally crossing her fingers, hoping she'd made the right call. Because making the wrong call would mean all those years of running away, all that hardship and awfulness, would have been for nothing. This was about self-preservation now and she would throw all the ammunition she had into the mix.

27

Mark woke a couple of hours later feeling groggy and muddleheaded, always the consequence of a daytime sleep for him. It did terrible things to his equilibrium and he tried to avoid it if possible. Today of all days, when he needed to be sharp, it left him feeling grumpy and agitated.

He stretched and yawned and decided a shower might freshen him up. Unfortunately, it didn't, his mind on an anxiety loop that was driving him mad. So many stupid what ifs and should haves. Why wouldn't his brain listen to reason?

At the centre of his worries was Holly. He was desperate to go and see her and make sure she was okay. Surely the police must have finished with her by now? Would forensics still be there, though, searching the house and the immediate area? How long would it take for the coast to be clear?

Hmm, when he thought about it, he supposed it might take a while. And he couldn't risk turning up at her house when the police were there, because he'd told them he was just a member of the public passing by. No connection to either her or Finn at all. Even though Mark's prints would be all over the chopping table in the outbuilding if they dusted it down. Would they do that, given he was found in the water? He tugged at his hair and did another lap of his room before deciding he was probably getting himself worked up about nothing.

He made himself a coffee and sat in the chair by the bay window, watching the traffic and the people going about their ordinary day while his had become surreal.

Finn is dead.

Obviously that was a big deal, but his main concern was Holly. If only he had her number. But then there would have been evidence of a direct connection between the two of them, and given the circumstances, that would not have been good at all.

Things are perfect as they are.

That was a favourite mantra he used when he was in a tight spot. He willed himself to believe it. If he could stop himself panicking and relax into the moment, his brain would work better. And he needed his brain to work because there were decisions to be made.

Maybe I should just go home to Wales?

The thought popped into his head, shocking him into still-ness. It was an option. A definite option, and one he needed to sit with for a little while, just to make sure he wasn't being stupid. Things were serious. A man was dead. He didn't need to be involved, did he?

He closed his eyes, thoughts of Holly flooding his brain. Her lovely smile, that laugh, her beautiful voice, the softness of her kiss. The undeniable spark between them. Did he want to throw away the chance of a relationship with this amazing woman? His heart was breaking at the idea this might be the end. *Isn't she worth the risk?*

He glanced at his watch and decided he'd give it another

hour, then it would probably be safe to go back and check on Holly. He'd take it step by step, knowing that he could bail out at any time. That was the way to do it. Feel his way forwards, then it wouldn't feel quite so scary. He took a couple of deep breaths, his heart rate slowing now he'd worked it through in his mind. The main thing was to stop catastrophising and keep a level head.

He had no idea how the police investigation might work, or what the timescales were likely to be. *Perhaps I need to wait a little longer than an hour?* He checked his watch again, heard his stomach growl and realised he was starving. He stood up and stretched, kneading the muscles at the back of his neck. He'd go and get himself a late lunch, then he'd be fortified and ready for whatever might unfold.

He had his hand on the door handle, about to leave his room, when a thought made his brain freeze in horror.

Oh God, the Insta messages. His legs felt suddenly weak and he leant against the door, fumbling his phone from his pocket. *The police can't see those.*

He deleted everything at his end, so there was no trace of their conversations, and a weight lifted from his chest. *Phew, that was close.* Ideally, he should have done it earlier, but hopefully it was soon enough for the police to never know there was a connection between him and Holly. Thankfully, he'd saved the video of them singing to his secure storage system at home, so it didn't matter if it wasn't on his phone or online any more.

Then he questioned himself, not sure of his facts. If he deleted the messages on his phone, would they still be visible on Holly's? Oh God, he had a feeling they might be. Hopefully she'd already deleted them.

His stomach gave another growl and he pushed his phone

back in his pocket, thinking there was nothing more he could do. He opened the door, startled to find himself face to face with two police officers.

28

The detective Mark had been speaking to earlier had a surprised look on his face, his hand raised in a fist as if to knock. But his surprise was nothing compared to the utter shock that Mark was experiencing. His heart almost jumped out of his chest and it was all he could do not to scream. He froze for a moment before managing to speak, hoping he didn't sound as horrified as he felt. 'Oh, hello Detective. I was... er... just going out to get some lunch.'

'Too late, sir.' The detective had a determined glint in his eye, his face set in an ominous frown. 'I'm arresting you for the murder of Finn McKinley.'

It took a couple of seconds for his words to register. Mark swallowed, blinked and finally managed to splutter an indignant reply. 'What? No, you can't do that. I had nothing to do with his death, I was just walking past the cottage, looked over the side of the bridge and there he was in the pool.'

The other officer shook his head and calmly read him his rights while Mark stared at him, his mouth gaping. 'Save whatever you want to say for when we get to the station,' DS Campbell said. 'You'll be formally interviewed and you can have legal representation.'

There was a detective on either side of him now, and one of them tucked Mark's arms behind his back before deftly fastening him in handcuffs. He'd clearly had a bit of practice at that particular manoeuvre, and they bustled Mark down the stairs and through the foyer, to the waiting car.

Mark's body was rigid, every instinct telling him to fight, to squirm, to wriggle his way out of this, but the sensible part of his brain told him to relax. Things would sort themselves out once he'd been able to have his say. After all, he wasn't guilty, was he?

Unfortunately, that thought provided little comfort, his brain listing all the miscarriages of justice that had come to light. People who'd spent years, even decades, in jail for crimes they hadn't committed. The police fitting the crime to the person they had in custody, rather than managing to find the guilty party.

He'd been trying to help a woman in distress and now it had come to this. Arrested for murder. *Oh God.* He wanted to cry, he really did.

29

The police went through all the formalities, taking his fingerprints and a DNA sample, before sitting him in an interview room, where he was allowed to speak to a duty solicitor. Almost three hours after Mark was taken to the station, they actually came to interview him. He'd almost fossilised in his chair, waiting for something to happen, and was shocked out of his stupor when the door was flung open and the two detectives walked in. They looked stern and sure of themselves, a folder thrown onto the desk with a practised flick of the wrist, before they both sat down and stared at him.

The door opened again and the duty solicitor hurried in, having excused herself for a fag break more than forty minutes ago. Angela, she was called, and Mark wasn't confident she'd been listening while he told her the same tale he'd told the police, almost verbatim. He'd wondered whether he should tell her the absolute truth, that he'd had an encounter with Finn in the outbuilding during the hailstorm, but he didn't in the end. He decided it was better to be consistent than completely honest. As it was, he'd dug himself a hole now and he would have to sit in it and hope.

His fingers tapped on the table, playing the melody from 'Fly Away', while the detectives went through the formalities for the benefit of the tape. He couldn't get that song out of his head and the words were so pertinent, it felt like an omen. Him and Holly in this mess together. Hopefully they'd get out of it together too.

'Can you stop that, Mark,' his solicitor said, putting a hand over his fingers, much like you would a child's to stop them fidgeting. 'We need you to focus.'

He flashed her an apologetic smile. 'I'm so sorry. It's a nervous tic.'

The detectives exchanged a look. 'And what would you have to be nervous about?' DS Campbell asked.

'Being arrested for something I didn't do.' He gave them an angry glare. Both of them. First DS Campbell. Then the other one, whose name he hadn't caught. Best to stand your ground, he'd learnt, however much your insides felt like jelly.

DS Campbell opened the folder and slid a photograph across the table. A picture of the boning knife with blood encrusted on the blade. 'Do you recognise this knife?'

Mark glanced at the picture and pushed it back across the table. 'No, never seen it before in my life.'

'Well, that's odd because your fingerprints are all over it.'

Mark started coughing and it just wouldn't stop, going on and on until he thought he would retch. His solicitor fussed over him, patting him on the back, as if that would thump his guilt out of him and allow him to breathe again. 'Can my client have a glass of water please? I won't let you interview him in this state.'

A glass of water duly appeared, Mark took a few grateful sips and finally, his coughing subsided.

'I might have omitted to tell you something,' he said carefully, ignoring the quizzical look on his solicitor's face. 'But I didn't think it was relevant at the time.'

The detectives exchanged another glance, obviously having a telepathic link that negated the need for words. 'Go on,' DS Campbell said, while Angela tugged at Mark's sleeve, trying to get his attention.

He turned to her. 'It's okay. It's better to be honest. When I was first interviewed, I thought it would just muddy the waters, so to speak. You know, complicate the whole picture and maybe send the police off down the wrong track. But I can see that was a mistake.'

'Honesty is always the best policy,' DS Campbell said, without a hint of sarcasm.

Mark almost laughed at that little nugget of wisdom. He sat for a moment, staring at his fingers splayed out on the table in front of him. *How much of the truth to tell?* That was the question.

'So yesterday... I was walking round the castle grounds and there was a massive hailstorm. I don't know if you can remember it? Anyway, I was coming back from the moors and it started when I was walking past the cottage. It was really intense, so I dashed around thinking there might be somewhere to shelter, otherwise I was going to get drenched. And those hailstones were huge, you know, they really hurt.'

He took another sip of water, three pairs of eyes staring at him, hanging on to his every word. 'There was no vehicle in the drive, no sign that anyone was home. Thankfully, the outbuilding at the back of the cottage was open. So, I slipped in there while I waited for the storm to pass.' He looked from one detective to the other, making sure he had their full attention. 'It was unlike any outbuilding I had ever seen. Dead birds hanging up, and I realised it was where someone must butcher the kills from the shoots. I'll admit I'm quite nosy, so while I was waiting for the storm to pass, I opened the drawers and I was looking at the knives, just for something to do.' He took another sip of water. 'To my absolute shock, the door opened and that man who died walked in.'

DS Campbell was staring at him so intently, Mark knew he couldn't make a wrong move, not a flinch or a twitch or a glance in the wrong direction. This was make or break time and he pulled on all his experience as a performer to steady his nerves.

'And what time was this?'

Mark shrugged. 'It was late morning, maybe lunch time. I can't be sure. I'm sorry, I didn't check. But surely the Met office would know when the storm came through.'

The detective nodded. 'Aye, okay, carry on.'

'I didn't think he'd be too chuffed at me messing with his butchery knives and I had that boning knife in my hand, so I slipped it up my sleeve, apologised for trespassing and made my exit.' He pulled up his sleeve, showing the cut on his arm stuck together with plasters.

'See, this is what I did to myself with that knife. So, I think you may find that the blood on the blade is mine, not Finn's. It fell out of my sleeve on my way to the car park and I was in such a hurry to get out of there, I didn't notice where I dropped it.'

The detectives exchanged yet another glance, this one involving a raised eyebrow and an imperceptible shake of the head.

DS Campbell took the picture of the knife back. 'Obviously the blood on the knife is being checked against the victim's. But we'll make sure to check it against your DNA sample as well.'

Mark couldn't work out if the detective believed his story or not. Beads of sweat broke out on his forehead and he swallowed, sure that he had nothing to hide in terms of the knife, but feeling a flood of guilt all the same. 'Of course, no problem.'

'Did you knock on the door of the house at all?'

Mark hesitated, wondering if this was a trick question. He thought it was. Had Holly told them he'd been there? His heart did a peculiar flutter, making him think for a moment that he might be sick. *Answer the question,* he told himself, aware that the silence had been a little too long for comfort. It was a simple yes or no answer but he dithered a moment longer. *Is this the right time to bend the truth a little?* Finally, after a surreptitious nudge from his solicitor, he made a choice. 'I did, yes, to see if I could shelter, but nobody answered.'

'That's odd. Miss Rhodes told us that a man had knocked on the door several times that day. She said he was persistent and wouldn't go away until her partner came home.' DS Campbell's gaze intensified. 'Was that you? Were you causing a nuisance? Were you involved in Finn's murder?'

Mark's eyes widened, blindsided for a moment. *She said what?*

30

That same afternoon, Holly was taken down to the police station to make her formal statement. She didn't think they had many murders in the area because everyone seemed to be a bit at sixes and sevens.

It was obviously a shock to the whole community because Finn was a larger-than-life figure, someone who was well known locally. He'd even been arrested a couple of times for being drunk and disorderly in his younger days, when he'd been involved in barroom brawls. He'd told Holly that with a certain amount of pride, and looking back now, she should have seen the red flag, the one that signalled a tendency to violence. But she'd believed him when he said he'd grown out of that behaviour, putting it down to a youthful surge of hormones and drinking too much.

Lots of people were charming before alcohol revealed a whole different personality. She'd already learnt that lesson, but... She sighed. There was no point dwelling on that part of her past.

During her interview, she stuck to her story of only being in

Finn's house for a couple of days and told them a tale about travelling round the UK before that, sofa surfing while visiting old friends. She'd left them with a ream of spurious people and addresses to check. It had been a risky strategy, but if she told the truth, and that led them to the hotel in Buxton, then she'd be in real trouble.

Thankfully, the interview didn't take long and she was told she was free to go. She hurried out of the police station, as fast as her bruised body would allow, happily aware that she was no longer the prime suspect. No, that would be Mark.

It was unfortunate, but she couldn't help the way the police had interpreted what she'd told them. They already appeared to have set their sights on a specific narrative, and seemed to think he'd been behaving suspiciously. Now she thought about it, perhaps it *had* been a bit weird, him chasing up here when they'd only known each other a couple of days and not spent more than an hour and a half together.

Of course, she hadn't told the police he'd done that because she'd sent him a picture of her poor face. Or even that she knew him. All she'd said was a stranger had turned up on the doorstep and Finn had found him in the outbuilding nosing around. *No, Officer*, she'd said, *neither of them knew who he was*. Or at least she didn't. She couldn't speak for Finn.

It felt bad to shift the blame on to Mark, when he'd been so lovely to her and all he'd been trying to do was to make sure she was okay. But the fact she'd been in Finn's house at the time when he'd died must have put her top of the list of suspects, so she had to deflect attention somewhere else. And she'd played up the severity of her injuries, making out she could barely walk after her fall, let alone attack a man who was six foot two, with arms as big as her thighs and solid as a tree.

In a way, by playing decoy, even though Mark wasn't aware

that's what he was doing, he was helping her more than he could ever know. They'd work out it wasn't him soon enough and then he could go back to where he came from, probably wishing that he'd never become embroiled in her terrible drama.

A sadness tugged at her heart. If they'd met at another time, Mark could have been the one. But any potential for a relationship with him was surely over. Her chin wobbled, tears pricking at her eyes.

What a terrible, terrible day this has turned out to be.

She still had to work out what to do now. The police had told her not to leave town, and that made her twitchy, just in case they *did* bother to check on that list of names and addresses she'd given them. *I can't stay, can I?*

31

In the interview room, Mark took another sip of water, his brain so busy his head felt like it was overheating. He glanced at his solicitor, needing support from somewhere but knowing he was on his own. He had to answer the question.

'No, Officer, you're wrong. I didn't kill Finn and I only knocked on the door once. But I did see a few other people out walking, so maybe it was one of them?'

The detective didn't look like he believed him. He leant back in his chair, arms folded across his chest. 'Am I right in thinking you drive a black Ford Focus?'

The change in tack threw Mark for a moment, but there was no point lying and it was a simple question. 'Yes, that's correct.'

'We believe a black Ford Focus was seen on the driveway of the gamekeeper's cottage at 10 p.m. yesterday. Was that your car?'

Mark reeled. Another question straight from the left field and his anxiety levels notched a little higher, an unpleasant question forcing itself into his head. *Am I being set up?* His gut instinct told him the answer to that was yes and it was like a stab to the heart. *What else has Holly told them?*

His fingers started tapping out the intro to another of the songs he'd sung with her, until his solicitor slapped a hand over his. The action startled him and he frowned at her, sensing she was feeling as uncomfortable as he was.

'Can you answer the question?' the detective asked.

'No, it wasn't my car,' Mark insisted. 'Of course it wasn't. Thousands of people drive black Ford Focuses. Why do you think it was me?'

The detective didn't answer, just came at him with another question. 'Can you account for your whereabouts at that time?'

The questions landed like physical blows. It was all getting a bit too intense for comfort and Mark locked his jaw, while his heart pounded. *Just keep answering the questions*, he told himself, *and eventually, they'll have to let you go.* He gave a frustrated sigh. 'I was at my hotel. People saw me.'

'At 10 p.m.?'

Mark frowned, a sinking sensation in his stomach as he realised he had no proper alibi. 'Well, no. I'm not sure anyone saw me at that exact time. I was in the bar, but I'd gone to bed by then.'

The other detective leaned forward in his seat and chipped in with a question. 'You've lied to us once already, so why should we believe it wasn't you that killed him?'

'Isn't there CCTV on the castle entrance? I'm sure one of you told me there was.'

DS Campbell grunted, his pen tapping on his notebook. 'There is, but apparently it's not operational at the moment.'

'That still doesn't mean it was me.' Mark shot a glance at his solicitor, feeling hemmed in by the barrage of questions. She gave him a nod.

'Detective, you're badgering my client now.' Angela gave the detectives a stern look; first one, then the other. 'He said it wasn't him. Can I suggest you check with staff at the hotel. They might have an operational CCTV system that shows he didn't leave the premises.' There was a weary, patronising tone to her voice and Mark decided he liked her more already.

It was becoming clear the police had jumped to an obvious conclusion without dotting the i's and crossing the t's. He'd explained the knife situation now and he was certain everything else they were throwing at him was circumstantial. *They have no actual proof.*

At that moment, the door opened and another officer leaned into the room. 'Can I have a word, boss?'

DS Campbell left the room for a moment and came back in with a face like thunder.

'Interview terminated at 16.04 p.m.' He picked up the file and pointed it at Mark. 'I'd like you to stay here for the time being. We'll be back shortly.'

Angela had a satisfied smirk on her face when the door shut and they were alone, like she'd enjoyed the fact they'd had to back off.

'I've got to ask you...' she said carefully as her eyes met his. 'Did you tell the whole truth then? This murder is nothing to do with you?'

Mark finished his glass of water, noticing his hand shaking. He'd never been interviewed by police before and that was more nerve-wracking than he could possibly have imagined. He felt so shaky he yearned to have a lie down but knew he could be here for quite a while yet.

He turned to Angela, needing her to believe him. 'Honest to God, that was the truth. It's my blood on that knife. Unless someone else picked it up and used it as the murder weapon.' He frowned. 'Have they even checked it's the murder weapon yet?'

'Hmm, I don't know. I'm going to see what they've got and try and get you out of here. They can't hold you on the basis that they might find something against you. But because it's a murder investigation they do have a bit longer than usual to keep you in custody.' She stood and put a comforting hand on his shoulder. 'I know this is easy for me to say, but try not to worry.'

She left the room and he was alone with his thoughts, going over the questions they'd asked him. Holly must have told them he'd knocked on the door. She'd landed him in it. But, in her defence, it was the truth and she didn't really know him. If her partner had been stabbed, he supposed it would be common sense to look at Mark as a potential killer. He couldn't blame her for that, could he? Of course she'd be suspicious. Anybody would.

The black Ford Focus car in the drive could potentially belong to the killer, so he hoped the police would now focus their attention on finding whoever it belonged to.

He laid his head on the table, so weary, his body was struggling to hold him upright. Half a lifetime later, the door opened and an officer came in to take him down to a cell to await the outcome of further investigations.

The following afternoon, when he'd been in police custody for over twenty-seven hours, Angela strutted into his cell, looking very pleased with herself. 'You can go. The blood on the knife is yours, not the victim's. The autopsy has been completed now and the pathologist says it's not the murder weapon. Not the right size or shape for the stab wound. And they located the owner of the black Ford Focus on the drive too – it was one of the victim's work colleagues.' She beamed at him. 'Come on, let's get you out of here.'

Mark burst into tears.

32

He walked back to his hotel, deep in thought. It had been a harrowing experience being interviewed by the police. Harrowing with a capital H, and he had no intention of going through that again.

As soon as he walked into the hotel, he sensed a change in the atmosphere, the landlady giving him a frosty glare.

'Is everything okay?' she asked, obviously curious to know why he'd been carted off in handcuffs, but not able to ask the question outright.

'Fine,' he said, with a tight smile. 'Everything's fine. Just a case of the police misinterpreting evidence, that's all. Thankfully they've realised I was just an innocent bystander.'

The landlady's face softened then. 'So, what's happened? I've heard all sorts of rumours, but have no idea what's true. People are saying there's been a murder!'

'That's right. The gamekeeper at Castle Drumlanrig. Finn McKinley. The solicitor was telling me everyone knows him round here.'

The landlady tutted. 'Aye, you're not wrong. That guy treads a thin line, always a whisker away from trouble.'

Mark sighed. 'Not any more.'

'And you're sure he's... dead?'

'Yes. I'm sorry to say I'm absolutely sure. I just happened to be there when the body was found.' He frowned, not really wanting to relive the events of the previous day. 'It appears somebody stabbed him and threw him in the river. Well, maybe they didn't throw him, I've no idea, but that's where he ended up. In the pool under the waterfall at the back of his cottage.'

'Never!' she exclaimed, eyes wide, her hands flying to cover her mouth.

'I'm afraid so.'

She sank into the seat behind the reception desk. 'Och, that must have been a terrible shock finding him.'

'It was. And then...' His lower lip started to wobble and for one awful moment he thought he might break down right in the middle of reception. He squeezed his eyes shut, pinching the bridge of his nose to keep his emotions in check. Thankfully, it worked and he was able to carry on. 'The police started jumping to conclusions, and that's been a pretty awful ordeal.' He gulped. 'And I just need a bit of a lie down.'

Her voice was full of concern now. 'Of course you do. That must have been a terrible experience.'

He made a move towards the stairs but she hurried after him and caught his arm. 'I take it you'll be staying a few more days then? It's just you only booked until last night. Shall I extend your booking for you?'

He gave her a weary smile. 'Yes, they've asked me to stay in the area for a little while longer and I'm happy to do whatever it takes to help their enquiries.'

She smiled at him. 'A couple more days, then?'

He nodded. 'Thank you. That sounds about right.'

She bustled back to the reception desk and got busy on the computer while he plodded up the stairs, wondering what this was going to end up costing him in hotel bills. He didn't have limitless resources and this trip was turning into an absolute car crash as far as his finances were concerned. He needed to lie down and focus, really focus, on his goal and what he could do now to achieve it.

His room was a cool sanctuary of calm and he closed the curtains and lay on his bed, relieved to have some peace and quiet at last. He decided he'd have a snooze and went to set the alarm on his phone, which the police had returned to him when he was released from custody.

The battery was dead. Of course it was. It was one of those days when nothing went right. He plugged it into the charger and waited for it to come to life. A whole series of pings alerted him to nine messages. He stared at the screen, not sure he could cope with any more surprises.

Oh God, he thought, as he began to scroll, *what fresh hell is the day going to throw at me now?*

33

After a short delay, a police officer gave Holly a lift back to the gamekeeper's cottage. The forensic work was now completed inside, although there was still a team finishing up outside.

She sat in the lounge, watching the sun dip below the trees, the shadows lengthening while her mind sought answers. *What do I do now? Is there anyone I can trust to help me?*

She thought about Sofia, who was more like an auntie than a boss, but she didn't dare speak to her after the incident with Greg, and then running off without telling her she was going. She'd be angry at being left in the lurch and, with the possibility of police involvement, Holly wasn't sure where she stood with her now.

There was one name she kept coming back to. Beth. The person who'd been her rock, her trusted advisor during the tumultuous years of her early adult life. Beth had been a youth worker in Birmingham, the place where Holly had ended up after running away from home when she was sixteen. It wasn't a conscious choice in terms of location; it was where the train she'd jumped on had terminated. At the time, it felt like a good place to get lost in. A place where she couldn't easily be found. *Yes, Beth might be able to help.* It was a long shot, but now Mark had been arrested, she was her only hope.

The police had packed up outside now and everywhere was quiet, the light beginning to fade. She peeked out of the window, checking she was alone, which wasn't necessarily a good thing because it felt pretty creepy. Finn had died here last night and the echoes of his death still reverberated in the air. She could hear snatches of conversation, his deep belly laugh, him shouting to the dogs, murmuring in her ear, telling her she was a bonny wee lassie.

A tear tracked down her cheek. Despite everything he'd done, regardless of the unpredictable monster he'd turned out to be, she'd never wanted him dead. All she'd wanted was to get away.

She heaved a sigh and pushed herself up from her chair, her body creaking after sitting there for so long. Her holdall was still in the hallway and she opened it up, unsurprised to find it had been searched through and re-packed. Of course it had. She took out the envelope that contained her important documents – her friend's birth certificate, National Insurance number, bank details. The letter from the passport office with her passport number on and instructions of what to do if it was lost. And her little address book.

It was old school, and there weren't many names in there, but she preferred to keep a paper copy of important numbers. Phones got lost, or had to be disposed of when you didn't want to be found. No point having all her contacts on there, just in case.

She rummaged in the holdall until she found her old pair of trainers and felt inside, pulling out the old socks she'd stuffed in there. Thank goodness she'd thought to stash her real birth certificate under the sole, and it was still there, apparently untouched. Her hand felt something hard in the sock and she smiled to herself as she tipped out her old phone. It didn't look like the police had found that either, which was very good news indeed. Because it meant they wouldn't be tracking her calls. There was just one problem, one major problem. No charger. She'd left it in the hotel in Buxton, in her haste to leave.

Oh wait... Her eyes widened as she remembered something magical. Finn had one of those multi-cable chargers in his truck. She remembered him telling her he had adapters for every make of phone, and the ones he didn't use were stowed in the glove box. *Oh joy!* She dashed outside, delighted that she'd remembered right, and there it was, the charger and its many attachments. It had a plug to fit in the car and another that would fit in the house. She found the right lead, grabbed the plug and hurried back to the kitchen, excited that she would soon be connected to the outside world again.

She leant against the worktop, staring at her phone as she waited for it to start to charge, but it was taking so long, she wondered if maybe the lead wasn't right after all. Then the phone beeped and the screen flashed to life. She let out a whimper of relief and waited until it was 10 per cent charged before she made her call.

'Hello, Beth here. Who's this?' The Brummie accent was enough to bring a tear to Holly's eye, the warm tone of her friend's voice like a soothing balm. Her mind filled with all the times that voice had calmed her down over the years and helped her sort out her problems. Beth was the one who'd helped her get a bank account and arranged proper accommodation. She'd even helped her to get her first job. She'd a lot to thank Beth for and she trusted her completely.

'It's Holly. Holly Rhodes. Remember me?'

Silence for a moment, then a laugh. 'How could I ever forget? This is a surprise, it's been so long. How are you?'

'I'm fine,' she said, before letting out a big sigh. She pulled a chair from under the table and sat, still tethered to the plug socket by the charging lead. Her shoulders folded forwards, the weight of her predicament bearing down on her. 'No, well, actually, I'm in a spot of bother. I hope you don't mind me ringing.'

Another laugh. 'Why am I not surprised? No, I don't mind, but I've retired now, so I'm not sure what use I can be.'

'I just need to talk things through, if that's okay? And I'm glad you've retired. That job was way too stressful, helping out stupid kids like me.'

'You were not stupid.' Holly stifled a laugh at Beth's stern tone, a welcome blast from the past. 'You just freaked out and didn't know what to do. That's a normal reaction at sixteen, so we'll have none of that talk. Anyway, what you been up to? Come on, fill me in. I've got a glass of wine here, TV is rubbish, let's see if I can help.'

Holly closed her eyes, letting her thoughts settle into some sort of logical order before she started to speak, giving Beth a concise version of her life story since she'd last seen her, almost ten years ago.

'Oh, my word, you're a magnet for unfortunate events, aren't you?'

Holly gave a frustrated huff. 'I know, it had to happen to me, didn't it?'

'It's not your fault, bab. Really, it's not, so don't go beating yourself up about it. You're just a bit impulsive, aren't you? See things in black and white and don't see the warnings.' Beth's sigh crackled down the line. 'It's because you have a lovely, trusting nature. That's your main downfall. People take advantage.'

Holly's emotions surged through her, tears streaming down her face. Beth always saw the best in people, whereas Holly's inner voice could only see the worst in herself. Unfortunately, kind words weren't going to solve her problems now.

She sniffed and blew her nose as she listened to Beth's advice. 'I think, at this stage, you've got to accept there are going to be things you don't want to do. But it's a matter of choosing the least worst option, because I can't see an easy way out of this one.'

'I know. But I'm so tired of running away. I was happy in Buxton until that stupid chef...'

'I can understand your response to that incident, especially if you reported Greg and nothing changed. But...' She sighed, quiet for a moment. 'I'm not going to judge because I wasn't there. What's done is done. We've got to look at how that changes things for you now.'

They chatted for over an hour and when Holly finally ended the call, her mind was made up. She knew what she had to do. It was just a matter of timing.

34

Mark didn't want to look at his messages, but he couldn't help scrolling through, speed reading before putting his phone down. It was a timely reminder that however much the police wanted him to stay locally, he had to get back home. Urgently. He'd been away too long already and had things to attend to that couldn't wait. Life and death type things.

He felt grubby and grimy after his experience at the police station and decided he'd have a shower, get himself packed and then try and sneak out when the landlady was busy serving the evening meal. That was only an hour away.

Although he knew it was the right decision, he still felt torn, unsure if leaving was going to get him into a heap of trouble. But that was life, wasn't it? A whole series of difficult decisions and moral dilemmas to navigate. At the end of the day, though, some things had to take priority.

The hot shower made a world of difference, followed by a cup of tea once he'd gathered his few possessions together. Now he was ready to face the world again and he'd made a decision. He was going to get Holly and take her with him. Sod the police.

How would they know where they were anyway? He'd watched that series on TV – *Hunted* – and had seen which tactics worked the best to make sure nobody knew where you were. Anyway, nobody was going to stop him from being with his love, not now that he'd found her. How could he leave her behind? How could he throw this opportunity for love away when it may never come again?

He managed to sneak out of the hotel without anyone noticing, making sure he was wearing his baseball cap to hide his face. He drove to the castle, relieved to see the car park was empty, and he hurried through the woods, his heart pounding in his chest. Would she come with him? That was the only doubt in his mind. He banged on the door, waiting for the twitch of the curtains, but everything was quiet. Very, very quiet. He banged again. No answer.

Unease churned in his stomach as he walked round the side of the house, the only sound the rushing of the river. No dogs barking. He peered through the kitchen window. It was dusk now but no lights were on, and there were no signs of movement. His heart sank, a feeling of emptiness hollowing out his chest. She wasn't there.

He heard his phone beep again with another message. He didn't even have to look at it to know what it said. He clenched his jaw, the weight of disappointment feeling heavy in his heart. *I've got to go home.*

35

He walked around to the front of the house and knocked again, even though he knew it was pointless. The place had that air of emptiness, the lack of a human spirit inhabiting its rooms.

He was loathe to head off without saying goodbye to Holly, or at least leaving his number, but he really did have to get back home. Yet again, he'd let his heart rule his head. It had been a silly, impulsive idea coming all this way for a stranger.

Emotion clogged his throat, his teeth grinding as his fist thumped the door. *Why can't this be my love story?*

In his head, he could hear the sound of their voices singing in harmony, could hear her laugh, see her wonderful smile. She was perfect. Absolutely perfect. He sighed, leaning against the door. It was fate that led him here, so he'd have to hope that fate would help him out when it came to finding her again.

It was hard to know if she was at the police station, or if she'd gone to stay with relatives or friends. How could he know where she was when she wasn't answering his messages? Realistically, she could be anywhere, but he felt that she was close. It was probably wishful thinking. In fact, the whole dash to Scotland could be filed under that category.

'You and your love stories, you're such a fool.' He could hear his mother's voice, scolding him, trying to stop him from looking for a life partner. She'd wanted him all to herself, that was the problem. Hadn't wanted Mark to have a stable relationship and scuppered any budding romances before they could really begin. Looking back now, he could see how she'd ruined any chance he'd had of finding romance and building his own family.

It had always been his heart's desire to get away from his mum's influence so he could be himself. But try as he might, he'd never managed to make it happen. He was like a yo-yo on a string and she'd been in control. Until recently. Things were different now and he still hadn't got used to his new reality.

She definitely wouldn't approve of this trip and if his mission had taught him anything, he was now certain that finding love was what he wanted most in life. Nothing else mattered. He would make it his top priority to reconnect with Holly but quite how he was going to do that he'd no idea. It seemed he'd just have to wait for fate to step in again, because if they were destined to be together as he believed, somehow it would happen.

With one last glance at the house, he crossed the road and made his way back to the car park, plodding along, deep in thought. The police had told him to stay locally, but he couldn't, and there was no way he wanted this drama with Finn to follow him home.

He'd got the impression the police were trying to nail him as the perpetrator, because that would be the easiest and quickest path for them to follow. Thank goodness for his solicitor. She'd worked a minor miracle getting him released and he'd been very grateful for her efforts. Luck had been on his side, she'd said, because the local force was currently being prosecuted for wrongful arrest, so she'd played on those sensitivities. However, looking at things from the police point of view, if he was the only person vaguely in the frame, it stood to reason they'd keep coming after him.

It was starting to drizzle and he pulled up his hood, only five minutes away from his car now. His mind was still whirring, wondering if he really could get away undetected. The police had his address, but it wasn't where he actually lived. It was an old address, his family home, where he'd lived with his mum until a couple of years ago. When his mum's health had become an issue, they'd sold up to release some cash and moved between rentals. He'd decided that he was happy to live his life moving around, experiencing new places where nobody had their nose stuck into his business. Anyway, all the nicest rental properties were holiday homes, which were often available for long lets over winter. He was presently living in a lovely cottage, tucked away in the hills near Bala, and he was pretty sure he'd be impossible to find.

Except... the police did have his phone number, so he'd have to get a new SIM card and change that over, but it was an easy fix. *Is that everything covered?* He thought so, but the idea of skipping off without telling the police where he was going was putting him on edge.

He'd drive back to Wales, avoiding the motorway so he didn't show up on the number plate recognition system. It would be a long, slow journey, but it meant he'd be lost to the police and hopefully he could live his life in peace without fear of their interference.

His mind was still running through the logistics when he reached the car park. It was dark now and his black car blended into the shadows. A stiff breeze had picked up, making the branches of the trees clatter together, the sound of the wind rustling through the leaves, reminding him of the roar of the waterfall and the dead body spinning in the pool below.

He leant against the car for a moment, resting his head on his arms as he tried to rid his mind of that image. But the death of Finn had him in its clutches, unwilling to let him go. Making him see the blood seeping through his shirt, the glassy stare of his lifeless eyes.

It's not my problem, he told himself as he fished in his pocket for the car keys, fumbling as he pressed the control to unlock the door. Noises echoed in the car park at this time of night, every sound having a twin, just a few seconds after. It was creepy as hell and he flopped into the driver's seat, wanting to leave. But that meant pressing pause on the chance of a relationship with Holly, which was proving hard to accept and made him hesitate. *That's all it is,* he told himself. *Just a pause while things sort themselves out.* At least he didn't have to worry about her being in danger from Finn any more, so he could cling to that as a positive while he waited.

With a sigh, he pulled on his seat belt and started the engine, singing the song that had brought them together in the first place as he drove out of the castle grounds. In his mind, he could hear her voice softly harmonising with his, could almost feel her breath on the back of his neck.

He glanced in his rear-view mirror as he drove past the turn-off to Dumfries and almost had a heart attack when he saw her face. Her real face, not just a memory in his mind. She was in the back seat of his car, sitting right behind him.

36

Mark could feel himself hyperventilating, his gaze stuck on the rear-view mirror, rather than concentrating on the road. Holly hung on to the back of his seat, fear in her eyes as the car swerved towards the kerb.

'I'm so sorry, I didn't mean to startle you,' she said. 'I just needed a way of getting out of the castle grounds without anyone seeing me.'

'Oh my God, I can't believe it,' he squeaked, his voice sounding strangled and not like him at all. 'I'm gonna... I just need a moment to...' He pulled into a lay-by, his hand on his chest, where his heart was pounding ten to the dozen, his eyes staring through the windscreen. He was feeling a bit dizzy and he wondered if he might pass out before he got his breathing under control. Thank God he'd pulled over.

Once he regained his composure, he twisted in his seat to look at her properly. 'How the hell did you get in the car?'

It wasn't an angry question, more incredulous and perfectly reasonable. He knew the car had been locked, so how had she done it? She had very lovely eyes, he noted as they stared at each other, and there was an innocence about her that he found more endearing every time they met.

'I was in the trees by the gate when I saw you drive in. I guessed you were coming to find me and honestly, I can't tell you how relieved I was when I saw you. I thought... well, I wondered if I'd ever see you again after I sent you away.' She was gnawing at her bottom lip, a nervous habit, he guessed, and it touched his heart. He didn't want her to feel anxious. He wanted her to feel protected.

'Anyway, I waited and followed you back to the car park. When you got in the car, I slipped into the back seat.' She laughed. 'Synchronicity.'

'Wow. That's a new level of sneaky.' He still couldn't fathom how he hadn't noticed. But then, he'd been distracted, lost in his thoughts, and when you were busy inside your head, you didn't always notice everything that was going on around you. 'I thought there was an echo. But how the hell did I not notice you getting in?'

She put a hand on his shoulder and her touch lit a fuse inside him. Did he care how she'd done it? No, he didn't think he did. She leant forwards and he could feel her breath on his face. 'Oh, you were away with the fairies. In fact, you looked really fed up. Your head was down, eyes on the floor.' She gave him a nervous smile. 'I don't think you were taking much notice of anything.'

He gazed at her, absorbing her presence, hardly able to believe his own eyes. *She's here in my car. Actually right here.* He put his hand over hers, his heart skipping a beat when her fingers curled around his. *She does feel it too. She really does.*

It was pretty weird how she'd sort of hijacked him though. She could have just called out to him, couldn't she? Why the secrecy? But maybe, after everything she'd said to the police, she thought he might be angry with her. Perhaps she'd thought he wouldn't want to help her any more. He couldn't work it out.

An undercurrent of unease stirred in his belly, but he chose to ignore it for now. He squeezed her hand. 'You're right, I was in a pretty miserable place. Because I thought you'd gone and I might never see you again and that was breaking my heart.'

'Oh, Mark. That's so sweet.' She visibly wilted, a sheen of tears in her eyes, and he felt it again, that magnetic draw towards her, but even stronger this time. Their eyes appeared to be locked together, neither of them wanting to look away. It was so lovely, like floating in a warm sea with nothing but blue skies above.

Finally, she broke eye contact, pulling her hand away from his as she leant back in her seat. She seemed twitchy, nervous, her eyes glancing out of the side window like she was looking for somebody, before focusing back on him. 'I'm sorry I had to send you away when Finn was around.'

He rolled his eyes. 'God, I wish I'd listened. He cornered me in the outbuilding and I can tell you I nearly pissed myself. He's a big guy. Was a...' He grimaced, looked down at his hands, twirling a signet ring round his little finger. 'Sorry. I'm sorry for your loss.'

She blew out her cheeks and looked out of the window again, her jaw tightening. The silence was palpable, a vacuum that was filled by his thoughts running riot, throwing questions at him that he didn't want to hear.

'Yeah,' she said eventually. 'Not a happy ending.'

'It's okay if you don't want to talk about it.'

She nodded. 'I'd rather not. If you don't mind. The whole thing has been major trauma. And then having to deal with police on top of that.' She sighed. 'Nothing but trouble, that man. And it looks like his trouble caught up with him in the end. He was into all sorts of shady deals. Not that I asked for any details, and he definitely wasn't open to sharing. But when you've got people turning up in the middle of the night, you know it's nothing legal.'

His eyes found hers again. There was a particular question he needed her to answer before they went any further. 'They arrested me on suspicion of his murder, you know.'

She chewed at her lip again, blinked a few times. He waited a moment, giving her a chance to say something, but she remained silent.

'Fortunately, their evidence wasn't what they thought it was,' he continued, when it was clear she wasn't going to speak, 'so they had to let me go. Told me to stay locally, but I know I'm innocent, and I need to get back home.'

'Home to Wales?'

He nodded. 'That's right. It's my... There are things I urgently need to attend to.'

'And... do they know where you live?' she asked cautiously. He could see what she was thinking, knew she was asking him if she'd be safe there. If the police would be able to find her.

He smiled at her. 'They think they do, but I gave them an old address.' His smile broadened. 'Nobody knows where I live.'

Her eyes lit up and she leant forwards again. 'I don't suppose... I could come with you, could I?'

He beamed at her, his heart exploding, like all his Christmases had come at once. 'Yes. Yes. If that's what you want. Of course you can.'

Fate had done it again. It was exactly the outcome he'd hoped for when he first set out on this mission two days ago, and he was tingling from the top of his head to the tip of his toes. The fact that she'd sneaked into his car really didn't matter. Neither did the answer to the question he hadn't dared to ask.

37

Mark grinned to himself as he set off again, advising Holly to lie down in the back for a while, so it looked like he was travelling alone. Just until they'd put enough distance between themselves and Dumfries. She was more than happy to oblige and the miles flew by now he was buoyed up on the remarkable fact that, for once in his life, things were going his way. Obviously, it would be better if they weren't both running away from the police, but that made the whole trip feel more romantic. Dramatic. Exciting. They were like Bonnie and Clyde. Fugitives on the run.

Mark had never felt so happy in his entire life, so happy he couldn't stop himself from bursting into song. Their song. Holly, his love, was in his actual car and had asked if she could come home with him. He belted out the words, incredulous that everything he'd hoped for with all his heart had somehow come about.

Holly sang with him, then she was quiet and he realised she was asleep. He hummed softly to himself instead, so he wouldn't wake her. He kept looking in the rear view mirror, making sure they weren't being followed, but he couldn't see anything obvious. No blue flashing lights, that was the main thing, but still his heart was racing.

She was so close, just lying on the back seat; if he stretched out his hand he could touch her, and he wanted to so much it was almost painful. But he kept his hands clamped to the steering wheel. He had to wait, let this romance develop organically, not force things too quickly. He'd made that mistake before and it hadn't turned out well. The main thing was, she was coming home with him and that, in itself, was a massive result.

After a couple of hours, his eyes were feeling scratchy and he stifled a yawn. There was something about driving on busy roads at night that was really stressful, but now the traffic was quieter, he could feel himself getting drowsy.

'I can drive if you're getting tired,' she said, the sound of her voice startling him. 'I mean, I haven't passed my test, but I know how to do it.'

He laughed. 'I don't think we need to risk doing anything else illegal at this stage. I'm okay. We'll just need lots of coffee stops. If you see me nodding off, just give me a nudge.'

It was a long time since he'd pulled an all-nighter, but he was so up for this he didn't think it would be a problem. Mind over matter. He was good at that. *Where there's a will there's a way.*

His repertoire of mottos went round on repeat in his brain, fortifying him for the ordeal ahead. He hated driving at the best of times, but in the dark it was easy to miss junctions and go the wrong way. Unfortunately, his car was old and didn't have satnav, so he had to use the one on his phone and he wasn't confident the directions were correct.

He waggled his phone in the air. 'Can you just check that

I've set this right to get us to Wrexham? I haven't a clue where
we are now. I'm assuming we're going in the right direction but I
have a horrible feeling we might be heading off east instead of
going south. There was a diversion a little while ago and the
instructions stopped making sense.' He frowned, studying a
signpost ahead of him, none of the place names familiar. 'I
think you might need to reset it. Make sure you tell it to avoid
motorways.'

'Sure thing.' She stepped over from the back, slipping into
the passenger seat next to him, something he was happy with
now they were out of Scotland. Their hands touched for a delicious second when she took his phone, sending a thrill zinging
through his body. She glanced at him and he knew from her
wide-eyed expression that she'd felt it too. He'd never taken
illegal drugs, but he imagined the buzz that touch of her skin
had given him was exactly the sort of high you might get. He
grinned to himself. *What a crazy world.*

She was busy for a few minutes. 'That's it. I think I've got it
sorted now.' She tapped a button and a robotic voice told him to
take the second exit at the next roundabout. His shoulders
relaxed a little. That was better. Someone telling you where to
go was so much easier than trying to study signposts as you
were flying past at sixty miles an hour. Especially when it was
dark.

She kicked off her shoes and sat cross legged, her eyes
closed. He wasn't sure if she was meditating or asleep. It was
hard to tell, but he didn't want to disturb her. In the silence, his
mind roamed through the events of the last two days and he
started to tense up again. There were things that needed to be
said, and maybe it would be easier to do that when it was dark
and they were driving and couldn't actually look at each other.

'I keep thinking about Finn,' he said into the darkness, eyes concentrating on the road. 'I found him, you know. In the pool at the bottom of the waterfall. I can't get that image out of my mind.'

She was silent for a long moment and he wondered if she was awake, but a quick glance told him she was staring out of the windscreen. 'I'm so sorry that happened to you. It must have been awful.' She sounded genuinely apologetic, not that it was her fault. But he supposed she meant if she hadn't sent him that picture of her slapped face, he wouldn't have come running to help, and then he wouldn't have had to witness the after-effects of a murder. Yes, that was definitely what she meant.

'It was horrible. And I got the shock of my life when the police came to arrest me. I mean, I'm just some random bloke. What would my motivation be? I couldn't see why they'd try to pin it on me.' He glanced at her, could see her eyes still focused on the road ahead and decided to press on, taking the conversation where it needed to go. 'You told them I'd been knocking at the door. I thought... and I know this is probably daft, but it crossed my mind you were trying to set me up.'

She seemed to shrink away from him, leaning against the door now. 'Oh, the bloody police!' She sounded annoyed. No, more than that. Angry. 'They twist everything you say, don't they? They completely misunderstood what I told them.'

'They did?'

'Yes, they absolutely did.'

'So, you don't think I killed him?'

'No, no, no. I never thought that. Not for a minute.' She was quiet for a moment before she gave a big sigh. 'We had a big row that afternoon. After you'd gone. I told him I was leaving.' She hesitated, a tremor in her voice when she spoke again. 'He threw me down the steps into the cellar and locked me in. Then a few hours later, when he let me out, he behaved like nothing had happened. That's what he was like.'

'He did what?' Mark gasped, his brain feeling like it was going to explode. 'Are you okay?' It sounded like things had escalated very quickly. Obviously, he'd read about men behaving like this towards women, but he'd never actually come across someone who'd experienced it in real life. Probably because it wasn't something people talked about.

'Just about.' She sounded a bit tearful, and who could blame her. 'Lots of bruises, but I'll mend.' She gave another sigh. 'It could have been so much worse.'

He desperately wanted to hold her and tell her she would never have to face anything like that ever again. He would give her his word that from now on, she'd be safe. Better than safe; she'd be loved and cherished and treated like the rare and lovely precious jewel she undoubtedly was.

They drove on in silence for a few moments before a question jumped into his mind.

'Did you tell the police about it? Him throwing you into the cellar?'

She snorted. 'No way. Christ, I'd be banged up by now if I'd told them that, because if there was ever a motive for murder that would be it, right there.'

'*Turn right at the next junction.*'

Mark followed the satnav's instructions, deep in thought. He hadn't considered Holly as a suspect in Finn's murder for some reason, but now he could see that was a bit of an oversight. *She* was the prime suspect.

38

The silence between them seemed to stretch out for days until Mark could bear it no more. He cleared his throat. 'You didn't kill him though... did you?'

Holly didn't reply immediately, her voice low and tinged with disappointment when she eventually spoke. 'I'm surprised you had to ask me that.'

'Just for the sake of clarification,' he said quickly, concerned now that he'd offended her. But every sane person would ask the same question, wouldn't they?

'Do you really think I'd stand a chance against a guy built like a brick shithouse when I'm already battered and bruised from falling down the stairs? I can tell you, I was in shock for the rest of the evening.'

'I'm sorry. I'm really sorry,' Mark blustered, concerned he'd ruined their budding relationship. 'I shouldn't have asked.'

'No, no, it's fine.' She flapped a hand. 'Better to get all this out in the open, isn't it? Especially if we're going to be together for a little while.' She paused. 'I mean, you wouldn't want to be travelling alone at night with a murderer, would you?'

He wasn't sure if she was being serious or if this was some sort of dark humour, and he was confused as to how he should respond. She could have stayed silent, he reasoned, so he took her willingness to speak as a sign of innocence. 'Ha, ha.' He gave a nervous laugh, hoping he'd read the situation right. 'Yes, so true. Full disclosure and all that.'

'So... after a few hours, he let me out of the cellar and he'd made me a lovely meal and there were flowers on the table and a bottle of wine. He knew he'd done wrong, was very apologetic, blah de blah de blah.' She gave a frustrated huff. 'I'm sorry if I'm not sounding like a grieving partner should, but things had morphed from bad to worse pretty rapidly and my feelings for Finn had changed. I was terrified of what he'd do next.'

Mark stayed silent, deciding it was better to let her talk. She puffed out her cheeks, the act of remembering clearly dredging up some difficult emotions. He could hear it in her voice.

'Before I went to the passport office, he'd never hit me. Yes, he'd shouted and grabbed my wrist a bit too tight, and that had probably been enough to make me behave how he wanted. But getting my passport was an act of defiance too far. He knew he'd blown it, so he resorted to violence.' She glanced at Mark. 'I was hoping you'd come back and then I was going to accept your offer of help.'

Oh, my word. She'd been thinking about him. She'd wanted him to save her.

Confirmation that she felt the same way he did sent his mind into a happy dance, relishing possibilities of a future he'd only dreamed about. Until he realised Holly had started talking again and tuned back in to what she was saying.

'Anyway, he went out drinking with his pals in the staff quarters and he came back with some guy. At least I assume it was a guy. I didn't see whoever it was, but their car was in the drive and they went to the outbuilding. I waited for Finn to come back in, but it got really late and eventually I couldn't stay awake. I was so exhausted after all the trauma from earlier.'

She paused. 'When I woke up in the morning, he wasn't there. The dogs were going mental and I knew something was off. But I didn't dare do anything.' Her voice became hard, saturated with anger. 'That's what domestic violence does to you. It makes you powerless. It paralyses you.'

Mark's heart was breaking for her. 'Oh my God, that's so awful. But it sounds like the guy in the black car is the culprit. He killed Finn.'

'Yeah, that's what I think. I told the police, but you have a black car too, and I think they took my earlier comments out of context, and two and two became five and maybe that's why they were so sure you were the murderer.'

Mark was thinking there were a few more reasons why they'd had him top of their list of suspects. Footprints in the mud behind the house. Fingerprints on what had seemed a very likely murder weapon. *Thank God for forensics and DNA.* In another time, he'd already be judged guilty and be hanging from a noose. Anyway, there was no need to tell her any more than she already knew. Why put doubts in her mind when things were going so well?

He loosened his grip on the steering wheel and stretched out his fingers, snatching a glance at Holly only to find her staring at him. His heart did a backflip, his mind racing ahead to another kiss, imagining what her bare skin would feel like against his. He cleared his throat, dragging his mind back to the conversation. 'Well, the guy in the black car is their only lead now. Hopefully they'll find him.'

'Finn was selling game meat illegally. I think it's to do with that. Probably had a row about money or something.'

'Did you tell the police?'

She gave another sigh. 'I can't remember what I did and didn't tell them. I was feeling so out of it when they interviewed me, I just don't know.'

He reached over and rubbed her knee, a warm glow in his heart. 'It's okay. You're safe now. I'll look after you.'

She put her hand over his and a tingle ran right up his arm. 'I know you will, Mark. I absolutely know you will.'

39

Holly woke up with a sense that something was different. It was quiet and still. The car had stopped. She was muzzy with sleep, and she blinked, rubbing at her eyes to try and wake them up a bit, scrubbing at her face with her palms. Gradually, she felt herself come to life and she squinted through the darkness, trying to work out what was going on.

They were in the middle of nowhere, not a streetlight to be seen, or any sort of light for that matter. It was pitch black and the absence of noise was unnerving. No sign of Mark either, the driver's seat was empty.

For a moment, panic gripped her, like some massive hand squeezing all of the air out of her chest. Had he dumped her? Decided she was too much of a liability? Frantically, she peered around, looking for signs of life. Thankfully, her brain clicked into gear at that point.

He's probably had to stop for a pee.

Or he's gone to get some fresh air and a walk around to wake himself up.

The scuff of footsteps made her head snap round, like a

meerkat on patrol hearing sounds of danger. The driver's door opened and Mark peered in at her before landing in his seat with a thump, like someone had thrown a sack of potatoes in the car. He looked completely shattered, his face pale and drawn, his eyes bloodshot slits, like he was struggling to keep them open. She reached out and put a hand on his arm, her brain fully alert now, giving her an idea.

Isn't this exactly the opportunity I've been waiting for?

'Hey, you look shattered, why don't you let me drive for a bit? Then you can have a nap.' He blinked, rubbed at his eyes. 'At least then we can keep going. I doubt they'll start looking for us until morning and we could be safely at your place by the time they realise we've gone.'

He wiped a hand down his face. 'I don't know. It's not easy driving at night. And if you haven't passed your test...' It was ironic that he thought letting her drive on deserted roads without a full licence was a problem. Hadn't they'd both just left town, following a murder, after the police had expressly told them not to?

'The fact that I haven't passed my driver's test doesn't mean I can't drive.' She gave him what she hoped was a reassuring smile. 'When I lived in the Peak District, I often drove the crew home from the pub. I don't really drink, you see.' She broadened her smile, sensing he was wavering. 'I've done lots of night driving along country lanes. Lots. And never had any sort of incident. Not once.'

He stared through the windscreen, his body hunched, his arms resting on the steering wheel. 'Hmm. I don't know. It feels a bit risky.'

Tentatively, she ran the back of her hand down his cheek, feeling the rasp of his stubble. He closed his eyes and gave a deep sigh. She rested her hand on his shoulder and he bent his head, nuzzling her skin with his cheek, just like her cat would do when she was young and still had a home to call her own.

Apart from their first kiss, this was the most affectionate contact they'd shared up to now and it felt like a giant leap forward. It had been a risk, but she knew now that she'd judged it right.

He put his head back against his seat, eyelids drooping, taking a moment to think. Or was he falling asleep? She ruffled his hair, wanting to keep the conversation going. Pushing for a decision. 'I don't think letting me drive is any riskier than you driving when you can hardly keep your eyes open.'

He flashed her a sheepish grin. 'Fair point. Okay, we can give it a try, but if you're making me nervous, you've got to stop and let me take over again.' Her hand was still on his shoulder and he bent and gave it a gentle kiss, looking up at her through his long lashes. A little shiver of pleasure ran though her. 'Promise?'

'Of course, but I think you'll be pleasantly surprised. Hopefully, you'll feel so safe you'll fall asleep, get a good nap and then after an hour or so, you can take over again feeling a bit fresher.'

He nodded. 'Okay, it's a deal. An hour will be plenty.'

They swapped places and adjusted seats until she was ready to set off. She might have exaggerated how often she'd been behind the wheel of a car. In reality, it was only a handful of times in her entire life, and her heart was hammering in her chest as she studied the controls, desperately trying to work out which levers and buttons did what and even how to start the thing. Why hadn't she paid more attention when Mark was driving? But then she hadn't been planning on taking control; she'd been more focused on putting a lot of distance between herself and Finn's dead body.

40

Holly had no option but to run away. No choice at all. Of course it was the right thing to do. *But what if they find me?* Then all that trouble at Buxton would rear its very ugly head. And surely, they'd decide, on the balance of probabilities, that Finn's murder was too much of a coincidence. They'd start looking at her more closely and everything would come out. All her stupid sordid past.

Oh God, it could take months for them to unravel that lot and because she'd always run away from trouble in the past, they'd assume that's what she'd do again. She'd be a flight risk and they'd remand her in custody. In prison for months and months, while they gathered all the evidence, deciding how many of her misdemeanours to charge her with.

The more her thoughts connected the dots, the more certain she was about her destiny. Her skin started to prickle, sweat making her shirt stick to her back. The police didn't listen to people like her. People with history. She knew that from the stories she'd heard over her lifetime. They made assumptions based on the type of life you'd led, the unlucky breaks you'd had to suffer.

Stop it. Stop it now! she instructed her brain. *You're catastrophising again. None of that might happen. Not if this works out.*

She did her breathing exercises, breathing in for five seconds, holding for five, breathing out for five. Guaranteed to work every time. Beth had shown her the technique when she'd first started working with her in Birmingham and had seen how prone she was to panic attacks. What a godsend that woman had been, and now she'd promised to help her again.

It was imperative she make the most of this opportunity to take control, and she straightened her back, concentrating on proving to Mark that she was a competent driver.

He was watching her every move, and even though she kept her gaze on the road, she could feel his eyes on her, his body language screaming that he was nervous. She sensed his legs moving a fraction before hers when she went to change gear or press on the brakes. His hand bracing against the door when they appeared to be rounding a corner too fast. He clearly wasn't going to be falling asleep while he was on edge like this and she chewed at her lip, wondering what else she could do to make him feel secure.

A few minutes later, the answer came to her and she started to sing. Slow, soft ballads, sung like lullabies. At first, he joined in, singing with her, but after a few songs, she could see in her peripheral vision that his head was nodding. Finally, his chin sunk onto his chest and he appeared to be asleep, but she waited a few more minutes just to be sure.

Now for the tricky bit...

Mark was snuffling in his sleep and she decided she could risk stopping for a minute or two while she adjusted their destination on the satnav app. If she could get to Birmingham and the safety of Beth, she'd be home and dry. She just needed new passport forms completing, then the process of getting a replacement could be underway, using Beth's address, while she was holed up in Wales with Mark.

She'd seriously considered Beth's offer to stay with her, but had decided Birmingham was too busy and there was CCTV everywhere. It would be too risky. Better to be in the middle of nowhere, in a place where nobody was likely to notice her arrival.

Once the new passport came through, she would be independent. No need for any man. That was the outcome she was aiming for. Okay, there were a few hurdles to navigate along the way, but you could only take one step at a time; no need to think too far ahead. It was definitely worth a shot and if it didn't pan out as she'd hoped, then she'd have to work out a plan B. Adjust and adapt as she always did.

She glanced across at Mark, the sight of him asleep and vulnerable tugging at her heart. There was no doubt she was attracted to this man. No doubt that he was ideal for her in many ways. But she didn't need another man right now, and look how wrong she'd got it with Finn. She couldn't trust her body's reactions to guide her. They'd deceived her before, her instincts caring more about primeval urges than measured assessments. Mark might well be lovely, but the idea of an independent future was more appealing. She just had to hope he didn't wake up too soon.

41

The drive was pretty straightforward and everything was going well until they got to a junction with traffic lights on the edge of a town. There were more vehicles on the roads now, more instructions to follow, and her nerves were absolutely shredded with the effort of driving and listening.

She stopped at the lights, but the junction was on a hill and when the lights changed and she tried to pull away, she stalled the engine. The car jolted to a stop. Mark stirred in his sleep, his head jerking up from his chest, eyes flickering open.

She swallowed a scream. *Not now, please, don't wake up yet.*

Telling herself not to panic, she put the car into gear and tried again, this time revving the engine harder, but she overdid it. The car leapt forwards and Mark was suddenly sitting bolt upright, eyes wide open, his hand braced on the dashboard.

'What's happening?' He glanced round, taking in their surroundings.

'It's okay, no need to panic, I just stalled.' She patted his knee. 'You go back to sleep.'

Unfortunately, he was awake now and looking out of the

window at the very moment they passed a large signpost to Wolverhampton. Her pulse rate spiked, hands tight round the steering wheel as she drove on, trying to appear unconcerned, like everything was exactly as it should be.

'Wolverhampton? Why are we going to Wolverhampton?' There was a note of suspicion in his voice. He turned in his seat to stare at her. 'You've gone the wrong way.'

She didn't answer, concentrating on the road.

He snatched up his phone and studied the map, then slapped it down on his leg. 'You've changed the destination.' He sounded incredulous. 'Why are we going to some town I've never heard of near Birmingham? The last place we need to be is on main roads.' He glared at her. 'Covert. That's what we're trying to be. Out of sight and out of range of any ANPR cameras.'

She ran her tongue round dry lips, trying to concentrate on driving but finding it almost impossible. 'I just need to do something...'

'What sort of thing?' he snapped, clearly flustered.

'I need to see somebody who can help me.' She was trying to sound unconcerned but even she could hear the vibration of panic in her voice.

'Oh, right. Somebody who will then know where you are and who you're with.' He'd progressed from bemused to angry now. 'No way, Holly. Absolutely no way.'

The unmistakable lights of a service station glowed in the distance.

He sighed and pointed up ahead. 'Look, let's stop there. I could use the toilet and get a coffee and a snack maybe and we can talk about it.'

His anger had disappeared as fast as it had arrived. Now he just sounded tired and she hoped she might still be able to persuade him to let her carry on. After all, it was just a detour she wanted. A short stop-over.

After driving for a couple of hours, she was absolutely shattered, so she pulled into the service station as he'd suggested. What else could she do? In all honesty, she wasn't safe to continue and if Mark agreed to take her to Beth's, then that would be the perfect outcome. If not, she'd have to think of something else. Maybe she could just get out and hitch.

She stopped the car, glad to climb out of the driving seat for some fresh air and to give her aching back a stretch. She watched him head off into the service station, wondering if she might have blown it. His sudden anger had surprised her but as she thought about it, she decided it was probably panic rather than anger. He was afraid they'd be seen.

Ten minutes later, he was back with two cups of hot drinks and some snacks. She took hers and leant against the car, blowing on her drink before taking a sip. It took a moment for her confused taste buds to register something was amiss.

'That's not coffee.' He was standing next to her, their shoulders almost touching.

'No, I got you a hot chocolate. That's what you had at the café when we first met.' He smiled at her and everything felt right between them again. He was such a thoughtful guy. And although hot chocolate was more likely to make her fall asleep than keep her awake, that wouldn't matter if he was taking over the driving again. 'I'll just drink this, then I'll be ready to go. You can have a rest now.'

'To Birmingham?' She gave him a beseeching look. 'Please, I really need to get an application for a replacement passport sorted and she's the only person who can help me. We won't be there long. She knows we're on the way.'

His eyebrows lifted. 'Oh, right. I didn't think anyone knew

our movements. You didn't say.' He stared at her for a long moment and she cringed inwardly, willing him to agree to the change of plan. He gave a shrug. 'If that's where you need to go, then that's where we'll go. But we'll have to be quick. I doubt anyone's looking for us yet, so we've probably got a few hours.'

She beamed at him. Thank God he wasn't like Finn, who'd be bawling her out right now for changing plans. Yelling at her for being untrustworthy. She reached out and grabbed his hand, gave it a squeeze and felt him return the pressure.

It was a nice hand. Not hot and sweaty, but pleasantly warm, soft to the touch. Not calloused like Finn's. Mark's hand felt gentle, reassuring, a hand perfect for holding. She had a strong urge to lean forwards and kiss him, remembering their first encounter.

Stop it! You're not doing that again, she reminded herself. *Keep your distance.*

They finished their drinks and she gave a yawn, stretching like a cat.

'Okay, let's go,' he said, holding out his hand for the keys, which she gratefully passed over. That drive had been stressful beyond words. At least she could relax now, knowing she was on her way to freedom.

There were more streetlights lining the route, more cars on the road, and Mark followed the satnav instructions. She was checking, just to make sure, and after a while she decided there was nothing to worry about. It would be good to see Beth again, an image of her mentor's face appearing in her mind before her eyes closed and she dropped into a dreamless sleep.

42

It was getting light when Mark pulled into the driveway of his home in Wales. The property was a detached, three-bedroomed cottage, built of local stone, attractive in its symmetrical dimensions. The whitewashed walls had just been re-painted, and Mark thought the place was looking much smarter now after all his hard work. It had taken him a while, because he was a bit of a perfectionist when it came to painting, but the end result had been worth it.

The track up to the place had seen better days, winding up the hill through fields and woodland, and every time there was a downpour, another layer of the surface stones seemed to wash away. That was something he'd tackle next, but he'd need the owners to stump up for that, because it wasn't going to be cheap. He had a whole list of maintenance jobs he wanted to tackle and he felt like he was the custodian of the place, rather than a mere tenant. To him, it was home.

The owners were an elderly couple who'd rented the place out for years. It had been their holiday home until their health had prevented them from doing the journey down from

Manchester. Their daughter had suggested that longer lets might be less trouble and Mark had spotted the advert at just the right time. The place was perfect, perched on the hillside with woodland at the back, fields at the front and only sheep for company. He thought he could probably stay as long as he wanted and made sure he paid his rent in cash, on time and was no bother at all.

This little corner of North Wales was largely forgotten. It was close enough to Bala for any shopping they might need, but a couple of miles off the main road. Few tourists ventured up this way at all, making it peaceful all year round. He climbed out of the car and looked up at the house. Was that a movement in the bedroom window, the flick of a curtain? He sighed. There was going to be trouble, that was unavoidable, but he had things to do before he went into the house.

He walked round the car and opened the passenger door, gazing down at Holly who was still fast asleep.

Carefully, he lifted her out and carried her up the path at the side of the house, enjoying the warmth of her body so close to his. This was the start, the beginning of a relationship he was sure would flourish, given care and attention. It was just a shame she'd made that silly decision to take a detour to Birmingham. But never mind, they were here now and hopefully no harm done.

She was going to have to learn that once a decision had been made, she couldn't just change it without telling him, or having some sort of discussion at the very least. That was rule number one. Life was unbearable when he was at the mercy of other people, but he'd reached a point where everything he could control in his world, he did. His life, his choices, and if Holly was to be part of his life going forwards, then she'd have to be willing to compromise.

He opened the gate into the back garden and felt her stir, mumbling something as her eyelids fluttered. *No, no, no, don't wake up.* He thought he'd crumbled enough sleeping tablets into her hot chocolate to keep her knocked out for a little while yet. He hardly dared to breathe in case it disturbed her, speeding up as he carried her down the path to the stone outbuilding at the end of the plot.

It had probably been accommodation for animals at some point, but it had been turned into a guest room by the owners when they were still doing holiday lets. It could only be described as bijou, and was basically a bedroom with an en suite and little more than that. No windows in the sides of the building, but it had big windows in the roof, so the room was nice and light and very private. He opened the door and carried her in, laying her carefully on the double bed, making sure she was in a comfortable position on her side.

It still smelt fresh in here, but he'd only cleaned it the day he'd left for Dumfries, so he knew everything was spotless. Fit for a princess. He smiled down at Holly, lying on the pristine white covers, looking so peaceful. Her hair was soft as silk and he wanted to bury his face in it and just breathe her in. But that wouldn't be right when she was asleep. All those delights awaited in the future, he hoped, and they'd feel so much better if he could experience them a little bit at a time.

The anticipation was almost as thrilling as the reality, he'd found. More so at times, if past experiences were anything to go by.

There was a little kitchenette in the opposite corner to the bed, with a small work surface, a sink, fridge and two rings for cooking. Not that she'd be needing those, and he'd cleared out all the cooking equipment and utensils a while ago. He walked over and filled a plastic jug with water, putting it by the bed with a plastic tumbler. There was nothing sharp in here. Nothing that could be smashed. Just in case. But it was a shame because the plastic was ugly and functional and she deserved to be surrounded by pretty things.

He stood back and checked that he'd thought of everything, leaning forwards to gently slip her shoes off and put them by the bed. He could bring her bag in later, but she wouldn't be needing it now and he had other things to do.

His phone pinged with a message and his mouth twitched. He sighed and turned to go, wanting to spend all his time in this room with Holly but knowing that he couldn't.

He left the building and looked up at the house, squaring his shoulders.

His jaw tightened as he had a familiar argument with himself. One he knew he couldn't win without feeling guilty. The thing was, he'd reached an age where he'd decided he had to put himself first for once, or his life would be over and he'd be left with nothing but regrets. He couldn't let that happen, could he? Surely he deserved a bit of happiness at some point.

It was true that managing his time was a juggling act, one he was finding harder to maintain, and he knew that soon he was going to have to make a big decision. Not today, though. He was too tired to even think about that today.

Everything's going to be okay. Of course it is. Nothing, absolutely nothing, was going to ruin his plans this time.

43

His nose wrinkled when he opened the back door of the cottage, and he gagged as the stench hit his nostrils, seeming to lodge on the back of his tongue. *Oh God, what's happened?* The smell was nauseating, like something had died. That's what his brain was telling him; this horrible smell was the sickly sweet aroma of death.

He nervously glanced round the kitchen to see if he could find the source. There was nothing obvious, no little bodies of dead vermin. It wouldn't be the first time wildlife had managed to get indoors, but he didn't think that was the problem.

His heart thundered in his chest as his mind sorted through the possibilities, some of them too unpalatable to consider. He hadn't been away that long though, only three days, and he'd prepared meticulously, putting contingency plans in place in case he was delayed.

Cautiously, he made his way into the living room, searching for the source of the disgusting smell.

'What you doing? What you doing? What you doing?'

He smiled, relieved to hear the voice of Archie, his African grey parrot, who was sitting on his swing in a tall, custom-built cage that took up a whole corner of the living room. The TV was on low, just as he'd left it, giving the bird some company. Archie hated being alone.

'Where you been? Where you been? Where you been?' the parrot scolded, sounding just like Mark's mother.

'None of your business,' he said, walking up to the cage. There was a pungent smell of bird poo, but that was better than the stench of death in the kitchen. He made a mental note to give the cage a good clean and let Archie exercise his wings. Once he'd dealt with whatever might be going on upstairs. At least there was still water in Archie's bottle and plenty of food left in the automatic feeder.

For a horrible moment, when he'd first walked into the kitchen, he'd thought it might have been Archie who'd died. He was always concerned for the parrot's welfare when he went on his trips away. He'd had him since his tenth birthday, so Mark had lived much more of his life with Archie than without him and would be desperately sad when he eventually passed away.

Archie knew all Mark's secrets. Every single one of them. There'd been long periods of time when he'd been Mark's only friend, his confidante, and their bond was as strong as siblings. At least Mark imagined it was, but he'd never had a sibling so he had no direct comparison. Suffice to say, Archie was a dearly loved part of the family.

The parrot bent his head and Mark poked a finger through the bars to give him a scratch. 'That's nice. That's nice. That's nice,' Archie said, twisting his head this way and that to get a complete head massage.

The only irritating thing about Archie was his habit of repeating everything three times when he was a bit stressed. Then doing it again until you responded. And once engaged in conversation, he was always reluctant to let you leave. But Mark had to find the source of the smell because if it wasn't Archie, there was a more significant possibility.

He poked his head into the dining room, which also doubled up as a music room, his keyboard pushed up against the far wall, sheets of music stacked on top. His computer, with his two screens, sat on the dining table alongside his printer. It was his workstation for the day job as a freelance content producer.

The floorboards above his head creaked and he looked up, not sure if he was relieved or disappointed. It appeared nobody was dead, which made the source of the smell even more of a mystery.

44

'Mum, I'm home,' he called as he plodded up the stairs, preparing himself for the inevitable onslaught.

'Where you been?' his mum screeched, her voice a carbon copy of Archie's. Or was that the other way round? Mark popped his head into his mum's bedroom. She was sitting on the edge of the bed in her pink nightie, the one she'd been wearing when he left, her grey hair sticking up in a frizzy mess. She was only fifty-eight, but she'd aged a lot in recent months and now looked closer to seventy. She glowered at him. 'I've been stuck up here for days, Mark. It's been days. You can't just go off and leave me.'

Oh, but I can, he thought to himself, with an inner smile as he kept his face straight. *Because I just did.*

Of course, he'd never say something like that to her face. It was more trouble than it was worth. Even if he would get a glow of satisfaction from seeing her shocked expression. It didn't do to rile her, though, because she could be such a nasty witch, and that just got him upset, because she knew how to land the psychological blows.

She'd always had that advantage, because she was his mother, the central figure in his life. Someone he'd depended on as a child, and he'd tried to love her even when he knew she was being mean. After his dad died, when Mark was six, she was all he had, so he'd tried to put a positive spin on things, telling himself she loved him really. He even let himself believe that her apologies were genuine and what she said about him was true: that he was a difficult child.

Now he knew different and over the years he'd learnt how to stop her behaviour from scarring him by avoiding fights. It was much better to keep things nice and calm, which meant concealing his thoughts and emotions. He'd learnt to keep his facial expressions neutral, even while he was raging within.

Ironically, it turned out to be a valuable life skill, one that had got him out of trouble several times in recent years, so he supposed he had her to thank for that. And the music. A teacher had suggested that learning a musical instrument might give him a positive focus for his energy, and stop him being disruptive. The fact that she'd used it as a punishment, not letting him eat until he'd finished his daily practice, was by the by. Music had given him joy, a career and, in more recent years, a means of finding love.

He delighted in life's little ironies, he really did.

'I'm so sorry, but I got delayed.' He went and sat next to her, put an arm round her shoulders and kissed her cheek. She batted him away, clearly annoyed, but he was used to her moods and didn't let it bother him.

'I'm so hungry. I thought you were going to leave me to starve.'

'I'd never do that, Mum. You know I wouldn't.'

He stood and went to check the fridge in the corner of the room. It was where he'd left a stock of ready meals and snacks for her while he was away, and there was a microwave sitting on top so she could heat things up. The fridge was empty, which was a puzzle, because he'd left her more than enough food for the few days he'd expected to be away.

'You can't be starving if you've eaten that lot.' He turned towards her, frowning. 'There was enough food for a week. I re-stocked before I went.'

She gave him a shifty look, her eyes sliding away from his, and he could tell she'd switched off combat mode for a few moments.

Unease gathered in a knot in the centre of his chest, and his frown deepened. 'What's going on?'

She sniffed, smoothed out her nightie against her legs and it took a while for her to answer. 'I haven't been so good. My digestive system. I think I've had a sickness and diarrhoea bug and everything I've eaten has just come back up. My legs have gone really wobbly and it's been a struggle just to get to the bathroom, let alone make myself food.'

She looked up at him with sunken eyes, which seemed too big for her scrawny face. 'I need a proper meal, not that heated up gunk. I think that's what's making me ill. I've had so much of it, just the sight of a cottage pie makes my stomach turn. Please, Mark, could I have something different for once? I know you don't eat meat, but could I have some bacon? Or eggs? Maybe a fried egg sandwich? That would be easy enough, wouldn't it?'

He took a deep breath, telling himself to be patient and kind. That was the way to minimise stress. He could have come back with a retort, something justified, like: 'If you'd bothered to feed me properly when I was a child, then I might be more prepared to make an effort for you.' But he didn't. He wasn't going to stoop that low. Not now.

He'd done that in the past and it had given him little satisfaction because his mother would then go on a long rant. Trying to justify her actions all those years ago, when food had been used as a weapon against him. 'I wasn't well,' she'd tell him. 'I didn't know what I was doing.' Or, 'It was the stress of being a single parent after your dad died, and not having enough money.' And, 'I wanted to keep you at a healthy weight. You've always been prone to being chubby.' Or, if she was feeling more honest about her motives, 'Food was the only weapon I had to try and make you behave.'

He'd heard all of that and he'd decided none of it was true. She'd been a dreadful, selfish mother. Overly strict, taking out her resentments on him because, as his mother, she had the power. She hated being a single parent, and without his father's influence to balance her out, she'd got worse and worse. He'd played up, fighting against the injustice of her punishments, and she'd retaliated with more punishment and they'd got themselves into a spiral of negativity.

God knows how they'd got through those years without killing each other, but, with the support of his piano teacher, who was like an uncle to him, he'd channelled his emotions into music. And he'd learnt a valuable lesson. Music was the portal to love. His route to a world that was his alone, which his mother could not enter or tarnish in any way.

He smiled at her. *Look how the tables have turned.* Food had been her weapon and now it was his. He was the one with all the power since his mother had developed an illness that was rapidly dragging her towards death. At least, he suspected that's what was happening. They hadn't been to the doctor, or seen any specialists about her recent bouts of ill-health because she'd said she'd had enough of that and didn't want them messing about with her body. Her words. So, he'd taken them literally and left her be.

He could have insisted, but he didn't. That was another thing he had power over. She'd deprived him of medical attention when he was a child on several occasions, believing she knew best. Or knowing that she'd be in trouble if she took him to the hospital. Once, he'd had a broken bone in his arm that had been left to heal on its own. He'd been seven at the time. Later, he understood it was a green stick fracture, caused when she'd twisted his arm to punish him for answering back. Thankfully, it hadn't affected his piano playing and it seemed to have healed up okay, despite his mother's neglect.

He was cheeky in those days, he'd admit that. But she took out her misery and resentments on him, like his life didn't matter.

If she refused medical attention then he wasn't going to persuade her. Her life, her choices. She'd set the standard and he was following her lead. How could she complain?

Eventually, she'd die of natural causes and that moment couldn't come soon enough. In fact, when he'd walked in and smelt that dreadful smell, he thought it might have already happened. But it seemed it was not to be just yet.

Her illness meant she was confined to upstairs. A fact that made his life a lot sweeter. He had the whole of downstairs and outside to himself and she couldn't interfere in his work or his hobbies, or anything else for that matter. She could scream the house down and nobody would hear.

His ancient mobile sat on a table next to the bed. It was her only means of communication because there was no landline in the house, and not much mobile reception either – you had to go into the garden to get a proper signal. But there was WiFi, so she could text him. And his was the only number programmed into the phone. Thankfully, she'd believed him when he told her they couldn't ring for emergency services from the house and he always made a point of telling her he had to go outside to make phone calls. The fact she'd never got up to speed on new technology was truly a blessing.

Once she'd understood that she was solely dependent on him for her care, she'd become a lot nicer. More polite, but then he insisted on a certain level of manners, just as she had when he'd been a child. If she was horrible to him, he took her food away for a day, a punishment he'd often suffered himself. Yes, she'd set the standard, so he had absolutely no qualms about doing it.

He went downstairs, opened the freezer and pulled out some more ready meals to re-stock the fridge upstairs. All of them were cottage pies because he knew she didn't like them. As a vegetarian, he would have preferred not to have meat in the house, but she was a meat eater and this was a means to an end. He took one and peeled back the lid, found his jar of herbs in the cupboard and put a generous sprinkling on the top, then added a bit more, before heading back upstairs. He re-stocked her fridge and put the meal in the microwave, standing watching it for a couple of minutes, his back to his mother. Then he took it out and stirred it, before putting it back in to finish heating up.

He turned to face her. 'I'll make something different later, but this will have to do for breakfast. I'm just a bit busy.'

Her shoulders were heaving up and down and he could see she was getting worked up, her eyes like two black coals in their sunken sockets. 'Busy doing what?'

He smiled at her. 'Things.'

They stared at each other until the microwave pinged and he took the meal out, put the container on a plate and held it out to her. 'You don't mind cottage pie for breakfast, do you?' He had to stop himself from laughing. Oh, he did enjoy his little power trips. Okay, so he knew it was mean, but it served her right. She went to grab it and he pulled it back out of her reach. 'Now, now. We don't want snatching, do we? What do you say?'

'Please can I have my food?' She glared at him, her mouth puckered like she was going to spit.

'And?' He cocked his head, mimicking her own movements as his mother when he'd been a child. Did she remember? Did she understand this situation was of her own making? He wasn't sure she did, but anyway, it was too late. There would be no redemption; he was set on a course that he would follow through to the end.

'Thank you for looking after me,' she mumbled through gritted teeth.

'There you go,' he said, a false cheeriness to his voice. 'Not so hard to be polite, is it?' He felt like tipping the piping hot food in her lap and leaving her to deal with it, but his nicer self stopped him. *Be the better person*, he advised as he left the room. And anyway, he had other things to do.

He still needed to find the source of the smell, and it was stronger up here; in fact, it seemed to be coming from his bedroom.

45

Mark stopped in the doorway of his room, appalled at the state of his bed. It was strewn with all the food that should have been in the fridge; cartons of cottage pie tipped out, packets of ham and cheese, slices of bread, all baking in the autumn sun that streamed through his bedroom window. His jaw hung open. *Why? Why would she do that?*

The stench was unbearable and he pulled his T-shirt up over his mouth and nose while he looked at the stinking mess. His mother had clearly lost her mind. She hadn't known how long he was going to be away, though, and probably thought he'd be back the day after he'd left. It must be some sort of protest, a rebellion, but it had backfired on her, hadn't it? Not only had she been forced to live with the awful smell, but she'd also been left with nothing to eat.

Stupid woman.

He bundled up the rotting food in the bedding, trying not to breathe as he took it outside and threw the whole lot in the bin. He gagged, the stench of it wafting up and hitting the back of his throat before he'd had a chance to close the lid.

He walked round to the back garden, putting some distance between himself and the bin, and took some deep breaths, filling his lungs with fresh air. He could have done without this palaver, but he just had to get on with it. At least he wouldn't be leaving his mum on her own for a while now, if things with Holly went the way he hoped.

Ah, Holly.

A beautiful warm glow spread through his body and he let his mind fill with sweet images of her lying asleep on the bed. Angelic. That's how she'd looked. At last, he had something to look forward to, something to counter the negativity of his relationship with his mother. Holly would show him what proper love was about and he couldn't wait for their romance to develop.

Unfortunately, the rotting smell was still with him, intruding on his lovely thoughts, souring his mood and bringing him back to the matter in hand. He stomped back upstairs and pulled a spare duvet from the guest room, making up his bed with fresh linen. Then he opened all the windows to allow the fresh air in and get rid of the lingering stink.

He was exhausted after the long drive and all the adrenaline of their escape from the police, but he thought they were safe now. Yes, the police had his old address, the one he used for all his important documents, but he was having his post redirected to a PO box in Wrexham to keep him nice and anonymous and he only checked it once a month. Not much came by post these days anyway. And he'd bought himself a new SIM card when they'd stopped at the service station, thrown his old one in the bin so the phone trail would stop there. In a way, the diversion towards Birmingham could turn out to be a good thing. A bit of misdirection if the police had been tracking his phone.

He leant on the windowsill, gazing out over the garden. Although it was autumn, there was still some heat in the sun and the odd patch of colour in the flower beds next to the lawn. From here, he could just see the ends of the raised vegetable beds he'd built further up the garden, in front of the outbuilding where Holly was asleep.

The building sat lengthways on to the house and he'd put up a trellis fence that stretched from the end of the outbuilding about two thirds of the way across the width of the garden, giving the place some privacy. It also created a sun trap, perfect for growing vegetables. He was sure the soil would be even better for growing next year, once everything had settled and the natural nutrients started to feed through.

He heard the floorboards creak, then the sound of the bathroom door closing, his mother retching. His lips twitched into a smile. *Is that very wrong? To be enjoying her discomfort like this?* He thought it probably was, but the witch deserved everything that was coming to her. You couldn't go around abusing your child and not expect some consequences further down the line.

Of course, the power dynamic hadn't always been like this. In fact, until quite recently, she'd still had the upper hand. He'd been a different person before she'd fallen off a step ladder putting up a hanging basket and broken her leg. It was a nasty break, a compound fracture, and not something that would heal quickly. Unfortunately, she'd had an infection, trips back and forth to hospital, bedridden for weeks, and it had severely weakened her.

Mark was obliged to step up to be her carer, and it took him a while to work out that the dynamic had changed. *He* was in charge now. He could 'forget' to give her painkillers, while telling her she'd had them. He could 'lose' half her supply of antibiotics while telling her she'd finished the course. No wonder the infection kept coming back. But she was tough and despite his best efforts, she'd got through it.

The upside of his 'care plan' was that she decided the doctors were incompetent, didn't know what they were doing and she'd had enough of their nonsense. She refused to attend her hospital appointments and he was happy to have nobody else meddling in her care. In fact, he considered it a win.

She wasn't an easy patient and didn't like the fact she relied on him, but she had no choice. She'd trained him his whole life to do as he was told, but now he was the one doing the telling and she was struggling to come to terms with the switch in status quo.

She hated it. He loved it. And now things were about to change again because he had Holly to think about and a whole new future ahead of him.

46

Holly thought she might be dreaming, but her eyes appeared to be open. It was like she was awake, but she couldn't be because she was in a room she didn't recognise. A nice room, but all the same, she couldn't comprehend where her brain had found the image. She was pleasantly comfy, and she dozed for a bit, her eyes opening then closing again, eyelids so heavy it was too much effort to stay awake. Finally, she felt a bit more alert and realised this wasn't a dream at all. She was in a strange room, with no recollection of how she'd come to be there.

Now that's a bit worrying.

She sat up on the bed, swinging her feet over the side, wondering how she'd transferred from being in the car on her way to Birmingham to this place. It was way too quiet to be in a city, and anyway, the architecture was all wrong. She glanced around, looking for a window to peer out of, but the walls were blank. There were two of those big windows that tilted on either side of the vaulted ceiling. She could see a blue sky, some fluffy clouds, a vapour trail from a plane and the branches of trees, hung with the remains of autumn leaves. Rural. She must be in an attic, she decided, listening for sounds of people in rooms below her, or outside. But there was nothing apart from birds singing.

Mark had obviously brought her here and she would bet that this was his place in Wales, not Birmingham where he'd promised to take her. She rubbed her eyes and yawned, still half in the grip of sleep. Well, she didn't have to stay here, did she? Her eyes scanned the room, looking for her bag, but she couldn't see it and she couldn't go without it. All her paperwork, her phone and her money were in there. The contents of that bag were essential to her survival.

She noticed her shoes had been taken off and put at the side of the bed. Mark must have done that. Surely she would have woken up if he'd carried her from the car into this room and then started untying her laces and messing about with her feet? Unease wriggled up the back of her neck, making her give an involuntary shiver.

This doesn't feel right.

It took a few seconds for her emotions to morph from unease to puzzlement through to disappointment, and ending with full-on anger. *Why do men always turn out to be the same control freaks? Why, for God's sake?*

Her fist thumped the covers, disillusionment making her body feel heavy and listless. Mark had seemed such a genuine bloke. Kind and charming and concerned. The fact that he'd rushed up to Scotland to make sure she was okay had shown her that he cared. At least that had been her interpretation, but it seemed she'd got it wrong.

She sighed and let her situation settle in her mind, finding it hard to accept that Mark might have done anything untoward. He was one of the good guys, wasn't he? Perhaps this was a minor setback, an adjustment to her plans that would turn out to be for the best in the long run. At least she was now well away from Dumfries, and the cops wouldn't be looking for her anywhere near here. That had to be a good thing, didn't it?

Maybe she should give Mark the benefit of the doubt for the time being. Perhaps something had happened when he was driving that got him spooked and made him head straight for home? She slapped her hands on her thighs, then her arms and her head, trying to wake herself up, wishing this fogginess would clear from her brain.

There's no point second-guessing, she told herself, eyeing the door. The best move would be to find him and ask.

Once she was standing, gravity made her aware that she was desperate for a pee and she spotted a door in the corner. *Is that a bathroom?* God, she hoped so. To her relief she found it was. A very lovely bathroom, newly fitted out and decorated. This en suite room was pretty special and she wondered what the rest of Mark's place was like. Maybe she didn't have to dash off just yet, maybe she could wait a couple of days and enjoy a bit of luxury. *Or would that be a mistake?* Didn't she need to get in and out of Birmingham as fast as possible before anyone thought to look for her there?

They won't though. Her connection to Birmingham was in the past, and she hadn't had a permanent address there for ten years now. Why would they choose to look there? In fact, they might not even know she was gone from the gamekeeper's cottage yet. Her evidence had been strong, she thought. They would be spending their time investigating the person in the black car rather than looking for her.

Thoughts were chasing round her head and she was unsure now what to do for the best. Stay or go? Would it really be such a bad idea to spend time with Mark? He was cute and there was no doubting their mutual attraction. What if he *was* 'the one'?

She washed her hands and splashed water on her face, but her brain was still sluggish and woolly, not like her at all. But then the last few days had been one big adrenaline rush and it wasn't surprising her body needed a bit of time to rest and recuperate.

It would be nice to stay but... there was something about this whole set-up that felt off.

Go and talk to him, she told herself, annoyed by her own indecision. Once she knew his side to the story, it might be easier to decide what her next step should be.

Her eyes scanned the bedroom, checking again for her bag, because if she could find that, and knew everything was present and correct, then she'd feel less panicky. But there was no sign of it. She slipped her feet into her shoes and hurried to the door, ready to be assertive and get the answers she needed. The door handle turned, but nothing happened, the door wouldn't open. She tried again, with two hands this time, but still the door wouldn't shift.

Her heart skittered in her chest, the realisation hitting like a hammer blow.

I'm locked in.

47

Mark decided he might as well get all the dirty jobs over with at once. So he closed the living room doors and let Archie out to have a fly around while he cleaned out his cage.

'Naughty boy. Naughty boy. Naughty boy,' Archie said from where he was perched on the back of the sofa, then laughed in a way that set Mark's teeth on edge. It was so like his mother's laugh it was uncanny and always caught him off guard. That particular laugh of his mother's was not a happy sound. It usually came after a put down, a signal that she'd successfully humiliated him, belittled him, made him embarrassed to exist at times.

'Nobody's a naughty boy,' Mark said, holding out his hand for the parrot. 'Not you and not me.' He felt Archie's claws digging into his skin as he landed, then the gentle nibble of his beak as he plucked at the hairs on the back of Mark's hand. It tickled, making him laugh and it felt good for something nice to be happening after the anxiety of the last few days. He held Archie up and kissed his head before launching him into the air. 'You have a bit of exercise while I sort this poop out.'

'I'll sort you out if you're not careful.' Archie was now perched on the back of an armchair. His mother's chair. *Ah, good. He only said that once.* It was a sign that his bird was calming down. Mark watched him strut up and down before Archie started speaking again. 'Go on, piss off, you snivelling little git. Get to bed. Get to bed. Get to bed.'

Hmm. Maybe he's still a bit stressed.

Mark recognised more of his mother's words and he wondered how much Archie understood about the sounds he made. He supposed he might sense the emotions, if not the meaning.

He frowned. 'Are you telling me off? I'm sorry I was away so long, and I promise it won't happen again.' Archie flapped his wings and did a bit of preening before flying his usual laps of the room, while Mark got on with cleaning out his cage. Then he tempted him back in with some tasty treats to try and make amends.

Once the cage was clean and the smelly jobs completed, Mark had a leisurely shower to rid himself of the awful smell that seemed to encase him, following him wherever he went in the house. Parrot poo and rotten food was not a great combination and it seemed to be embedded not only in his clothes, but his skin too. He already felt grubby after that long journey and he'd never needed a shower more. Who was it who said cleanliness was next to godliness? He'd no idea but his mind always felt sharper after a shower and today, he needed to be sharp. There were a number of things he had to get straight in his mind.

He dressed in his new grey chinos and a navy patterned shirt, wanting to be presentable when he saw Holly again. He desperately yearned for her to like him, a feeling so strong it was like an ache in his heart. If he was being honest with himself, he didn't want her to just like him. He wanted her to fall in love with him. That was the bottom line, his goal, and he couldn't relax his efforts to make a good impression.

He made a coffee and took it out into the garden with a bowl of cereal, looking forward to having a moment to himself to mull over everything. The coffee was strong and bitter, just how he liked it, and he wolfed his breakfast down so he could sit and enjoy his drink.

He gazed at the outbuilding. There was something about Holly niggling at the back of his mind and now he was sitting quietly, it pushed its way into his thoughts. *She'd tried to trick me into going to Birmingham.* So, what had been her plan when they'd got there? Would she have dumped him? He had a nasty feeling that's exactly what she'd had in mind, using him like a taxi service. Someone of no consequence.

Thinking about it now, he remembered catching a sly look when she'd been suggesting she could drive to give him a chance to rest. He hadn't been able to nail it down at the time, but now, with the benefit of hindsight, he could see that she'd tried very hard to persuade him to let her take the wheel.

He sighed, overwhelmed by a wave of disappointment. *I can't trust her, can I?* Not now, not ever; but hadn't he known that about women? None of them could be trusted.

They said one thing and did another, or acted one way and said something contradictory. Behaving like they mean yes and then saying no. How was a bloke supposed to work out what a woman really meant? It was too confusing and he'd got it wrong on a number of occasions, with horrible consequences. He shook the thoughts out of his head, not wanting any of that past trauma invading his headspace. There was enough to think about without any of that negativity butting in.

He blinked, tears of frustration stinging at his eyes. He'd had such high hopes for Holly and knew their connection had been real, but that didn't mean she wasn't using him. It broke his heart to think that might be the case. Was he merely the provider of a getaway car to distance her from trouble?

His mind stopped at the word trouble, another connection slotting into place in his brain. It wasn't a savoury thought, but he had to ask himself why Holly was running away. He remembered her excuse, that she'd be the automatic suspect, but didn't running away smack of guilt?

48

Holly hammered on the door, rattling the handle and shouting at the top of her voice. This was like being locked in the cellar all over again and she felt as helpless now as she had then. The only positive was the environment she was trapped in this time was a hell of a lot nicer.

After ten minutes of yelling and banging, her voice was hoarse, her hands were stinging like crazy and she had to give up. Nobody was out there. Nobody could hear her. She had no idea where she was in the house or even if there were neighbours. Maybe there weren't any. Maybe she was as isolated as she'd been in the gamekeeper's cottage. The thought sent a sudden chill through her body.

Why has he locked me in?

The obvious answer was he thought she'd run away if the door was unlocked. But could there be a more sinister explanation? Was he planning on doing horrible things to her? It happened, didn't it? Women abducted and sometimes kept for years in hidden rooms, nobody knowing they were there while their captor raped and tortured them. A bead of panic lodged in her chest while she tried to push the awful images from her mind. Images that culminated in a painful, ultimately death.

She leant against the wall, her eyes scanning the room for another way out, but there was just the one door. She was a prisoner.

Hitching a lift with Mark had seemed a safe option for her escape from Scotland, but she appeared to have jumped out of the frying pan into the fire. Wasn't that just typical of her luck? In fact, it was a metaphor for her whole life, if she was being honest.

Why me? Why does it always have to happen to me?

Confused and alarmed by the latest turn of events, she trudged back to the bed and lay down. There was nothing she could do except wait and although her body was happy to rest, her brain was scurrying around, looking for explanations.

Her nan had once said she'd been born unlucky. It had alarmed her when she'd first overheard her say that in a conversation with her grandad. She didn't know why she'd formed that opinion, had no idea what she'd done in her nine-year-old life to merit such a comment, and she'd never liked to ask. Firstly, because she didn't want to believe it was true and secondly, because she shouldn't have been listening at the door.

She'd admit her decision-making had been less than perfect at times, but who never made a mistake? That's how you learnt, but she'd had a run of bad luck recently and whenever there'd been a critical choice to make, a fifty-fifty decision, she'd taken the wrong path.

Isn't that why I'm here? All those months ago, she could have chosen not to go home with Finn. But he'd seemed like the easy option. She could also have chosen to make her own escape without relying on Mark for a lift. But again, she'd taken the

easy option. And she'd believed him when he'd said he wanted
to help her.

Ha! The hard way is the easy way. That was a saying her nan
had been fond of but Holly hadn't really understood what it
meant until recently. Even now, she hadn't learnt that lesson,
always relying on someone else to get her out of a mess she'd
found herself in, thinking that was the easy option.

There's nobody to help you now. She puffed out her cheeks.
There really wasn't. She was going to have to work things out on
her own because if she couldn't trust Mark, she only had herself
to rely on. *You've done it before,* she reminded herself, and it was
true, she'd got herself out of a few tricky situations. But what
use was that when it had ultimately led to this?

And this could be the end, the very end, if she couldn't work
out how to escape.

Her heart raced as her internal monologue whittered on,
telling her how stupid she was, how ridiculous to think she
could run away from the Finn situation and the police.
Wouldn't it have been better to sit it out? But she didn't dare.
That was the truth of it. Just in case they decided to pin his
murder on her. And then she'd be in prison and the last fifteen
years of running away would have been for nothing. It was a
thought she couldn't bear.

Shut up! Just shut up.

She didn't want to hear another word and started singing to
block out her thoughts. Words she wanted to believe covering
words she didn't. Lenny Kravitz singing about getting away
because that's what she needed to do. That's what she needed to
focus on, rather than berating herself about past choices she
could do nothing to change.

Her eyes travelled slowly round the room again, taking in
every little detail, looking for a way to get herself out of there.

Unlike the cellar, this room was not somewhere you put people to punish them, she realised. It was a well-appointed guest room. There were lovely, thoughtful touches, like the fluffy towels hanging on a rail, a thick towelling robe on the back of the bathroom door, a little vase of flowers by the bed. The furnishings were lovely and tasteful and feminine. Everything smelt fresh and clean. Care had been put into preparing this room.

That in itself was a puzzle, because Mark hadn't known she was coming back with him.

She tucked her hands behind her head and a waft of stale, acrid sweat from her armpits assaulted her nostrils. Feeling decidedly grubby, she swung her legs off the bed and sat up. She might as well have a shower while she was waiting for Mark to show up, and the shower was where she had all her best ideas for some reason. It could only help. She checked the drawers in the hope of finding clean clothes and found some cotton pyjamas that might fit. That's all there was, which seemed a bit random. They were new as well, still in their packaging. Two pairs. One pink and one grey, organic cotton and a brand she recognised as being outside of her normal budget.

Her head was throbbing and she thought it was probably because she was dehydrated. She eyed up the jug of water next to the bed. Everything else in the room was thoughtful and kind rather than sinister, so should she risk it?

Nope. She took the tumbler over to the sink and filled it from the tap, gulping it down in a couple of mouthfuls. She refilled it and drank that as well. If she wanted to be alert, she had to avoid being dehydrated. She'd seen a programme on this recently with a famous TV doctor, the message being that nobody drank enough water and it affected your body chemistry in many subtle ways. It dulled your thinking, confused your logic and she needed hers to be working.

The shower was wonderful and she stayed under the steaming cascade of water for ages, just letting it flow over her while her thoughts ran free. Perhaps there was a good reason for Mark locking the door. She shouldn't jump to conclusions, just wait and see how everything played out. For the time being, she was safe from the police at least and if Mark turned out to be more of a threat than she'd thought, then she would deal with that when the time came. No need to get stressed about it now.

She was sitting on the bed in the fresh pyjamas, fidgeting with her nails, when she heard a rattle at the door and her head snapped up. Mark walked in with a big grin on his face, like nothing untoward had happened. Like it was normal to lock a woman you hardly knew in a bedroom in an unfamiliar house.

'You're awake,' he said, unnecessarily.

She knew she should smile at him, play nice, but found that she couldn't, a sudden anger roaring in her chest. 'You lied to me,' she snapped, glaring at him as he walked towards her. 'You said we were going to Birmingham, but that's not where we are, is it?'

He sighed and came and sat next to her, reaching for her hand. But she moved away, jumping to her feet to put some distance between them. She caught a flicker of hurt on his face, but she was distracted by something in her peripheral vision. A sliver of light, like the door hadn't shut properly. Her brain went into overdrive and she edged closer to the exit, her back to it now, her eyes fixed on Mark. Here was her chance to escape.

She could see his lips moving, realised he was talking and made herself tune in. 'No, we're not in Birmingham because there was a news report on the radio about Finn's death and it mentioned the police were looking for a suspect.' He was gazing straight at her, their eyes locked together. 'And then they gave your description.'

Holly gasped, her heart leaping up her throat as her hands covered her mouth. 'No.'

Mark nodded. 'Yes. You were asleep, so I couldn't tell you what was going on. And I thought the last thing we needed was to be anywhere near a city where people might recognise you.' He shrugged, looking concerned. 'Did I do the wrong thing?'

Holly's brain went numb, unsure what to think any more. Perhaps she'd read this whole thing wrong. 'But... You locked me in.'

Mark laughed. 'Well, not really. The door's a bit dodgy, it keeps opening and I thought you'd want some privacy, so I locked it.' He looked over towards the door, the gap wider now as the breeze pushed it open. She could see the green of plants, the grey of slate paving, the brown of wood. It looked like she was in an annex, maybe. Definitely not in an attic as she'd originally imagined. 'The weather was pretty awful when we arrived as well and I didn't want the rain getting in. Or you getting a chill.'

'Ah, okay.' She crossed her arms, caught his eye, and his gaze was so clear and untroubled, she knew he was telling her the truth. She'd been seeing suspicious things where there weren't any. A flush warmed her cheeks and she looked away, embarrassed by her outburst.

He held up her bag. 'I thought you might want this, but I see you found the pyjamas.'

She looked down at her clothing, feeling quite vulnerable in such a flimsy outfit, and crossed her arms over her chest again. 'I hope you don't mind.'

He smiled at her. 'Of course I don't mind. It's a guest room.

Everything here is to be used by my guests.' His smile broadened, his eyes travelling up and down her body. 'I'm happy that they fit.'

She was feeling awkward and a bit stupid, thinking she'd built the whole situation up to be something it wasn't. It just went to show that you had to get your facts straight. But the unease swirling in her gut made her realise that something still wasn't sitting quite right with her. Not that she could articulate exactly what that might be. For now, though, she'd give him the benefit of the doubt, while proceeding with caution.

She smiled at him and reached out to grab her bag, clasping it to her chest. Home and dry, she thought to herself. At least now she could make her own plans. She wasn't dependent on anyone and that made her feel a whole lot better.

Mark was gawping at her like a lovestruck teenager, which was rather sweet and absolutely non-threatening. She'd been worrying about nothing, because it was clear from his expression that she was the one with the power. He wanted her to be comfortable and happy and despite all her reservations, she still felt that tug in her heart when he looked at her.

It would be rash to run off when she had such a strong ally in her corner. Especially if the police had started looking for her. Wouldn't his house be a great bolthole until all the fuss had died down over Finn? If the whole place was decorated to the same finish as this bedroom, it would be a very comfortable spot to stay and rest up while she decided what to do next.

You're taking the easy road again, a voice in her head was telling her, that unease still clamped to the back of her neck.

He pointed at the door. 'I've just got a few things to attend to. Shall I lock the door again? Give you some privacy for a few minutes if you want to get changed. Or you can stay in the pyjamas, it's up to you.'

She felt herself relax a little. *He wants me to feel comfortable, that's all.* And hadn't she seen the door blowing open earlier? His explanation rang true. Nothing to worry about, she told herself, just a practical thing. 'Okay. Give me ten minutes, then you can come and unlock it again.'

'Right-ho. Whatever works for you. I'd give you a key for yourself, but it's just a bolt on the outside, not a proper lock.' He pulled an apologetic face. 'I had to take the original lock out because it jammed up and I haven't had a chance to buy a new one yet. I wasn't expecting visitors, you see.'

'That's fine.' She shooed him away, keen to get herself dressed.

The door closed, the bolt slammed into its housing and she heard his footsteps walk away.

49

Mark grinned as he strode back to the house. He was picturing Holly in those cute pyjamas, thinking how pretty she looked, delighted that he'd picked the right size from his stash of women's clothes. Some things had worked out perfectly and he told himself he shouldn't beat himself up about the things that hadn't quite gone to plan.

Yes, but... what about... He gave a grunt of annoyance, frustrated that his brain refused to focus on the positives. Okay, so he had to address the things about her that perturbed him. The fact that she had two birth certificates in her bag was more than a little odd. It would appear she was using a false identity, so there were obviously shady things in her past.

Everyone makes mistakes.

Yes, that was true. He'd made pretty huge mistakes, but he'd never had to change his name. It would take something spectacular for him to need to do that, so what the heck had she done?

The insistence on going to Birmingham hadn't made sense either. And who was in Birmingham that she was so desperate to see? He was going to have to ask a few more questions to understand exactly what that agenda might be.

It wasn't quite adding up. Was there another man she was going to meet? It was clear she hadn't been 100 per cent honest with him and not only was that hurtful, it was also very disappointing.

He sighed and looked up at the bedroom window. Holly hadn't been the only person who'd been bending the truth though and he wished now that he hadn't told her that his mother was dead. Because she clearly wasn't and, as soon as Holly came into the house, she'd find that out for herself. Trust was such a delicate thing; he couldn't afford for her to doubt him.

There was still a decision to be made about his mother. And therein lay his biggest problem. It turned out that wishing for something, and then actually making it happen, were two very different things.

As he got closer to the house, he could hear a knocking sound. He frowned, the muscles in his shoulders pulling at his neck. *What is she up to now?* He opened the back door and walked through the kitchen towards the stairs. Then he heard the knocking again and realised it wasn't his mother at all; there was someone at the front door.

His heart gave a little flip.

Nobody came to the door. In the year that he and his mother had lived here, they'd had two visitors and those had been the landlady's children, doing a routine check of the place. They'd only visited a few weeks ago, giving him the green light for the re-decoration and telling him they were delighted with the way he'd been tidying the place up. They'd been especially impressed with his renovations of the garden and the creation of the raised beds. Model tenants, they'd said. And yes, they'd been happy to let them renew the lease for another year.

The knocking came again, more insistent this time. A proper rat-a-tat. He broke out in a cold sweat, panic scuttling round his brain. *Oh God...* He froze in place, like a statue. *Is it the police? It can't be.* But there was a possibility, his brain said. A definite possibility. Especially with them venturing so close to Wolverhampton on the way home. Those ANPR cameras were hidden everywhere these days. His pulse raced a little faster.

His car was in the drive, which strongly suggested he was at home. *I'm going to have to answer, aren't I?* He took a couple of deep breaths and made a conscious effort to arrange his face into a neutral expression before he opened the front door, surprised to see a middle-aged couple on the doorstep.

The man was tall and rake thin, with stooped shoulders, his grey hair arranged in a comb-over. The woman was short and round, her hair like a bleached blonde helmet, cut just under her ears. *Like Humpty Dumpty.* If she happened to trip and fall, he imagined her rolling all the way down the track. The idea of it made him smile and they beamed back at him.

The man waved a leaflet. 'We've come to talk to you about our Lord Jesus. Do you have a few moments to spare?'

He stifled a sigh. *Jehovah's Witnesses.*

'I'm so sorry, I appreciate you coming all the way up here, but I'm afraid I'm an atheist.' He moved to close the door, but the man stepped closer, his hand curled round the door frame. It was a clever move because Mark couldn't close the door now without trapping the man's fingers.

'Then you're exactly the person who needs to hear what we have to say.' The man's smile broadened. 'That's why we're here today.' He exchanged a smug look with the woman, who was presumably his wife. 'Our Lord has brought us here to talk to you and save your soul. It's never too late, you know.'

'That's very kind of you but my soul doesn't need saving.' Mark closed the door a little bit more, peering through the crack. 'I'm so sorry you've had a wasted journey, but I'm trying to work and I really need to get on.'

'Oh, but your soul *does* need saving,' the dumpy woman said, peering through the closing gap. 'All of us need redemption.'

'HELP!'

Mark jumped, the scream loud and piercing and coming from upstairs.

50

The man pushed at the door, looking alarmed, trying to peer inside. 'Was that someone shouting for help?'

'It was my parrot.' Mark fixed a rictus grin on his face, hoping to God these people would accept his explanation.

'Your parrot?' the woman repeated as the couple exchanged disbelieving looks. 'It sounded like a woman shouting. A distressed woman.'

'Oh, he's got quite a repertoire.' Mark forced a laugh. 'He loves to watch dramas on the TV.'

'HELP ME! PLEASE HELP. I'M A PRISONER.'

His mother's voice was crystal clear and Mark could feel himself starting to panic. His scalp seemed to shrink over his skull, clutching his head in a vice-like grip.

He gave a hollow laugh. 'We were watching an old TV series last night. It obviously made an impression.'

The man's frown deepened, his jaw set. 'And which series would that be?'

'Funnily enough it was *The Prisoner*. Have you seen it? You know, the one they filmed at Portmeirion.'

The woman tutted. 'I've watched that several times and I'm pretty sure nobody shouts like that.'

'Yes, well, he makes up his own dialogue from the sounds he's heard.' Mark was getting exasperated now and it was coming through in his voice. 'He's a parrot,' he snapped. 'Nuances are lost on him.'

The couple exchanged another look before the man spoke again. 'Well, I think we need to see this bird, don't we, Ruth?' His wife nodded. Mark didn't move, his body blocking the doorway. 'Or we'll have to call the police. We can't just walk away after hearing that. It wouldn't be right, would it, love? I'd never forgive myself if we found out later that—'

'I'll bring him to you.' Mark put the chain on the door so the couple couldn't force their way in and gave a silent scream, his fists clenched, wanting to punch the pair of them. What right did they have to just turn up on the doorstep and demand anything? It was a gross invasion of privacy. But he knew, in his heart, that they had a point and he couldn't have the police coming round.

He went to the lounge, calling Archie over to his hand and clipping a leash to his leg, which he then attached to his wrist so he wasn't able to fly away. 'I want you to shout help, okay?' he whispered, keeping his voice low so the Jehovah's Witnesses wouldn't hear. 'Just that word. Help. Really loud.' The parrot looked at him, cocking its head to one side.

'Just that word. Help,' the bird repeated, in a hoarse whisper, copying Mark. 'Really loud.'

His heart sank. This wasn't going to work, was it?

He heard a knocking at the door again and knew he had no choice but to take Archie to meet the couple and hope for the best. Sweat was popping out on his forehead, his shirt damp under the arms, his heart beating so hard it was making him shake. Surely they'd notice?

He pinned a smile to his face as he swung the door open and stepped outside, forcing the couple to move back. 'Here you go. This is Archie.' He bent his head towards the parrot. 'Say hello to these nice people.'

'Bugger off, bugger off, bugger off,' Archie squawked, hopping about on Mark's hand and flapping his wings.

He cringed. The woman had gone pale and was now one step behind her husband, as though using him as a shield.

'I'm so sorry,' Mark said, fighting to keep his emotions under control. This encounter was going from bad to worse and he wasn't sure whether he was about to burst into a fit of hysterical laughter or start sobbing. He calmed Archie down, taking a moment to collect himself, his voice. 'He has no manners. But as you can see, he can speak. And that's what you heard earlier.' He turned, ready to take Archie back to his cage.

'HELP ME!'

They all looked up at the bedroom window where his mother was now banging on the glass. Mark sighed, rocked back on his heels, his choices limited to one. 'You'd better come in,' he said wearily. 'Let me explain.'

51

Holly changed into a fresh pair of jeans and a T-shirt, folded up the pyjamas and left them on the bed. She wouldn't be needing those again because she'd decided that she wasn't staying. As much as the rest of the house might be palatial, and her heart was drawn to Mark, that unease was still present and her gut was telling her she needed to go.

Quite apart from doubts about Mark's motivations and behaviour, there was another thing that worried her. What if there had been ANPR cameras somewhere in the urban areas she'd driven them through? What if the police could track Mark's car back here? The very thought of it made her feel shaky and she knew she wouldn't be able to relax if she was constantly listening for the cops to arrive. She'd learnt from experience that was no way to live.

No, the only solution was to move on and as soon as Mark came back and unlocked the door, she was going.

She checked the front pocket of her bag and pulled out the envelope with her paperwork inside. It was a relief to see it was all there. She also had a spare passport application form, having picked up two in case she made a mistake when she was filling the first one in. She had no idea how it worked if your passport was completely destroyed, but Beth would help her with that.

She frowned, realising something was missing from her bag. *Where's my phone?*

A rummage in the rest of her bag came up with nothing. It wasn't there. She tried to visualise when she'd last had it and could distinctly remember charging it and tucking it in the front pocket before she'd left the cottage. There was only one possible conclusion to be drawn: Mark must have taken it. Her unease amplified. *Now why would he do that?*

She couldn't come up with a palatable answer.

It had been a bad mistake to fall asleep in the car. She'd been so close to her goal, not more than thirty miles away, but now she was here, in the back of beyond, if Mark's description of the place was anything to go by. She frowned. Talking of Mark, where was he? He said he'd only be ten minutes and it was way more than that now.

She walked to the door and gave it a rattle. Still locked. And that didn't feel right. Mark had come up with a reasonable explanation, she supposed, but there was something unnerving about the way his eyes shifted when he'd been explaining his rationale for locking the door. It made her doubt he was telling the truth. And if he was lying about that, what else had he been lying about?

Her situation was beginning to feel more than a little precarious. His behaviour sinister.

The recognition that she might be in danger made her pulse race. *How stupid have I been?* She'd thought she was being clever by hiding in Mark's car to get herself out of the castle grounds without being seen, but it appeared to have backfired in the worst possible way. Once again, she'd been too trusting, judging everything on face value. Her mind took her straight to the worst-case scenario and she whimpered, imagining reports about her on the news. A body found in the woods.

Nervously, her eyes scanned the room, fixing on the windows in the sloping ceiling. They were her only possible escape route. But they were pretty high up and she couldn't work out how to reach them. Her eyes trawled the room for a possible solution.

There was no chair, but if she put the bedside cabinet on the worktop and stood on that, would she be able to reach? It looked feasible, and given it was the only thing she could think of, it had to be worth a try.

The cabinet was fairly light and although her bruised body objected to doing anything physical, she gritted her teeth against the aches and pains and managed to stand it on the worktop. Getting *herself* up there took a little longer, but eventually, with a lot of huffing and puffing, she managed to clamber up. The slope of the ceiling made the next manoeuvre more precarious, but by kneeling on the cabinet and leaning backwards, she could just reach the bar that opened the window.

She pulled it wide open, hooking her elbows over the bottom edge of the window frame, just the balls of her feet keeping contact with the cabinet. The view was stunning. Trees and fields and dry-stone walls. The dip of a valley to her left. The ridge of a hill to her right. Mountains in the distance. Below her was a vegetable patch and apart from the house to her left, not another building in sight.

A shout made her hold her breath, straining to hear. There it was again. A woman's voice. 'Help me!' she was shouting.

Holly's blood ran cold. The woman sounded scared. Frantic. Now she knew her gut instinct had been on the money. This wasn't right. Not right at all.

52

Mark tried to appear unconcerned as he let the couple into the house. If the Lord had led them here, as the lady believed, then the Lord was responsible for whatever happened next.

The man had a stern, self-righteous look on his face, his wife appearing a little fearful as they pushed past him, like they were some rescue force on a mission.

The man was about to head upstairs when Mark put a hand on his shoulder. 'Let me just explain the situation first. Then you can go upstairs.' He smiled at him. 'Let's have a cup of tea, shall we?' The man looked at his wife, who gave a small nod, and they followed Mark into the lounge, where he put Archie back in his cage. 'Have a seat,' he said pleasantly, indicating the sofa. 'And I'll get the kettle on. Tea alright for both of you?'

Having established that tea was fine, he hurried into the kitchen and pulled the large teapot out of the cupboard, filled the kettle and flicked it on. He opened another cupboard and took out a small tin caddy with 'Tea' painted on the side. He peered inside and could see a good amount of dried leaves. Not tea, but his special mix of herbs, which would be effective in an infusion. He tipped the contents into the teapot along with a couple of tea bags to disguise the flavour. He calculated there was enough to do the job. More than enough to do the job, he decided once he'd double-checked his maths.

Standing sideways on to the worktop, he could see the couple through the open door and made an effort to keep them talking. 'You must be thirsty after walking all the way up here. Where did you leave your car?'

'In the lay-by at the bottom of the track,' the man replied. 'It seemed the sensible thing to do because we weren't sure we'd get the car up here.'

Mark laughed. 'Yes, wise move. The surface is a bit rough at the moment. It's one of the jobs on my list.' He poured boiling water into the teapot and gave it a good stir. 'It's funny, you're the first people to knock on our door for months. We don't get visitors all the way up here.'

'The Lord brought us to your door,' the woman said, her voice ringing with fervour. 'I firmly believe that. I said to Frank when we were driving past that we needed to come up because we haven't been in this area for a while. I felt it, you see. I felt His guiding hand pulling us in this direction.' Her mouth was a line of grim determination. 'And make no mistake, we will help whoever that poor lady is upstairs.'

'That's my mother,' Mark said, rummaging in the utensils drawer for the tea strainer. He pulled three mugs from the hooks that hung underneath the cupboards and made a coffee for himself. He'd never been much of a tea drinker and if he'd ever needed a caffeine hit, it was now. He waited a few moments before taking the strainer and pouring tea into the two other mugs. It looked the right colour. He bent and gave it a sniff, smiling to himself. Yes, that would do nicely.

He found a tray and emptied a packet of chocolate digestives onto a plate, pouring some milk into a jug and tipping some sugar into a little ramekin dish that would have to do as a sugar bowl. He surveyed the tray. Teaspoons. He found a couple that matched and put them on the tray as well, satisfied that he'd now remembered everything. It paid to have good manners, and a bit of hospitality went a long way. He was hoping it might sort out this particular problem anyway.

'The truth is my poor mum has dementia,' he said as he passed his guests their tea, encouraging them to help themselves to milk and sugar. They were perched next to each other on the sofa, both of them sitting ramrod straight, knees together, looking decidedly uncomfortable. He took the armchair next to Archie's cage, sat back and crossed his legs, cradling his mug against his chest. 'She keeps forgetting where she is, that's the problem we're having. And who I am, for that matter.' He sighed and took a sip of his drink. 'It breaks my heart to see her so scared.'

He blinked and squeezed his eyes shut for a moment before turning his gaze to his guests. 'I also have to lock the bedroom door because she wanders and I'm worried about her falling down the stairs.' He leant forwards to grab a biscuit. 'Help yourselves,' he said, offering them the plate. 'She had an accident about five months ago now. A really nasty fracture of her leg and it got infected and just hasn't healed properly. She's too unsteady to get down the stairs.' He gave another sigh. 'So, we're in a bit of a bind at the moment. I have to lock her room so she doesn't fall down the stairs, but she thinks I'm a prison officer keeping her locked up.'

The woman tutted and reached for another biscuit. The man took a sip of his tea and Mark held his breath for a moment, waiting for a reaction, his heart leaping when there wasn't one. Not a shudder or a facial expression that said he was desperate to spit out the tea but politeness prevented him.

'Oh, I see,' the woman said. 'I suppose that does explain things. I have a dear friend who has dementia and her suffering has been terrible to witness. But she does like us to visit because she still recognises the Lord's word, even if she doesn't recognise us any more.' The woman raised her mug to her mouth. Then lowered it again, her eyebrows pinched together in a quizzical frown. 'Can I ask you what sort of tea this is? It smells a little... different.'

'Oh, it's Lapsang Souchong,' he lied. 'Mum's favourite. I hope that's alright. I suppose it's not to everyone's taste but Mum likes it.'

The woman took a tentative sip and gave a small smile. 'I've never had it before but it's actually rather nice.' She turned to her husband. 'What do you think, Frank?'

'I can honestly say it just tastes like tea.' He took another sip. 'But then my taste buds haven't been the same since Covid.'

They chatted for a bit longer until the tea was finished and half the plate of biscuits was eaten, their conversation punctuated by his mother's intermittent cries for help.

Mark put his empty mug on the coffee table and stood. 'I'll take you up to meet her, shall I?'

'Yes, please, if you don't mind,' the woman said, springing to her feet. 'It would be on my conscience if I didn't see her for myself.'

'I quite understand,' Mark said, thinking how rude it was to come into someone's home and basically tell them you thought they were a liar. He led the way upstairs and opened his mother's bedroom door.

'Oh, thank God you've come to rescue me.' His mother was sitting on the edge of the bed. 'Take me with you, please, I beg you.' She held out her arms like a child wanting to be picked up. 'Take me away from this man.' She looked like a gargoyle and sounded demented, her hair sticking up all over the place, her eyes sunken, lips tinged a bluey-purple, like she'd been eating blackberries.

'Now, now, Mum.' Mark went and sat beside her. He tried to put an arm round her shoulders but she shrugged him off, slapping at him until he stood up and moved away. 'These people have just come to say hello and to tell you about Jesus. They're Jehovah's Witnesses. Isn't that lovely?'

He could hardly look at her because he anticipated what her reaction would be. Mark's mum wasn't just an atheist, she was vehemently anti-religion and he'd expected her to be horrified that he'd let these people into the house.

'Take me with you,' she pleaded, a bony hand clutching at the woman. 'He's trying to kill me.'

Hmm. That wasn't the reaction he'd been hoping for. But the woman shrank back, her mouth dropping open. The man just stood there, arms dangling by his sides, a pamphlet clasped between his fingers.

Mark shrugged and gave the couple a 'what can you do?' look.

'I'm so sorry, but I don't think this is good for Mum,' he murmured, ushering the couple towards the door. 'She's getting herself very distressed. Let's go back downstairs, shall we?' He followed them out of the room, locking the door behind him, before they all headed back down the stairs.

'I told you she was confused,' he said when they reached the front door. 'She really doesn't understand what's going on no matter how many times I try and explain.' He sighed. 'It's distressing for both of us as you can imagine.'

'I think we need to inform her GP,' the lady said to her

husband. 'She needs medical attention.' She pushed her shoulders back. 'I worked in a nursing home for thirty years, looking after people like your mum. I know what a challenge it can be and you're obviously doing your best, but I think she should be in hospital. There's a problem with her liver. You can see it in the eyes and the colour of her skin.'

Mark gave what he hoped was a benign smile while inside he was seething. Bloody do-gooders. 'Really? Maybe that's what the problem has been. She has a phobia about the hospital, though. Can't stand all the messing about with blood pressure and temperature and doing tests. She says it's exhausting and intrusive and demeaning and she won't subject herself to it any more.' He sighed again. 'She thinks *they're* trying to kill her too. And last time she was on a ward, they had to put her in a side room because she kept trying to escape.' He shook his head. 'Believe me, I really have tried everything.'

The woman frowned at him, clearly unconvinced. Would she take matters into her own hands and interfere? Would the authorities turn up at the house? That's what he'd been afraid of when his mother had called out the first time. It had given him no alternative; at that point, the fate of the couple had been determined. It was a shame but what could you do? He had to protect himself, first and foremost, and give himself a chance of a future with Holly. He wasn't going to let these do-gooders or his mother ruin that for him.

'I think Ruth's right,' her husband said. 'It can't do any harm to speak to the doctor, and it might make her more comfortable. I say it's worth a try.'

'Okay,' Mark agreed. 'If you think that's what needs doing, I'll make the call tomorrow.'

'No. You should do it now,' the woman insisted, jabbing a finger at him. Implying she didn't trust him to do it tomorrow.

God, she was annoying. *But karma is a wonderful thing,* he thought, trying to keep his emotions at bay. *The stupid woman doesn't know what's coming for her.*

'I can see you're worried.' He pulled his phone from his pocket, found his contact list and pretended to dial a number. He glanced up at her. 'It's the answerphone,' he lied, leaving a message asking the GP to make a house call as a matter of urgency. He slipped his phone back in his pocket. 'There, happy now?'

The woman stared at him, a suspicious look in her eyes. 'I suppose so. But we would very much like to come and check on her again.'

Mark could hear his teeth grinding but gave her a smile like there was nothing he would like better. 'Of course. That would be absolutely fine.'

'Let us pray,' the man said, reaching for Mark's hand. His clasp was dry and firm and Mark knew it would be better to just give in at this stage. If that's what it took to get rid of them, then he would play along.

He had to endure ten minutes of fervent prayers, husband and wife acting as a tag team. When one seemed to be winding things up, the other would start, muttering pleas for God's mercy and help for his mother and Mark and even the parrot. Finally, after effusive thanks and reassurances that he'd follow up with the GP if he didn't hear anything, he managed to get them out of the front door.

He watched them walk down the track, the woman in full flow, casting glances over her shoulder towards the house as she talked to the man. Oh, how he wished he could hear what she was saying. It was clear from her body language that she wasn't happy with his explanations and reassurances. Wasn't it just his luck that she was a retired care worker?

Nerves stirred in his stomach, his fingers tapping out a melody on the door casing as he watched the couple disappear out of sight.

These people were dangerous, of that he had no doubt. As soon as his mother had called out, his intuition had told him he needed to act and he'd learnt to trust his instincts. The woman wasn't going to let things lie, he could tell by the way she'd insisted on seeing his mother, making him call the GP, telling him they would return to check. Unfortunately, he felt she had the upper hand in her marriage and he couldn't rely on the husband to calm her down and keep their noses out of his business. She was going to cause trouble.

Thank goodness he'd taken decisive action. But was it going to be enough?

53

Mark cleared up the tea things, making sure he gave the cups a thorough wash. The whole encounter with the couple had created a rush of adrenaline that now left him feeling completely drained. But although his body wanted nothing more than a lie down, his mind was jittery and distracted, asking him question after question.

What if the couple decide to phone the doctor's practice themselves?

Or call for an ambulance?

Or, God forbid, the police?

He stood at the front window, tapping his knuckles against his chin. His nerves were in shreds, his plans turned upside down. He sat on his piano stool, his fingers on the keyboard, playing a song, any song, in an effort calm himself. How was he ever going to make the right decisions when his mind was in disarray? But the music wasn't working, the questions getting louder.

The need to know what the couple were doing became so

strong he couldn't stop himself from dashing out of the house, and following their route down the track.

He did mental calculations as he walked, hoping that he'd got it right in terms of the potency of the herbs. But there were other variables at play, things outside his control. They could have made a call as soon as they'd left the house and were out of sight. Although, he did know that cell phone reception was patchy in the trees, so maybe not. But then again—

It might already be too late.

A strangled scream caught in his throat, his hands balled into fists as he walked. The track twisted and turned through the edge of the woods before crossing a field full of sheep, and ending at a gate which opened out onto the single-track road. If you turned left, you eventually hit the main road that led to Bala. If you turned right, the road circumnavigated the hillside, creeping ever higher, past three more holiday homes before ending at a derelict farm a couple of miles further along. Would they be carrying on to spread the word of Jehovah along the whole road, or might they be on their way home now? Via the police station? Or the GP's surgery?

He jogged across the field, glad to see a silver car parked in the lay-by at the bottom of the track. He slowed to a walk, trying to get his breath back.

Now he was closer, he could see a figure bent double by the bonnet of the car. It was the man, judging by the size and shape of him. His body was heaving, like he was being sick. Mark slowed and crept behind a wall, watching for a moment. The figure staggered before falling forwards, sprawling face down on the road.

Ouch, that would have hurt. Mark winced and waited. No sign of movement. He couldn't see the woman. If she'd seen her husband fall, surely she would have come to help him? It looked like the tea had done its job and he allowed himself to feel cautiously optimistic. He waited a little longer until he was certain there was no movement, then he sauntered down the last bit of the track to the road.

He crouched next to the man, put a finger to his neck to feel for a pulse. *Oh dear, he seems to be dead.* He stood and walked round the front of the car, looking for the woman. The back door of the car was open and he found her sprawled on the seat, a pool of vomit on the floor. She looked like a rag doll, limbs hanging loose. He checked for a pulse and found that she too appeared to be dead.

With nobody around to watch what he was doing, he checked the bodies but could find no sign of a mobile phone. There was nothing in the car either. He supposed not everyone carried one, although it seemed a little foolish when you were intending to travel off the beaten track. Still, each to their own. Maybe they imagined God was looking out for them and they had no need for modern technology. At least that was one less thing to worry about. They hadn't rung anyone to report their concerns about his mother, so he'd successfully nipped this threat in the bud.

His work was far from done, though. To make sure there were no questions asked when the bodies were found, he needed to plant some evidence.

He hurried back up to the house and pulled a pair of medical gloves from the box under the sink. Then he scooted out into the back garden, making his way to the little stream that ran down the right-hand edge. He knew exactly where to find the water hemlock he was looking for, and he clipped off a few sprigs, before collecting leaves from the lamb's lettuce and watercress that he often used in salads. Foraging was a healthy option if you knew what to look for... and what to avoid.

He dropped the leaves into a ziplock freezer bag and ran back down the track to the road. Thankfully, nothing had been disturbed. He pulled the water hemlock from the bag and poked a tiny bit of leaf into the man's mouth. Then he did the same to the woman, leaving the bag of leaves hanging from her hand.

Hopefully, the whole scenario would be taken for a foraging expedition gone wrong. The poor misguided individuals mistaking the poisonous hemlock for parsley or something similar.

He ripped off the medical gloves and shoved them in his pocket. Now, he had a decision to make. Should he call for an ambulance himself? Then he could get the questions over with down here on the road, where he was in control of the environment, rather than waiting for them to come up to the house. Or should he let somebody else find them?

In reality, there was nothing to suggest they would have been up to his house, so maybe the police wouldn't bother him at all. But then, once they saw the religious leaflets in the car, they might work out why they were here.

It was a difficult choice. He pulled his phone from his pocket, tapped it against his lips. What to do?

54

Holly could feel her arms slipping from the edge of the window, her feet barely touching the top of the bedside cabinet, and she knew she couldn't hang on for much longer. Her muscles were quivering with the effort, her brain screaming at her to get back down before she fell and did herself a serious injury. Broken bones, twisted ankles, head injuries. All of these were possibilities. Then she'd be completely stuffed. Now was not the time to be impulsive.

Carefully, she reversed the moves, clambering back on top of the bedside cabinet, down onto the worktop and back onto the floor. She flopped onto the bed, her body shaking, and that nugget of unease she'd been feeling, ever since she woke up in this room, had grown to a lead weight, sitting on her chest. The belief that she was in danger had intensified from a low hum to a blaring alarm, urging her to get out.

She looked at the open window, not sure she could even get herself back up there again, but what choice did she have? Mark had been gone over an hour now and he'd promised ten minutes. That just showed she couldn't trust him, didn't it?

For a moment, she wavered, because staying here and waiting for him to come back was a much easier option than trying to climb out of the window. *What about the woman shouting for help?* The skin prickled at the back of her neck as she remembered the frantic shouts, and her resolve hardened.

I am not going to be that helpless woman.

She'd managed to reach the window once and she could do it again, couldn't she? It was time to face up to her reality, however challenging that might be – she was a prisoner, not a guest.

She shrugged her backpack onto her shoulders again and clambered back up on the worktop, adjusting the position of the bedside cabinet to make it easier to reach the window. Her muscles protested at every move, but she made herself push on through. The window was her escape route, and she'd probably only get once chance. But she had to be quick because Mark could be back any minute.

Grunting with the effort, she crouched on the bedside cabinet, glad now of all those times she'd allowed her friend in Buxton to drag her to the climbing wall. Who knew any of that exercise would ever have a practical application? Gingerly, she straightened up, her heart leaping up her throat when she felt the cabinet start to slide beneath her. Thankfully, she managed to grab the edge of the window and haul herself up again, but the force of the movement sent the cabinet skidding across the worktop before crashing onto the floor below.

Suddenly she was hanging there, her legs dangling in space, her full weight on her arms, which were hooked by the elbows over the edge of the window. She looked down the slope of the roof and knew if she could just get herself out of the window, she could slide down and jump off into the vegetable bed below.

By her estimate, the walls were only seven or eight feet high, so it was definitely feasible and unlikely to cause her injury.

Trying not to panic, she steadied herself, thinking about the bouldering wall she used to practise on. *I've done harder moves than this,* she told herself as she worked out what her body needed to do.

In her mind, it seemed a straightforward manoeuvre, but when she actually tried to do it, the physics eluded her. There was nothing for her feet to push off and she kept shifting her weight, cursing as she tried and failed to heave her body up and over the edge of the window. No matter how hard she tried, she just couldn't get gravity on her side.

Her strength was starting to fade and if she didn't make her move on the next go, she knew she was going to end up falling to the floor. From where she was hanging, that looked like a long way down onto a hard, bone-breaking surface. She gritted her teeth. *I've got to try something different.*

She visualised the new movement in her mind, the swing of her legs, hooking a foot or a knee into the gap next to her elbows. Her teeth were clenched so hard her jaw was aching, but she counted herself down. *Three, two, one.* And she launched her leg as high as it would go.

Her toe found a purchase and she wriggled as if her life depended on it. Which could well be the case. Then her ankle was over the lip and her knee and now she was certain she wouldn't be falling back inside. Because she was stuck, jammed in the opening with her sinews screaming at her to stop whatever she was doing before they snapped.

55

Mark plodded back up the track, his phone in his hand, still unsure about his next move. He'd decided to leave the bodies of the couple where they were. It could be days before they were found because nobody really came up this road apart from Mark, and that was only once a week when he went out to do a grocery shop. They didn't get any post because he used a PO box in town, and the other houses on the road were holiday homes, so very little post for any of them either. The recycling was collected weekly, but that was four days away. It would be a while before anyone knew they were there.

Looking at it from an outsider's perspective, there was no reason for Mark to be down on the road to find the Jehovah's Witnesses. The longer he left them, he reasoned, the more convincing the staged deaths would be and the harder to determine exactly what had gone on.

Also, in terms of timing, it would be much better if he could sort out the situation with his mother before he had to deal with the emergency services. He couldn't risk her yelling for help again.

It was vital to focus on one thing at a time because, at the moment, there was far too much going on.

Currently, he was spinning three plates – his mum, Holly and now this couple. His brain was overloaded and he wanted things to calm the heck down because the stress was getting to him. The last thing he needed, when he was so close to his goal, was to start making mistakes.

He'd been using a stealthy approach with his mother, her bouts of illness being a mystery to the medical profession, while she gradually became more incapacitated. The time had come to just get the job done, he decided, clear her out of his life and then he could turn his attention to Holly. And if his mother had gone before he let Holly out of the outbuilding, then she wouldn't know he'd lied about her already being dead, and—

Oh God, Holly.

He'd told her he'd be back in ten minutes and that was ages ago. She'd already been nervous about being locked in so what must she be thinking now? He gave a frustrated grunt and picked up his pace, forcing his muscles to work harder on the steeper uphill section. This was another reason for speeding up the demise of his mother. Once she was out of the way, he wouldn't need to lock Holly in and everything could be more normal. He'd just have to think of an excuse to keep her in the outbuilding for a little while longer.

Beads of sweat trickled into his eyes, the salt making them sting. He stopped and wiped his face with his T-shirt, annoyed that those stupid people had turned up. It had all been under control until they came knocking at the door. And he could have got rid of them if his mother hadn't started shouting. So really, it was her fault.

He carried on walking, hoping he could talk his way out of

the situation with Holly. He was good with words. A little bit longer wasn't going to make much difference, was it?

Panting hard, he arrived back at the house, hurried into the kitchen and gulped down a glass of water, then filled the kettle and flicked it on. He studied the jar of herbs that he'd been sprinkling on his mum's food. It was a mixture of dried hemlock and foxglove and it had been perfect for the slow poisoning he'd been implementing. Unfortunately, there wasn't enough left to finish the job. He'd have to go out and collect some more.

While the kettle was boiling, he pulled on a fresh pair of medical gloves, dashed out to the stream and grabbed a fistful of hemlock. Back in the kitchen, he opened the fridge, trying to remember what he had in there. A block of mature cheddar and a packet of spinach and ricotta pasta. Perfect.

He diced the hemlock into small pieces on a special board he kept on top of the cupboard. Food hygiene was very important when you were dealing with poisons; no room for sloppiness. He took off his medical gloves and washed his hands before opening the packet of pasta and putting it on to boil. In a saucepan, he melted some butter, spooned in some flour, made it into a paste and added some milk, stirring until it was thickened. To finish, he grated in a generous helping of cheese and seasoning.

He drained the pasta and returned it to the saucepan, before tipping the cheese sauce over and giving it a stir. He spooned half of it into a dish for himself. Then he tipped the chopped hemlock into the pan with the pasta, and gave it a good stir before spooning it into a dish for his mother. He'd chopped the hemlock so fine you could hardly see it, and he could tell his mother it was spinach. Her eyesight wasn't great these days and he really didn't think she'd notice.

With the meals ready, he then made a pot of tea with the

remaining hemlock and a tea bag, pouring his mum a mug. Finally, he put everything on a tray and carefully carried it upstairs, resting it on the floor while he unlocked the door to his mum's bedroom.

He smiled to himself, thinking how delighted she'd be that he'd made her a fresh meal rather than giving her cottage pie again. She'd be so grateful, he was sure she'd wolf it down. And then... well, he didn't want to think about specifics, but it wouldn't take long for the poison to work. And finally, his mum's frustration and suffering would be over. As would his. It would be a mercy for both of them.

He wouldn't miss the critical voice that could never say anything good to him. The chatter that undermined him, day in, day out. At last, he'd be free and at liberty to develop a loving relationship with Holly. The thought of it filled his heart with a warm glow and his smile widened. He should have done this years ago.

The door swung open and he picked up the tray. He only took a couple of steps before he halted and looked around, his heart skipping a beat. *How strange.* His mother wasn't in the bed where he'd left her. In fact, the room was empty.

56

Mark did a double-take, completely dumfounded. It wasn't possible. He'd locked the door; she had to be here. He rushed into the room, setting the tray on the bed while he scanned the space. Perhaps she'd fallen out of bed, on the other side where he couldn't see her. He hurried round, sure he'd see her crumpled, helpless body. Perhaps his work was already done and the old witch was no more.

The slam of the door made his head snap round. The clunk of the key being turned in the lock made his breath hitch in his throat. *Goddammit. How did she do that?* It seemed impossible that she could be that nimble, but she must have been hiding behind the door and snuck out when his back was turned. It had never occurred to him to even look there, sure she was too frail to move far without his support. Now she'd locked him in.

He hammered on the door. 'Mum, what are you doing? Let me out.'

She gave a harsh laugh. 'What? Do you think I'm dumb? Why would I let you out?' He could hear her raspy breathing, knew the exertion would be draining her, but she seemed determined to have her say. 'I know what you've been doing. I know you've been trying to kill me. Poisoning my food.' Another cackle. 'I worked it out, you see. When you were away and I spoiled all the food, and yes, I was hungry, but my God did I feel better. Then the first meal you made me when you came back I was sick. That's when I knew.'

A chill ran through Mark's body and he realised he'd seriously underestimated his mother. Got a bit too far ahead of himself and taken his eyes off the task. It was the thought of love distracting him. The thought that someone, somewhere, would be happy to live with him. Unlike his mother, who was impossible to satisfy.

'I don't know what you're talking about, Mum.' He banged on the door with his fist, wanting to punch through it, grab her by the throat and strangle the life out of her. But he needed to calm down and put a lid on his aggression. Otherwise, he had no chance of talking her round. 'Come on,' he wheedled. 'Let me out and let's talk this through. The doctor said your medication might make you feel a bit disorientated, didn't she?'

They hadn't said that, but he could persuade her that they did.

Silence. *Is she still there?*

He held his breath and listened, could still hear her breathing, the rustle of her movements, could sense her on the other side of the door. The malevolent presence of her dark soul tainting the atmosphere, like an unpleasant smell. He imagined her as a shapeshifter, her blackness seeping under the door, forming a hand and grabbing his ankle. He took a step back, had a mental regroup and tried again.

'I just made you a lovely lunch. One of your favourites, you know, with the spinach pasta and cheese sauce.' He slapped the door. 'Come on, Mum. I'm worried you're going to fall down the stairs and hurt yourself. You know your legs aren't strong. You don't want to end up back in hospital, do you?'

'Well, if I eat whatever it is you've made for me, I'm going to end up in the morgue,' she snapped. 'And I'd rather avoid that, thank you very much.'

He stifled a howl of frustration. Christ, she thought she was clever. And she had definitely beaten him this time, but it was just one little battle and he was confident he would win the war.

'Anyway, my legs are stronger than they were. I've been doing my physio exercises. Practising while you were away.' She laughed again, clearly delighted with herself. 'I can even get down the stairs. You think I'm stupid, well, who's the stupid one now?'

'Mum, let me out. Please. This is silly. You know you need me.' He leant his head against the wood, at a loss to know what to say. He had a terrible sinking sensation in his stomach, a feeling that his world was unravelling and there was nothing he could do to stop it.

He made his voice as gentle and reasonable as he could. 'I've only been trying to look after you. Why would I want to poison you? You're my mum. I'd never want to hurt you.'

'Why would you want to poison me? Ha! It's obvious. I'm a burden, a blockage, a barrier. Call it what you will. You want me out of the way because it'll make your life easier.'

'No, Mum. You've got it wrong. I want you to get better. Then we can go back to the way things used to be.'

Another long silence.

Then he heard the slow thump, thump, thump as she made her way down the stairs.

Clearly, she wasn't going to let him out, but no matter, this old mortice lock on the door was something he could fiddle open, with the right tool and a bit of patience.

She thinks she's won but she hasn't got a clue.

It didn't matter how his mother met her end. The poisoning would have been relatively benign, but there were plenty of other options open to him and after this little escapade of hers, he no longer cared how she died. It just had to happen.

He opened the drawer of her bedside cabinet and rooted around until he found a couple of hairgrips. He smiled to himself as he held them up triumphantly. He thought there might be something like this lying about. Her hair had been long until fairly recently, when he'd given it a trim, fed up with having to help her to wash and brush and maintain it. For years she used to wear it tied back, using hairgrips to keep the wispy bits under control, and he'd been sure they'd still be here. His mother threw nothing away and thank goodness for that, he thought, even though it was a habit that irritated the hell out of him. He hated clutter but she insisted on keeping all of her 'things' and there were boxes of stuff in the spare bedroom that would never see the light of day.

It didn't take him long to jiggle the lock, smiling when he heard the mechanism give a satisfying click. He opened the door as quietly as he could, not wanting his mother to know that he was free.

Now she'd worked out that he'd been trying to poison her, the scenario had changed. She'd ambushed him once and, in a way, she had the upper hand at the moment, because he had no idea where she was. He'd heard her go downstairs, but she could be hiding round any corner, ready with something heavy to bash his head in. Or she could have pulled a knife from the block on the kitchen counter.

All the while, he was very aware that the clock was ticking and Holly was still locked up, no doubt wondering why he hadn't come and let her out. Angry tears pricked at his eyes. His mother was ruining everything.

Can this day get any worse?

He crept down the stairs, eyes raking the area in front of him, looking for clues as to where she might be. She wasn't in the hall, and he sneaked out of the front door and round the side of the house. His plan was to come back in through the kitchen and arm himself with a knife. As he rounded the corner into the back garden, he detected a movement in his peripheral vision, pulling his attention to the outbuilding. His heart stuttered, his jaw dropping in horror when he realised that his day could indeed get worse. Because Holly was climbing out of the window.

57

Holly was unable to move in any direction, half in and half out of the window, when she looked down and her eyes met Mark's. Her heart skittered and the bony hand of fear grabbed her neck and squeezed. She whimpered, tears of frustration springing to her eyes.

'Holly, what on earth are you doing?' He rushed towards her across the garden. 'You're going to hurt yourself.'

'You didn't come.' She swallowed, blinking back tears. 'I was... I was frightened.'

'Oh, Holly. You don't need to be frightened of me.' He gave her a gentle smile that made her wonder if she'd overreacted. 'I had these people at the door. Jehovah's Witnesses, and I couldn't get rid of them. And then—' He flapped a hand. 'I'll tell you about it later, but let me help you down from there before you have a nasty accident.' He held up a finger. 'Hold on while I go and get the ladder.'

She watched him hurry towards a shed in the corner of the garden, relieved that he seemed more flabbergasted than angry.

Had she misjudged him in all this? Was she creating problems where there weren't any?

A woman was screaming for help, she reminded herself. *Did I imagine that?*

No, she'd heard it not just once, but several times. And she remembered he'd told her he lived on his own. *So who is the woman?* Having caught him in a lie, she had to ask herself how many other lies he may have told her.

Her pulse was racing, adrenaline pumping round her body readying her for fight or flight, whichever one of those she needed. Once she was out of this window and down on solid ground, she was going to take off, and she wouldn't let him stop her.

He came out of the shed with a set of ladders and leant them against the roof, taking his time to make sure they were set firm before he started to climb up towards her.

He frowned and tutted, standing with one foot on the ladder and one on the roof. 'How on earth have you got yourself stuck like that?'

There was nothing sensible she could say, so she didn't reply, her mind fixed on escape and how she was going to do it.

'If I can take one of your hands, then maybe I can pull you a little bit until you can get your leg onto the roof. I think you'll be in balance then. What do you think?'

She didn't move, not sure she wanted him pulling her. *What if it's a trick?*

He held out his hand. 'Come on, I promise I won't let go. You're not going to fall. And once you're out of there you can slide down the roof and climb down the ladder.' He grinned at her and she felt herself wavering. Nothing about him was threatening in any way and she wondered why her body was refusing to move, resisting his help.

You've got no choice, she reminded herself. *You're stuck, and he's the only one around.*

Reluctantly, she did as he suggested, and as he gently pulled her arm, she was able to heave more of her body out of the window. Finally, she could move her leg out of the excruciating position it had been stuck in, but her muscles were wobbling and she had little control over any of her limbs.

Mark beckoned to her. 'Come on, let's get you down.'

She shook her head, thinking it might be better to sit on the roof for a little while, to let herself recover, before trying to get down a ladder. 'I'm not quite ready.'

'Well, let me shut the window, so you don't fall back inside.' He stepped onto the roof and slammed the window shut. He was behind her now and suddenly she was slipping, gravity pulling her downwards. She screamed, her arms grabbing for anything she could get hold of, but it was happening too fast. A blast of fear sheared through her body, but there was nothing she could do to stop herself falling, flying through the air for a terrifying couple of seconds before landing in the vegetable bed below.

'Oh my God!' Mark shouted. Then everything was quiet, apart from the sound of his feet, scraping down the rungs of the ladder. Time appeared to have stopped as she lay there, immobile and winded. Thank goodness the soil had been freshly dug and provided a relatively soft landing. If she'd been a little to the left, she would have landed on paving slabs and then the outcome would have been quite different. Christ, it didn't bear thinking about.

'Holly, what happened? I thought you were safe there?' Concerned eyes met her own as he crouched next to her. She could feel his breath on her cheeks as he spoke. 'Are you okay?'

She couldn't make her body move, or get her mouth to form

words, her brain dazed with the shock of the sudden fall. He picked her up, one arm round her torso, the other under her knees, and she found herself surprised that he seemed to be carrying her so easily. He was obviously stronger than he looked. Her head flopped against his shoulder, her thoughts too jumbled to make sense.

Gently, he eased off her backpack and laid her on the bed. Then he walked away, shutting the door behind him. She heard the scrape of the bolt.

It took a moment for her to realise the significance of this sequence of events. A moment for her brain to understand she was right back where she started. Locked in. And that's when she knew one thing for certain. *He pushed me.*

58

Mark locked the outbuilding door with a sigh of relief. His heart was pounding so hard he was seeing stars, and he crouched against the wall for a few moments, his back leaning against the cold stone. God, that was close, but at least Holly was safe for now. If she hadn't been stuck in the window, she'd have been away from here and he would have lost her.

He ran a hand down his face, as if he was washing away the fear that thought stirred in him. Never did he imagine she'd try a stunt like that. Nobody else had ever tried to climb out of the window, but they were all different. Except in one thing. *Why did these women always want to run away?* He treated them like princesses, did his best to pamper them, yet none of them wanted to stay.

It baffled him, tugged at the sadness that lay crumpled inside him, like a discarded blanket. Even Archie the parrot wouldn't stay if he wasn't on a leash. Tears of self-pity welled inside him, emotions constricting his chest. His hands covered his face while he tried to push his desolation away, but it wasn't working this time and his disappointment in Holly's desire to leave threatened to overwhelm him.

Why can't people love me like I love them?

How many times had he asked himself that same question? But it was the story of his life. He had no idea what more he could do, what more he could give to make Holly realise he only wanted to love her. Was that so bad?

Give it time, she'll come round. That was the voice of the eternal optimist in him, but he wasn't feeling it today. Not after everything that had happened. His life was imploding and his energy was waning at an alarming rate.

He could hear her crying now. Not gentle sniffles, but anguished wails, sounding like cats fighting. It wasn't a ladylike sound. In fact, it rather grated on his nerves. A piece of him found it distasteful, his image of her shifting slightly, his desire cooling a few degrees.

He puffed out his cheeks, weary with the way his day was panning out. Holly would have to wait because he had a more important problem to resolve. His mother.

Given her health issues, it was unrealistic to imagine she'd be able to escape, so he'd no idea what she thought she was going to achieve apart from pissing him off. Did she really think he wouldn't be able to get out of that room? Is that how useless she thought he was? And if she genuinely thought he was trying to kill her, why would she want to make him angry?

There was no logic to it. Basically, she'd signed her own death warrant, the silly witch. She always had to have the last say, but this time that wasn't going to happen. His words would be the last words she'd ever hear. This was their final battle, the end to their war, and for once in his life, where his mother was concerned, he was going to win.

Even his bloody mother couldn't love him. And that thought turned his sadness into a molten fury that rose within him, making him clamber to his feet and head towards the house. This situation, his life and how it had turned out, was *her* fault. And her fault alone.

If she'd been a better mother, if she'd cared for him properly and shown him a modicum of compassion and understanding, things would have been so different. She was a monster, and monsters deserved to die, didn't they? He would be like one of the heroes in *The Avengers*, ridding the world of evil. Yes, right was on his side.

His fingers flexed, opening and closing into fists, while his brain fired ideas at him, ways to engineer her untimely end. A fall down the stairs would be an obvious solution. Except she wasn't upstairs any more and it didn't make sense to drag her up there just to throw her back down.

Hmm. Perhaps he didn't have to stage anything. Better to think this through a little, not be hasty. It wasn't about making her death look like an accident or natural causes. The fact was, he couldn't have the ambulance coming up here, could he? Not with the Jehovah's Witnesses dead in their car. That would look suspicious right from the off. He shook his head, frustrated at the tangled mess she'd made him create.

Really, it would be better if there was no official record of his mother being dead. She could disappear, and if anyone asked, he could say she was off visiting a friend in London. Who was going to check? Who was going to care? Nobody.

His fingers started cramping, his fists clenched too tightly, and he stretched out his hands, wincing while the cramp subsided. God, he was tense. It wasn't good. This was when he made mistakes, and his mother was a wily old bag, especially if she'd been pretending to still be ill when she'd actually started to recover. Foolishly, he hadn't credited her with being that sneaky.

He reached to open the kitchen door and then snatched his hand back. The kitchen was the last place he should be going, with all those knives in there. And his mother could be waiting for him behind the door. She'd done that once already. In fact, he needed to just stop and think for a moment. At the very least he needed to arm himself *before* he entered the house. His eyes landed on the garden shed and he hurried towards it.

59

Mark scanned the inside of the shed, wondering which of the tools would be most use. Now he'd moved on from the idea of engineering a natural-looking death for his mother to just getting the job done, he didn't need anything subtle. All he had to do was disable her. Then he could finish her off however he liked.

His rage burned brighter, filling his head until he felt his brain was expanding, the pressure inside his skull throbbing in time with his pulse. His eyes fell on the spade. The *perfect* multi-purpose tool.

He could use it to knock a weapon out of her hand, keeping her far enough away from him to prevent her from causing him any damage. Then he could use it to swipe her off her feet, break limbs, smash her skull... The images came thick and fast, bringing with them a surge of emotion so strong he had to bend over and catch his breath. This desire to end her had been inside him for so long, it had developed a life of its own and now it was consuming him. It was repulsive and compulsive at the same time, gaining a momentum he felt powerless to stop.

He reached for the spade, happy with the weight of it in his hand. So many things he could do with just the one tool and, once she was dead, he'd use it to bury her. Out in the woods where nobody would notice. Not ever. She'd be gone and forgotten like she'd never existed and he would be free of her poisonous words, her disparaging looks, her confidence-shredding malevolence. He propped the shovel by the shed door and grabbed the wheelbarrow because he'd be needing that too.

It felt like there was an electrical current fizzing through his brain, his senses so alert and sharp everything seemed amplified. The sound of the birds singing, the whisper of the wind in the trees, the banging of the door.

Wait... He stopped in his tracks, listening hard. *What door banging?* There shouldn't *be* a door banging. He glanced towards the outbuilding, but the door was still firmly bolted and the back door of the house was shut, which could only mean... He jettisoned the wheelbarrow in the middle of the lawn, grabbed the spade and dashed round the front of the house. A weight landed in his gut when he saw the front door swinging backwards and forwards on its hinges, caught in the wind. He knew he'd shut it behind him.

He looked down the track, wondering if his mother had gone down that way, although she was nowhere to be seen.

He marched down the track, but pulled himself up after about fifty yards and turned around, heading back towards the house instead. His mother would know he could easily catch her, would know it was a fool's errand to even attempt to run away. *I bet she hasn't gone anywhere.* This was a bluff. She was trying to fool him into heading off on a wild goose chase while she did what?

He frowned as he tried to work out her game plan. She couldn't call for help because there was no landline and she couldn't make calls on the old mobile he'd left her. His phone was in his pocket. He patted his jeans, his heart doing a wild flip when he realised his phone was not in his pocket at all. He stared at the house. His phone was in there with his mother. At this very moment, she could be searching for a signal so she could ring for help.

60

Holly's gaze settled on the smashed remains of the bedside cabinet, scattered across the floor. She groaned with the horrible realisation that she'd broken her only means of reaching the window, the only way to escape. But escape she must, because Mark was not the man he appeared to be. He'd pretended to help when really, he just wanted her back in her prison cell.

It was incredible that his innocent and harmless facade hid a person so cunning and manipulative. She couldn't trust a word he said. Not one word. And she hoped she could get her idiotic brain to remember that fact, furious with herself for ignoring her gut instincts.

She curled into the foetal position on the bed, her brain replaying the montage of terrible things that Mark might do to her. Images that she'd had in her head and dismissed only an hour ago. She sobbed until she was all out of tears, telling herself that crying wasn't going to help her get out of there, but the release of emotion did make her feel better.

You are stronger than this, she told herself. *Remember every-*

*thing you've done to get through the tough times. Remember where
this started, when you were just fifteen.*

She stared at the ceiling as her mind took her back.

* * *

The day when everything went wrong for Holly, or Erin as she
was then, had started off as the most exciting day of her life. She
was meeting Carl, the lead guitarist she was so smitten with, in
the afternoon and they were going back to her house. Nobody
would be there and she was bunking off school to have sex with
the love of her life for the very first time. She was a few weeks
away from being sixteen. Sex was almost legal, and anyway, who
would know?

Unfortunately, the answer to that was the girl next door. She
was an obnoxious toad of a person, who'd been off school for
some reason, and had seen her sneaking Carl through the back
door. Seen the bedroom curtains close. She'd taken pictures,
threatening to tell Holly's parents unless she agreed to help her
out with a little job that needed doing. Just a delivery. But it
wasn't just the one delivery, like she'd promised. It turned into
at least one delivery a day. Sometimes two. And sometimes it
involved bringing the pouches of pills to school to pass on to
some other kid.

On one of these occasions, Holly's best friend had seen the
pouches in her school bag. The little pink pills had a smiley face
stamped on them and they looked harmless enough if you
didn't know better.

It was a hot summer day and they were sitting outside on
the grass, eating their packed lunches, Holly gazing at the sky
rather than paying attention to what her friend was doing.

'Ooh, what are these?' her friend had said, slipping her

hand into Holly's bag before she could stop her. She held up the pouch, studying the contents. 'Are these the pills everyone's talking about? The one's that make you feel amazing, like you can do anything?'

Holly snatched the pouch out of her hand and stuffed it back into her bag, her cheeks burning, having been caught redhanded. 'I don't know,' she mumbled, wishing the ground would open and swallow her up.

Her friend was staring at her, eyes narrowed. 'You must know. Or why would you have them?'

'I'm just... I said I'd...' She swallowed and zipped up her bag, putting it out of reach. 'I'm looking after them for somebody.'

'I've been dying to try one,' her friend said, leaning over to grab Holly's bag, attempting to pull it towards her. But Holly snatched it up and scrambled to her feet, clasping the bag to her chest.

'You can't,' Holly snapped. 'I told you. They're not mine.'

'Why have you got them, though?' Understanding dawned in her friend's eyes. 'It's Bella, isn't it? That girl who lives next door to you. I've seen you huddled together and I did wonder why. Because you've always said you can't stand her.' She raised her eyebrows. 'In fact, I'm sure you said you found her a bit scary.'

Holly crumpled then, unable to lie any more. She sank to the ground and told her friend everything, relieved to get the secret off her chest. It had been going on for months now and the strain of the constant lying was starting to affect her schoolwork. She couldn't concentrate, was always on edge and she hated having to do the deliveries.

'You can't tell anyone. Promise me.'

'But she's blackmailing you,' her friend said, obviously concerned. The bell rang for the start of the next lesson and they scrambled to their feet. 'Tell her you won't do it any more.'

Holly sighed. If only it was that easy. 'I can't though. I've got myself stuck. She'll tell Mum and Dad that Carl's been round to the house and you know how they'll react to that. They'll probably throw me out. I mean, we're not getting on great as it is and I'm pretty sure that would be the final straw. And now she's got pictures of me handing out packets of drugs to people and taking money.' She blinked back tears, her voice cracking. 'She says she owns me and it's true.'

Her friend put an arm round her shoulders and whispered in her ear. 'You could still let me try a pill, though. Nobody will know there's one missing.'

'No,' Holly snapped, pulling away, wondering if her friend had really been listening. 'I can't risk it.'

The next morning, her friend was found unresponsive in her bedroom. She'd sneaked some of the pills out of Holly's bag without her knowing and now Holly was responsible for her death. The whole train of events had got so completely out of hand, her brain was paralysed by fear. She didn't know what to do, her thoughts clouded by guilt and grief and regret.

Whatever happened, she would still be owned by the toad girl next door for the foreseeable future. In fact, the death of her friend meant Bella's power had increased, because she knew Holly's secret. But that was the least of her worries. If the truth got out, she'd be charged with drug dealing, maybe manslaughter, and sent to a young offender's institution. Her friends would ostracise her and her parents would never forgive her. The nightmare had developed into a full-blown horror story and she couldn't live with the lies any longer.

There was only one solution she could see.

She ran away.

Not only did she run away, but she took the drug money with her, to give her something to live on until she found a way to earn some money. In hindsight that had been one of many stupid mistakes, because that money was not just owed to Bella next door. It was owed to people further up the chain and those were people you didn't want to mess with. That's what Bella had told her. One guy who didn't pay had been stuffed into a drain headfirst, just his feet sticking out, and he'd drowned. That was a future she couldn't risk. So not only was Holly homeless, she couldn't use her real name either, because if she did, they might find her and punish her.

She'd messed up so thoroughly she could never go back.

61

Holly thought about the struggle she'd had as a teenager living on the streets of Birmingham. But she'd found the right people to help, and life had taken a turn for the better. Taking her friend's identity seemed like the best way to keep herself hidden, because she was so terrified the drug gang would be looking for her. Yes, it was illegal, but if she was genuinely scared for her life, why not?

She was reluctant at first, but the more she thought about it, the more it made sense. She was over a hundred miles away from her hometown and nobody would link her assumed name with a schoolgirl who'd died of an overdose. It hadn't even made the national news. It allowed her to be somebody new, to reinvent herself and swear she would never again let people take advantage of her like that. Using Holly's name was a constant reminder that she had to do better.

Now, as she lay on the bed in the outbuilding, she thought about her friend and the promise she'd made herself that she could have a life worth living. Fear was something she'd lived with for years, that was the thing. *I've been through worse than this and come out the other side.* Admittedly, she'd hoped that she'd never be in that situation again, and she wouldn't have been if it hadn't been for Greg, the new chef at the hotel where she'd worked in Buxton.

That incident had given her a whole new set of fears.

* * *

Over the six weeks that he'd been in the kitchens, he'd touched her up a few times when they'd been prepping for evening service. He did it to the other girls as well, but none of them wanted to say anything, scared they'd lose their jobs. Holly decided she wasn't going to put up with his behaviour and complained to her manager, Sofia, who'd been appalled. He'd been reprimanded, but nothing changed. He seemed to think he was impervious to sanctions for sexual harassment because quality head chefs were as rare as hen's teeth.

One night, it was just the two of them in the kitchen. She was prepping vegetables when he came up behind her and started caressing her bum. She stopped what she was doing, knife poised in the air.

'Get your hands off me,' she'd snarled.

'You don't mean that.' His voice was silky smooth and guaranteed to make her cringe. 'I know girls like you.' Rather than stopping his assault, he was now closer, pressing himself against her back. One hand on her bum, his fingers creeping downwards.

'No, you do not. You don't know anyone like me.' She elbowed him in the chest. 'Leave me alone!'

He laughed, leaning his chin on her shoulder, his garlicky breath hot in her face. 'Playing hard to get, aren't you?'

He leant forwards, his hand on the chopping board on the

edge of the workbench, pressing himself harder against her. That was the moment she snapped, her endurance at an end. The point of the chopping knife she was holding slammed down into his hand. It was as though the thing had a mind of its own. She didn't consciously think *I'm going to impale him on the chopping board*, but that's what happened.

She didn't know exactly what damage she'd done. There was definitely blood. Lots of blood. And screaming. Hers as well as his, until she got a grip and ran out of the kitchen and up to her room, throwing stuff into her bag. She didn't have time to pack all her possessions, only the essentials. There was going to be a charge of GBH to answer for and she couldn't risk getting mixed up with the police in case they found out her true identity, and her past misdemeanours.

Once again, she'd found herself running away, ending up with Finn. And that disastrous relationship had led her to here. This prison.

Laying it all out in her mind made it easy to identify the weaknesses, the things she had to stop doing. But it also made her realise that she'd got through all of that by using her own initiative.

So why can't I do that again?

She wiped her face on her sleeve and swung her legs to the floor. It was defeatist to sit and wait for whatever fate Mark had planned for her. She was going to get herself out.

Her eyes scanned the room again, looking for inspiration. The window really was the only exit and now the bedside cabinet was broken, she had nothing to stand on to open the damned thing.

There was very little furniture. The bed was pine framed, the chest of drawers and wardrobe to match. There was a rug next to the bed. Then the fitted corner unit and worktop with a sink. That was it. The wardrobe would be too heavy for her to move so she had to discount that. The chest of drawers was too low to give her the height she needed and there was no way it would fit on the worktop even if she had the strength to get it up there. Her eyes came back to the bed.

She'd had a similar one as a child and it had a slatted base. A memory popped into her head of moving the furniture around to decorate her bedroom and she recalled being surprised at how light the bed frame was once they'd taken the mattress off. Could she prop the frame against the worktop and climb on top of it? It would be like climbing up a ladder, using the slats to help her get height.

Her pulse quickened. *Oh my God, it might just work.*

She pulled the mattress off the bed, happy to find the frame on its own was not too heavy. Yes, it was going to be a bit of a struggle, but it wasn't impossible. She pulled it across the room and with a great deal of grunting and groaning, managed to get the foot of the bed resting against the worktop, then she moved round and shoved the head of the bed as close as she could, so the foot end reared up into the air. The headboard was flat on the ground now and stopped it from tipping over. She gave it a wobble, deciding it felt stable enough.

I've got to give it a try. It was, after all, her only hope of escape.

Carefully, she climbed up the slats using the worktop to steady herself. Climbing up the last few slats felt precarious, like if she shifted her weight at all, the whole thing would slip away from her. But she held her nerve, moving slowly, imagining she was doing a hard move on the climbing wall, making sure she was always in balance until she could reach up for the window catch.

She pulled the window open, relief fizzing through her when the breeze hit her face.

There was no way she could risk getting stuck again and needed to refine her approach. This time, she decided the best way was to just launch herself head-first out of the window, like diving into a pool. If she could get enough of her body out of the window to tip her centre of gravity forwards then she could wriggle down the roof, and even if she fell off, she knew there was a soft landing in the vegetable bed. At least the fear of falling had diminished now it had already happened once, and really, what choice did she have?

Oh God, oh God, I'm so close, she thought, as she dithered, unable to make herself leave the relative safety of the bed.

Her hands were slick with sweat, her clothes sticking to her body after the exertion of moving the bed, and climbing up to open the window. One of her legs was starting to tremble, her muscles not used to standing in such an unnatural position. The bed frame rattled beneath her and all her instincts were telling her to get the hell down from there before she went crashing to the floor.

Fear paralysed her. *Do I really have to do this?* She wanted the answer to be no, but her mind wasn't letting her off that easily, giving her another question to answer. *Why would any man, a stranger, want to imprison a woman?* The answer had to involve sex, didn't it? Rape. He might be into kinky sex, might want to hurt her, strangle her—

She brought her thoughts to a screeching halt, took a deep breath, and launched herself towards the open window.

62

Mark crept through the front door and into the hallway, the spade held in front of him, all his senses on high alert. He could hear his mother's voice, talking.

Oh God, she's on the phone.

All his nerve endings seemed to be screaming, setting off a buzzing in his head as he imagined his mother ruining everything he'd been working towards. She could only be calling emergency services and that would signal the end for him. *Is it already too late?*

The lounge door was closed and he pushed it open, standing in the doorway, reluctant to venture in until he knew what was awaiting him.

'Naughty boy, naughty boy, naughty boy,' Archie squawked as he flapped towards Mark and landed on his head, claws digging into his scalp, his beak pulling at strands of hair.

'Ow! Get off me!' Mark shouted, a hand smacking at the bird, no patience to deal with his parrot when he had to get that phone off his mother. It didn't occur to him, at that point, to ask himself why his bird was out of his cage. And when, a few seconds later, the significance actually registered, the bird had flapped away from his grasping hand, flown out of the front door and was a diminishing speck in the sky.

He's gone. Mark's gaze followed the bird's flight, helpless to do anything. *Archie's gone.*

The pain was so sharp, he thought he might be having a heart attack, his hands clasping at his chest while the spade clunked to the floor. His mother was sitting in the chair next to the bird's cage, facing him. She was laughing, pointing at him. 'That's the last you'll see of that bird and you've only yourself to blame. What were you thinking leaving the front door open like that?'

Mark's mouth opened and closed, a whole stream of words all jammed together, unable to separate themselves into sentences. He tried to calm himself down and just think. That's all he had to do, but his head was exploding and the pain in his chest was getting worse.

He glared at his mother. 'Who were you talking to?' He couldn't see his phone, but she could easily have hidden it down the side of the chair or something. He bent down and picked up the spade from where it had fallen on the floor, thinking the sight of a weapon in his hand might encourage her to tell the truth.

She shrugged, looked away through the patio doors. 'I wasn't talking to anyone. It was that bird talking to me.'

'I don't believe you,' he snarled.

'You don't have to believe me. Anyway, what difference would it make who I was talking to?'

He glared at her. 'Where's my phone? I know you've got it.' He moved closer, the spade held in front of him, ready to strike out should she make any weird move. He couldn't discount the possibility she had a knife tucked away somewhere and he scanned her body, looking for anything suspicious. But she didn't look suspicious, just a middle-aged lady in a nightie, her hands resting on her knees as she sat back in the armchair, legs crossed at the ankles, slippers on her feet.

She looked about as dangerous as a rabbit. But he could see the fire in her eyes and knew he couldn't underestimate her. *None of this is real.* It was all an illusion, staged, a big pretence. She was toying with him, trying to throw him off balance and make his head spin with doubts.

If she *was* telling the truth and she *had* been talking to the parrot, he still needed to find his phone, just to put his mind at rest. He turned and stomped upstairs, thinking it must have fallen out of his pocket when he'd been fiddling with the door lock in her bedroom. Sure enough, there it was lying on the floor. He heaved a sigh of relief and returned his phone to his pocket, glad that he didn't have to worry about the emergency services turning up unexpectedly. *All that panic for nothing.*

His grip tightened on the spade as he hurried back downstairs ready to face his mother again.

'You think I don't know what you've done?' she said as soon as he walked through the lounge door.

What I've done? That could be any one of a number of things at this stage.

For a moment, he couldn't work out exactly what she might mean. His eyes caught sight of the raised beds in the garden, and suddenly he couldn't speak, his vocal cords paralysed, his heart skipping about in his chest like a squash ball bouncing off the walls of a court. *No, she can't know.* She was bluffing, goading him again.

'I don't know what you're talking about,' he snarled, hating her just a little bit more. He glared at her and she glared back and a sudden thought struck him.

If she really thinks I'm trying to kill her, why is she just sitting there?

It didn't make sense. He tightened his grip on the spade, his heart so full of loathing he could taste it in his mouth. Bitter and rancid and something he needed to expel before it poisoned him.

Do it, he told himself. *Just finish it now.*

He could, couldn't he? He could swing his arm back and swipe at her head like he was knocking a cricket ball for six. That would do it. He nodded to himself, his hands clasping the spade so tight now his fingers were aching. In his mind he was doing it, could even see the blood splatter up the walls, but his body was not responding. He was standing there at the ready and nothing was happening, like he'd been set in stone.

His mother smirked at him. 'I know what you're thinking, but you can't, can you?' She pointed a finger at him. 'Because you're a coward. You're a pathetic, weak man and you know that without me, you wouldn't survive.' She laughed. 'That's your problem, isn't it? You know you need me. Because if you didn't, I'd be dead by now.' She gave a satisfied nod, folded her arms across her chest. 'We both know that's the truth.'

'You're wrong,' he snapped.

But of course, she was right.

He *couldn't* bring himself to do it. Having these ideas in his head was very different to actually doing the deed. She was his mum for God's sake, and despite all the torment she'd put him through over his life, however much he wished her dead, he couldn't actually bring himself to kill her in cold blood.

The gradual poisoning had been different. He'd never given her enough to finish her off, just enough to make her feel unwell, and that had seemed okay. Like she deserved a bit of discomfort in her life, a bit of payback.

When she'd broken her leg, it was the first time he'd ever had any power over her and he'd enjoyed seeing her feeble and distressed. Enjoyed being in control. But killing her with the spade? *No. I can't do it.*

63

Holly landed with a thump, a little more than halfway out of the window. This time she could lever herself forwards with her arms and managed a less than elegant slide, head-first down the roof before her hand caught the gutter, bringing her to a halt. From there, she managed to swing herself over the edge before dropping onto the slate slabs below.

She crumpled to the floor, overwhelmed by the exertion, and the fact that she'd only gone and bloody done it. She was out and her route to freedom looked like a short one. A quick dash across the garden then she could climb over the wall and scoot off down the fields to wherever that may lead.

It took a moment for her to catch her breath and feel ready for the next stage of her escape. She would be a bit vulnerable when she was getting over the wall, very visible on her high perch, but she wasn't planning on being up there for long.

She made the dash across the garden and had her hands on top of the wall, figuring out which stones she could use to climb up, when she heard shouting coming from inside the house. At this point, she was no more than ten feet away, partly hidden by a large shrub. She glanced towards the patio doors and saw a grey-haired woman, lit up in the sunshine, like it was a spot-light, picking her out. She was sitting in a chair by what looked like a cage. A very big cage, which seemed like a strange thing to have in your living room.

Their eyes met. This must be the woman who'd been shouting for help, the one who'd alerted Holly to the danger she might be in herself.

'It's not my problem,' she muttered as she found her first foothold and started to climb, desperate to make her bid for freedom.

If you were in that woman's shoes, what would you be hoping for?

The voice in her head was stern, disapproving, telling her off. She took a step back down. How could she, in all conscience, leave without at least checking the woman was okay? If the people who'd helped Holly over the years had turned their backs, where would she have been?

She crouched behind the shrub, parting the leaves to give herself a view of the house. Mark came into focus and... Oh God, he was waving a spade around like he was going to use it to club the poor woman to death. Holly's heart started to gallop, her brain telling her she had to act quickly. She slipped her holdall off her shoulders and prepared to make her move.

Mark had his back towards the window and while he couldn't see what she was doing, Holly dashed across the garden towards the back door. She opened it a crack, listening as she crouched on the doormat.

'I want you to be dead,' Mark sobbed. 'With all my heart, I wish you didn't exist. You've ruined my life. Ever since Dad died. And you've enjoyed doing it, I know you have.' He carried on talking through his tears. 'You are a sick, twisted, evil excuse for a human being and I hate that you're my mother.'

He sounded so distraught, it made Holly hesitate. And then she remembered he'd told her that his mother was dead. Her jaw clenched. It just confirmed that he was a liar, completely untrustworthy, and now his emotions were running high it was clear that his mum was in danger. He'd just admitted he wanted her dead, hadn't he? Her heart raced faster, her body tensing for action. She couldn't be a witness to murder.

She crept into the kitchen, leaving the back door open as an escape route, and inched towards the door into the lounge. She peeped round the door frame and the older woman's eyes widened a little when she saw her. Holly knew she'd have no chance of overpowering Mark. She wouldn't be strong enough to fight him. Whatever action she took had to be based on cunning rather than strength.

Her eyes glanced round the room and in an instant, she knew what she had to do. But she had to act fast, before he moved and the trajectory became all wrong. A small smile played on her lips, determination firing through her body. *This guy has no idea who he's up against, no idea at all.*

His back was towards her and she bent low, charging him with as much force as she could muster, driving with her legs like she was in a rugby scrum. He yelped as she hit the back of his thighs, catching him completely by surprise. He dropped the spade, arms flailing to try and keep his balance, but she carried on shoving him with all her might, until she drove him into the cage and shut the door.

'There's a padlock over here,' his mother told her, waving something in the air. 'Otherwise, he'll get out.'

Holly slipped it through the mesh of the cage, snapping it shut.

64

Mark couldn't understand what had just happened. One minute he'd been having an argument with his mother, the next he'd been barged by an unknown force and locked in Archie's cage. He clambered to his feet, his hands grabbing the wire mesh as he turned and stared into the face of Holly.

His jaw dropped open, his brain stuttering like a car running out of fuel. *It's not possible.*

The last thing he knew, she'd been imprisoned in the outbuilding, the door bolted in place. He glanced into the garden and saw the window pushed wide open and his mouth snapped shut. He'd been sure she wouldn't be trying that caper again, but here she was. The woman was a bloody Houdini.

His body deflated, and he clung to the wire of the cage to keep himself upright. The day had gone from bad to worse, on a downward spiral, just when he'd thought he was finally winning. He rattled the mesh, knowing it was pointless, but frustration making him do it anyway.

The cage was a sturdy construction. He'd made it himself, the wire mesh nailed onto a solid wooden frame. He leant his forehead against the wire, trying to summon his powers of persuasion in the same way he'd like to summon a genie.

'Holly, let me out,' he said, fighting to keep his anger in check. 'I really need to explain. Whatever you might have seen or heard, it's not what you think.' He glared at his mother, wishing his eyes were laser beams that could fry her brain with just one look.

Holly was panting hard, leaning forwards, her hands on her thighs as she gazed at him. There was something in her stare, a hardness in her eyes that surprised him. She looked different to the willowy songstress he'd fallen for. She looked feral with her hair all mussed up and dirt smeared on her face. And the fact she'd managed to find a way out of the window told him she was resourceful, crafty. Worry pinched the muscles at the back of his neck.

She straightened up, took a step closer, hands on her hips, her eyes fixed on his. The defiance in her gaze was unnerving and Mark understood in that moment that he might have severely underestimated this woman.

'I heard you saying you wanted to kill her and I'm not sure how anything you say can change what that might mean. Especially when you had a spade in your hands and looked like you were going to hit her with it.'

Mark sighed, trying to keep his voice gentle. The last thing he wanted was to come over as confrontational. What he needed most was for her to understand.

'Me wanting to kill her and actually going through with it are two very different things, as my mother well knows.' He shot his mum a glance, annoyed to see she was smiling, sitting in that chair like she was watching a favourite drama on TV. His fingers tightened round the wire as he switched his gaze back to

Holly. 'I'm sure you've told people in your life that you wanted them dead and not meant it.'

He saw a flicker of doubt flash across her face and in that moment, he dared to hope there was a chance he could persuade her to let him out. If he could keep his focus and not let his mother get to him. 'She knew she wasn't in danger, or why would she have just been sitting there? Didn't you hear her laughing at me?'

Holly frowned. 'I didn't hear any laughing. What I heard was you shouting. And I saw you threatening her with a spade and it looked like you were going to smash her head in.'

He puffed out his cheeks, almost too weary to argue. But he had to, because his mother was dangerous. Look at the situation she'd created, him locked in a cage. Who knew what she'd do next? *Oh my God, what if she gets Holly to call the police?*

He closed his eyes, unable to consider that as an option. She wouldn't do that, would she? His whole life was in danger of collapsing, like it was being sucked down a sink hole. It was time to take a different tack. Find something that might make Holly change her mind about his mother, and cast him in a more sympathetic light.

'I made her a lovely lunch and you know what she did? She tricked me and locked me in the bedroom. I'd still be there if I hadn't been able to pick the lock.' Holly appeared unmoved, but then, he supposed he had locked her in the outbuilding. He threw up his hands in frustration. 'Holly, listen to me. Please, just listen. She's had ample chance to escape and she didn't. Instead, she came down here and what did she do? She let my parrot out of his cage.' His emotions surged at the thought of what he'd lost and it was a struggle to get his words out. 'And he flew out of the front door and now he's gone.' He sniffed. 'That bird has been my companion and friend for over two decades. Can you imagine what losing him means?'

Holly folded her arms across her chest, casting a glance at his mother, but she didn't reply. She needed more. 'My mother let him out, then waited for me to open the front door, knowing he was going to escape. She made it my fault. As usual. She always does that, twists things round.' His chin started to quiver, and for a moment it was too hard to speak. 'Can you imagine how it feels, losing my friend like that?' He pointed at his mother. 'She's cruel. She's always been cruel.'

Holly's mouth worked from side to side, like she was chewing over his words, and a glimmer of hope ignited in his heart. This was not over. Not yet.

'I heard her calling for help earlier,' Holly said, glancing at his mum again. 'She sounded frantic.'

'He's been slowly killing me for weeks,' his mother said, venom in her tone. 'Don't you listen to his excuses, he's a smooth talker. That's how he gets himself out of trouble.' She heaved herself to her feet, grabbing the back of the chair as she wobbled, clearly unsteady. 'I think we should go. We can take his car.' She looked at Holly. 'You can drive, can't you, love?'

Holly looked unsure. 'What, and just leave him here, locked in a cage?'

'Yes. He deserves nothing more. I'm done with him.' She gave a dismissive flap of her hand, her back towards him as she headed for the door. 'I regret the day he was born.'

Holly's face was a picture. She definitely hadn't liked that comment and he told himself there was still a chance he could turn this round.

'Shouldn't we just ring the police or something?' Holly looked nervous, unsure.

'I don't have a phone that works properly,' his mother

pointed out. 'There's no landline in the house and he's not going to let us use his mobile, is he?' She frowned at Holly. 'You don't happen to have one, do you?'

Holly shook her head. 'No. I think he took mine.'

'Right, well, we'll have to go to the police station then, won't we?'

'Mum, don't do this,' Mark begged. 'Don't get the police involved.'

'It's too late,' his mother spat. 'It's time you were properly punished. And I'll feel safer once you're locked away...' She walked back towards the cage and jabbed a finger at him. 'In prison where you belong.' She grabbed Holly's arm and led her into the kitchen where he'd left the car keys on the worktop. 'Come on, we need to go.'

Mark heard the door close as they left the house, a voice in his head screaming at him for not bashing the old witch with the spade when he'd had the chance.

65

Holly's heart was still racing when she reached Mark's car, parked on the driveway at the side of the house. She got his mum settled in the passenger seat and was about to open the driver's door when she realised she'd forgotten something.

She hurried round the front of the car pointing to the back garden. 'I've just got to go and get my bag. I left it by the wall.'

She jogged up the drive and across the lawn, picking up her holdall from where she'd left it behind the shrub and looping the straps over her shoulders. The sun was still slanting into the lounge, and she couldn't help looking through the patio window. Mark was standing there in the cage, fingers clinging to the wire, his head bowed. He was a picture of despair. A poster boy for misery. And something about it made her hesitate.

She couldn't just leave him locked in a cage, could she? Not when she wasn't sure if she really *was* going to go to the police. It could compromise her own freedom. No harm had come to her, or his mother for that matter, so maybe she should just back out of the whole scenario and fade away. But then, who would find

Mark before he died of dehydration? Maybe she should make an anonymous call, but she didn't know the address and wouldn't be able to direct the emergency services here even if she wanted to. And she wasn't sure she trusted his mother. Her attitude to Mark, the way she spoke to him, had been awful.

There were so many questions buzzing round her head and she needed answers before she decided what to do. She opened the back door and walked through to the lounge.

'I'm not sure about leaving you locked in,' she said, and his head lifted, a flicker of surprise in his eyes. She chewed at her lip, hesitating before walking closer. 'Is your mother telling the truth? Have you been poisoning her?'

Mark sighed. 'Unfortunately, my mother is bitter and twisted and downright mean.'

'I... didn't like the way she talked to you.'

Mark gave a derisive snort. 'Oh, she's always spoken to me like that. And she's always told lies. She's the sort of person who never takes responsibility for anything, just shoves the blame on to somebody else. Usually me.'

Holly frowned. 'Then why haven't you left home, if she's so awful? Why are you still living with her at your age?'

'Because she needs looking after and she's my mum, isn't she?' There was a note of frustration in his voice. 'However bad she's been as a parent, she fed me and clothed me and gave me a roof over my head when I was a child. When my dad died, she struggled to cope, and somehow that was my fault too, even though I tried to help her every step of the way.' He gave a hollow laugh. 'I suppose that's always been the dynamic between us. But you've seen what she's like. Her body and her mind are failing and she lives in a fantasy world half the time. She can't manage on her own and I feel it's only right that I should be here when she needs me.' He shrugged. 'It's what any decent person would do, isn't it?'

He gazed at Holly with those lovely eyes of his and she had to pull herself away, concentrate on the questions she needed answering. Her eyes fell onto the padlock key, lying on the coffee table where she'd left it, and she stuffed her hands in her pockets to stop herself from reaching for it.

She took another step towards him and his eyes lit up, but then she hesitated, still conflicted. *He locked you in and pushed you off the roof.* How could she possibly think of giving him his freedom?

His fingers tightened round the mesh of the cage, his voice a little tetchy when he spoke. 'Why can't you see that it's my mother who's the evil one here? She's playing you for a fool. Do you really feel safe getting in a car with her? Because I wouldn't.'

Holly snorted. 'She's a middle-aged lady in a nightie. I can't see she has any weapons hidden about her person and she appears to be pretty frail, judging by the way she walks.' She poked a finger at him. 'And anyway, I don't feel safe letting you out of there. Not when you lied to me. You told me your mother was dead. And you pushed me off the roof.'

It was satisfying to see the shock register in his eyes. He'd thought she hadn't noticed the pressure on her back, sending her hurtling into a freefall. It was unnerving how this benign persona he presented kept fooling her.

'But also, I'm confused, Mark. I want an answer to this at least... Why did you kidnap me and bring me here?'

His mouth dropped open, his eyes wide with indignation. 'I did not kidnap you! *You* were hiding in *my* car, remember.'

She took a step closer, her anger mounting. 'But we were

supposed to be going to Birmingham. You promised, and then I woke up here.'

He looked at her with puppy dog eyes as if she was doing him a great injustice. 'I was keeping you safe. I thought it was too risky getting that close to a city, and then there was a police car behind me with flashing lights and I just panicked. I knew you wanted to escape from the police and I thought bringing you here, for now, would be the best thing. Just until everything calmed down.'

Her eyes narrowed. He'd changed his story. He'd told her earlier he heard a news report but now it was a police car making him panic and bring her here. She folded her arms across her chest, thinking she'd let the conversation roll on a little and see where it might take them. 'You were keeping me safe, were you? Well, locking me in a room is not the way to make me feel safe.'

'I told you, I had to lock you in because the door wasn't shutting properly.' His voice was whiny now, pleading. He rattled the mesh in a sudden burst of irritation. 'Come on, let me out so we can talk about this properly.'

'I don't believe anything you're telling me.' She shrugged. 'And we are talking properly.'

He was getting more irate by the second, frustrated with her for standing her ground, and she could see a vein popping out on his forehead, his skin taking on a reddish hue as he rattled the wire of the cage again. 'Look, Holly, I think you owe me a favour. A very big favour. If it wasn't for me sorting Finn out, once and for all, you'd still be in an abusive relationship.'

It took a moment for his words to register, her brain freezing when she understood.

He sorted Finn out. Is he saying... Did he just admit to murder?

66

The shock was like a physical blow, stunning her for a moment, and when Holly finally found her voice, it was hard to say the words. 'You... killed Finn?'

'I saved you from a situation that could have killed you. That's what I did.'

Holly felt herself sway and grabbed the back of a chair. My God, how had she got it so wrong? Mark was a murderer. A cold-blooded murderer.

There's nothing more to say.

She took a deep breath, turned on her heel and left, slamming the back door behind her before stumbling back to the car. After that last revelation, perhaps she believed his mother more than she believed Mark now.

She played his words on repeat in her head, appalled that he'd just admitted to killing Finn. And the police had questioned him and let him go. Unbelievable. She had to tell them. And at the same time, she could report him for her own kidnapping and false imprisonment. And the attempted murder of his mother.

Her mind spun, telling her there was no evidence. It would be her word against his and would they really believe her when she was wanted for assault in Buxton? And once they discovered all the other stuff from her past, her word would hold no weight at all. It would be a waste of time, not to mention a waste of her freedom. If she could get a new passport sorted out and leave the country, she could draw a line under everything and start again. Wouldn't that be a better way forward?

His mother, though... Yes, well, she could make her own accusations. That was between her and Mark and nothing to do with Holly. She'd just arrived at an opportune moment. No, she didn't need to get involved in any of that.

But Finn... There must be evidence that would connect Mark to Finn's murder. Concrete evidence. Could she really let him get away with something as terrible as that?

She heaved her bag off her back and threw it in the boot before opening the car door and getting in. Mark's mother was watching her every move, a look on her face that Holly couldn't quite decipher. Something about the woman made Holly very uneasy and she was hoping they wouldn't have to spend too much time together.

'Sorry, let's go, shall we?'

'That took you a while,' his mother said, leaving Holly in no doubt she knew she'd been talking to Mark.

Holly nodded and started the car. 'Yes, well, I had to make sure I hadn't forgotten anything.'

The thing she'd definitely forgotten for a moment in there was common sense, and his admission to murdering Finn had given her a flash of clarity. Locking him in a cage was the only thing they could have done, and he wasn't going to die in there in the time it took for the police to arrive. It was merely a matter of containment. He was perfectly safe and secure until he could be taken into custody, and she was mightily relieved to be leaving him behind.

She drove carefully down the track, her knuckles white as she clutched the steering wheel, concerned that she might veer off into the undergrowth round the tight bends. She'd never driven on such a rough surface, or one that was so steep and twisty. It took a lot of concentration and she wasn't sure how much battery power her brain had left.

There was something about the woman sitting next to her that was making her skin crawl. Was it the way she was staring at her, or the fact that she emanated bad vibes as strong as any odour? It was nothing Holly could really put her finger on, or describe with any clarity. It was more of a feeling. A very strong feeling.

Mark was clearly one of those people who used his words like a snake-charmer, hypnotising her and confusing her as to what was real. But she had to wonder about his mother's part in all this. Had he been born bad or been shaped that way by his mother's behaviour?

Perhaps it wasn't a case of one being good and one being bad. Perhaps mother and son were as evil and rotten as each other, but in any case, that wasn't the issue. Her primary concern was getting justice for Finn. He wasn't a good man, and he'd made some big mistakes, but he *hadn't* deserved to have his life taken from him. And Mark *did* deserve to be locked up for what he'd done.

'I'm Jean by the way,' his mother said into the awkward silence. 'And you're... Holly, is that right?'

'Yes.' Holly nodded, not keen to get into conversation when she was trying to think about driving.

'Thank you for saving me,' Jean gushed. 'I thought I was going to die, you know.' Holly thought about the scene she'd witnessed through the window, the conversation she'd over-heard. But then she thought about Mark's words, his insistence that it had been an empty threat. Had his mum really needed saving?

She stayed silent, not responding to Jean's comment, because she wasn't sure what she believed any more.

'You had a lucky escape as well, you know. The last girls didn't. Both of them died.'

67

Holly slammed on the brakes. Her brain was misfiring, trying to compute what she'd just heard, and she didn't feel in control of her body, let alone the car. She stared at Jean. 'What do you mean, the last girls?'

Jean pursed her lips. 'I think there have been two, but I don't know. There might have been more. He brought the first one home a little while ago, just after I'd broken my leg. He thought I didn't know, but even though I couldn't get down the stairs, I could see out of the back window in the spare bedroom. I kept hearing him going in and out of the back door, disappearing off for hours and I couldn't work out what he might be up to, so I started spying on him, just for something to do. I saw him carry a woman into the outbuilding. He kept her locked up, just like you.'

Holly's blood ran cold. Did this mean he'd brought Holly home specifically to... kill her? The thought chilled her to the bone, like someone had poured freezing water through her veins.

She cleared her throat. 'How... did she... die?'

Jean thought for a moment. 'I don't know. He wouldn't talk about it, denied everything. I just saw him making the first of those vegetable beds, which struck me as odd because he's never really shown any interest in gardening. And then he wasn't going to the outbuilding every night, like he was doing before. He was sulky for a while. Distant, and I knew the signs. Knew he'd done something terrible. Then it happened all over again and the second vegetable bed appeared.'

Holly couldn't believe what she was hearing, or the way in which the news had been delivered, in such a calm voice. Like Jean had been talking about something she'd seen on TV, not a real, live human being dying at the hands of her son. 'And you didn't think to tell anyone?' she gasped. 'You didn't think to call the police?'

Jean's mouth pressed into a thin line, a frown creasing her forehead. 'Don't you go judging me,' she snapped. 'He's kept me like a prisoner as well, you know. I've not been allowed near a phone. And I've been fighting for my life.' There was a brittleness to her voice, fire smouldering in her eyes. 'Like I told you, he's been poisoning me.' She put a bony hand on Holly's arm and squeezed hard, making her wince. 'Do you understand what I'm saying? Because you don't seem to be on my side somehow. He's been slowly killing me. The doctors knew something was wrong but they couldn't work it out.' She barked a laugh. 'But I worked it out when he went away this last time and I started feeling better. That's when I knew I had to find a way to escape or he was going to finish me off and put me in a vegetable bed, just like those girls.'

Holly crumpled, her forehead leaning against the steering wheel, her face cupped in her hands. This was too much. Way too much, and it was a good few moments before she could gather her thoughts into any coherent order. She flopped back in her seat, staring out of the window, not able to look at the woman beside her. 'You're honestly telling me he brought two girls home, killed them, and buried them in the vegetable beds?'

Jean nodded. 'That's right. But I couldn't say anything because I thought if he could kill them, he could kill me.' She gave a snort. 'Little did I realise he was already doing it.'

Holly's mind flashed back to falling off the roof, landing in the freshly dug earth. Her stomach heaved, her hands covering her mouth. She'd been lying on a poor girl's grave.

'I've been so scared living with him,' Jean continued, crimping the fabric of her nightie between her fingers. 'He's never been right, ever since he was a child. In fact, he's been a worry to me from when he was an infant.' She sighed. 'He seemed to live in a different world, you see? For many years he had an invisible friend and anything he did wrong was always their fault. It was never him. Then when he got Archie, he blamed the parrot for everything, even when it was obvious a parrot couldn't have done half the things he was accused of.'

She huffed, staring out of the windscreen. 'I made appointments to see psychologists, but he would never talk to them, not a word. And when he got older, he refused point blank to attend any appointments at all.' She heaved another big sigh. 'He's my son. What am I supposed to do? It's my job to look after him.'

Holly frowned. This conversation seemed to be the mirror image of the one she'd just had with Mark. Something didn't quite ring true and it all felt a bit... manufactured. Mark had been emotional, quite distressed when he was talking. But Jean was calm as you like, no emotion whatsoever, even though she was talking about young women losing their lives and struggling to deal with a mentally ill child.

He'd complained of her cruelty and now she was beginning

to see a coldness that made her wonder if Mark's version was the truth. Maybe theirs was a toxic relationship and they somehow needed each other in a weird way. Whatever was happening, it brought Holly's skin out in goosebumps. She didn't want to be involved, couldn't even think about it now.

Get the hell out of here, her brain was shouting.

She was even more uncomfortable at being in the same car with this woman now. Talk about twisted morals. Instead of trying to protect other women from her son, she'd allowed him to carry on. What sort of person would do that? Or was she being unfair if Jean's version of events had an element of truth in it?

She shook her head as she started the car again, her thoughts so tangled she didn't even know where to start to make sense of it all. It was easier to just concentrate on the driving, the final bend leading them out into a field where the track evened out. There was a gateway and a cattlegrid where the field joined the single-track road, and as they travelled towards it, she realised there was a problem.

A very big problem.

An ambulance was blocking the road and a police car was parked across the gateway.

68

At the very moment she registered they were stuck, with no way out, a police officer spotted them, holding up a hand as a signal to stop. Holly didn't know whether to feel relieved or scared, but it was clear there was no running away now. Fate had dealt her this hand and she was just going to have to make the most of it.

She stopped the car and lowered her window as the officer approached, her heart thundering in her chest.

'I'm sorry, but you're not going to be able to get out.'

'What happened?' Jean asked, leaning forwards. 'Is it a car accident? It's a bit of a blind bend here, isn't it?'

The officer shook his head. 'There was a call for an ambulance. An elderly couple got taken ill, very suddenly by the caller's account, but when the ambulance arrived, unfortunately they'd passed away.'

Jean's jaw dropped open, eyes bulging out of her head. 'An elderly couple?' she whispered.

The officer frowned and leant a bit lower so he could see Jean better. 'That's right. I don't suppose you know them, do you?' He looked towards the lay-by where they were parked.

'There are a lot of leaflets in the car. Jehovah's Witnesses, by the looks of things.'

Jean grabbed Holly's arm. 'Oh my God. They came to the house earlier. I heard them at the door and I shouted for help to try and get their attention.' The officer looked startled, which was not surprising with Jean gabbling like a madwoman, bone thin with her hair sticking up all over her head, sitting there in a pink floral nightie. 'He gave them tea, I'm sure he did. I heard them talking downstairs. Then they came up to see me and I asked them to take me with them, but he told them I had dementia and whisked them back downstairs.'

Holly understood now why Jean had been shouting, at least that was making a bit more sense. She had wondered why she would be calling for help when there were no neighbours to hear. The officer glanced at Holly, a questioning look in his eyes as if asking if he should believe what she was saying.

Jean leant across Holly, banging on the steering wheel to make sure the officer was paying attention. 'It was him. My son.' She pointed back up the track. 'You need to go and arrest him. I think... he might have poisoned them. And he's definitely been poisoning me. We were just on our way to the station to report it.'

Holly felt sick. Was that the fate she'd escaped?

The officer straightened up, clearly taken aback by this new information. He glanced towards the road. 'I'll just go and have a word with my boss. You stay here, I'll be right back.'

Jean settled in her seat. 'That'll be the end of it now,' she said, almost wistfully.

Holly supposed it must be a hard thing to do, shopping your son to the police. Even harder to know they were a murderer and they'd been slowly killing you. What sort of person would poison two innocent people though? People who'd come in the name of God. It seemed hard to fathom. But she supposed Mark was getting desperate at that point, trying to protect himself against scrutiny.

Holly was feeling queasy and opened the car door, stepping out into the field to get some fresh air into her lungs. Nerves swirled in her stomach as she thought about the conversations she might be having with the police in the not-too-distant future. Her eyes scanned the field, noting the woodland bordering both sides. Plenty of places to hide if she decided to just take off and avoid police scrutiny altogether.

I should have jumped over that wall, she thought. *Then I'd be long gone.* But if she'd done that, Jean could be dead by now, Mark would be at large to strike again and Finn and the murdered couple wouldn't get their justice. Although running *seemed* like the easy option, was it really? Had experience taught her nothing? She nodded to herself as a familiar phrase came into her head. *The hard way is the easy way.*

Just tell them the truth. Everything. Get it all out in the open and deal with the consequences. Only then would she truly be free.

It was a bit of an epiphany, her whole life flickering in front of her eyes, the bad decisions and the consequences that had left her homeless and in dire situations. Yes, she'd always managed to survive, but there was no doubt those experiences had left their mental scars. All her adult life she'd been running away from something, ignoring the rules of society to save her own skin. It was a pattern that seemed to be on repeat as she staggered from one catastrophe to another.

If you always do what you've always done, then you'll always get what you've always got. It was another of her nan's sayings, and she understood now exactly what she'd meant. If Holly wanted her life to be different, she had to stop running away from diffi-cult things. That habit had landed her in so much trouble, she couldn't face thinking about it all. If she'd stayed at home and been honest when her friend had died, she would at least have had some integrity. If she'd faced up to her wrongdoing then, her life could have been very different. And she might still be part of a family.

Not only had she run away from the truth as a teenager, she'd also disrespected her friend. She'd told herself she was keeping Holly's memory alive by taking on her identity, but that was one of the biggest lies she'd ever told herself. It was convenient, nothing about respect. If she'd respected her friend, she would have stayed, told the truth, and the people who'd been dealing those drugs would have been caught and put in prison, saving other young people's lives.

Sometimes, she hated herself for the web of lies that held her life together. Wasn't it time to face up to the truth, whatever the consequences? If she hadn't gone to get her passport behind Finn's back, she would never have met Mark and he wouldn't have followed her to Dumfries and Finn would still be alive. All deceitful actions had consequences, even if you couldn't see it at the time.

She watched the officer walking back towards her with a smaller man beside him. There was a confidence about him, an authority that ramped up her nerves. Her decision now would change the rest of her life. *Are you really going to do this?*

69

The men stopped in front of Holly. 'I've got a lot to tell you,' she said, before the man could even introduce himself. 'I need to report a kidnapping and a false imprisonment and attempted murder,' she gabbled, desperate to get the words out before she changed her mind. The officers glanced at each other. 'And Mark, the man who is responsible, is locked up in the house. The key to the padlock is on the coffee table and—'

'Hold on a minute,' the smaller man said, clearly surprised by her outburst. 'Let's just do this one thing at a time, shall we?' He showed her his ID. 'I'm Detective Inspector James Pritchard and this is Detective Sergeant Gethin Jones.' He put his ID away. 'We're investigating what may have caused the unexplained deaths of the couple in the silver car over there.' He paused, frowning. 'I understand you believe the couple may have been poisoned by a man who is still in a property at the top of this track. Is that correct?'

Holly nodded. 'That's right. And he—'

DI Pritchard held up a hand. 'I realise there's a lot going on, and there are other crimes you want to talk to us about, but our first priority is getting him in custody, okay? Everything else we can deal with later, but right now, we need you to come with us, and show us exactly where he is.'

Go back up there? The idea struck horror into her heart, her brain going into meltdown. She stared at the officer, her mouth hanging open, no words coming out.

'I can see that's a worrying prospect, but we have back-up arriving any time now and I promise you won't be in danger. It'll just help with the logistics.' She nodded her agreement, thinking she should do whatever was needed to get Mark safely into custody.

He pointed at the car. 'We just need you to move off the track so we can get our vehicles up there when they arrive.'

She grimaced. 'It's not my car. It's Mark's. I'm not even insured to drive. I haven't passed my test. I was only driving so Jean could be safe and to get help.'

The officers moved away, having a whispered conversation before DS Jones went over to the car, asking Jean to get out. He helped her over to where Holly was standing. 'You might want to sit down for a minute while we get things sorted. Hopefully we won't keep you too long.'

Holly helped Jean to get comfortable on the grass, before moving a little distance away, still wary of the woman. She watched DS Jones move Mark's car off the track, then have a good look inside and in the boot, bagging up bits and pieces as he went along.

A little while later, another ambulance arrived and two more police cars, followed by a van. The field was starting to resemble a car park and was a bustle of activity, providing a welcome distraction. She watched Jean being led to the ambulance by a paramedic, saw them help her inside, and that was another task completed. The woman was not her problem any more.

Tiredness was starting to overwhelm her, creating a strange, out-of-body experience, like she was watching from above. It was the weirdest sensation, but it came with a wonderful sense of calm. Perhaps it was because she'd finally given herself over to telling the truth, not caring what the consequences might be. Knowing for certain that living a lie was no life at all.

'Holly, are you ready?'

The voice of DS Jones broke into her thoughts, bringing her back to the present and the job at hand. She blinked, trying to get herself focused on what they were going to do. *It'll be good to see him arrested,* she thought, clambering to her feet. It would give her a sense of closure if she was certain he was safely locked away. He'd definitely be kept on remand, given the crimes he was accused of, and it was now her job to guide the police to him.

Three cars were parked on the track and she was shown to the first one, DS Jones holding the back door open as she slid into the seat behind DI Pritchard. They travelled up the track at a careful speed, rolling over the lumps and bumps, Holly rocking from side to side in the back. She was glad she didn't suffer from motion sickness because this would have been a challenge, and as it was, she had to open the window and gulp in big breaths of fresh air.

Finally, the house came into view and the car pulled up in the parking space alongside it. Holly leant forwards. 'I don't actually have to come in, do I?'

'Not initially. Just explain the lie of the land and where you left him and anything you think we might need to know.'

'As you can see, the front door is open. I know the back door is unlocked, because that's how we came out. That takes you into the kitchen which leads into the lounge. And that's where he is. In the parrot's cage. I know that sounds ridiculous, and unlikely, but it's an extremely large cage. There's a padlock and the key is on the coffee table.'

Holly watched as two officers positioned themselves on either side of the front door and the others went round the back. She could hardly breathe, but was surprised when DS Jones walked through the front door only a few minutes later, and spoke to the two officers who disappeared back into the house with him.

'You're so stupid. Bugger off.'

Holly's head snapped round. It sounded like Jean but it couldn't be because Jean was in an ambulance at the bottom of the hill. A shiver crept up her spine. She saw a flash of grey in the trees next to the car, a rustle of branches.

'You're back.'

That was a man's voice. It sounded like Mark, or was she imagining that too? A sudden fear rippled through her and she didn't want to be in the car on her own any more; she needed to be with people.

She'd been expressly told to stay in the vehicle, but the sound of the voices had unnerved her, together with the distinct impression she was being watched. It didn't feel safe on her own. She opened the door and slid out, running full pelt round the back of the house, where she found DS Jones standing in the middle of the lawn. He was talking into his radio and looked up, startled, as she slid to a stop in front of him.

'He's gone, hasn't he?' she panted, pointing back towards the car. 'I heard him, in the trees over there. I heard him.'

All hell broke loose then, police climbing over the wall into the woods, leaving Holly with a terrible sinking feeling in her gut. Somehow, he'd escaped.

70

Much later that evening, after spending hours at the police station, Holly was weary beyond belief. The officers had quizzed her relentlessly and, at first, she wasn't sure how much of her tale they actually believed, especially with Mark nowhere to be seen. Finn's murder, the kidnap, false imprisonment, the murder of two women before her and witnessing the attempted murder of Jean. It was quite a list. But once they'd corroborated her version of events with Jean's, and made calls to the police team in Dumfries, they seemed more inclined to take her seriously. When news came through that their officers had found human remains in the vegetable beds, they were definitely listening.

She wasn't under arrest for anything at that point in time, just helping them with their enquiries and being treated as a victim. At this point, she'd only told them part of the story. Nothing about the attack on the chef in Buxton, or that she was using a false identity. All of that was to come, and she'd asked for a duty solicitor to support her. Now she had to wait for them to arrive before they could go any further.

In the meantime, she'd been allowed a phone call, and she was chewing nervously at a fingernail while she waited for someone to answer. When she heard the voice on the line, her heart skittered.

'Hello, Sofia? It's Holly...'

The woman on the end of the line gasped. 'Holly? Is that really you? Oh, thank God. I was terrified something awful had happened to you.'

Holly burst into tears, the sound of a familiar, friendly voice tipping her over the edge. 'I'm fine.' She sniffed. 'I mean, it's been pretty awful, but I'm fine.'

'Oh, Holly. You don't sound fine. What happened? Where did you go?' Her voice was warm and sympathetic, and Holly knew if Sofia was in the room with her, she'd be giving her a hug. The questions came in quick succession and Holly couldn't answer any of them, too choked up to speak. She fumbled in her pocket for a tissue to blow her nose.

'Tell me where you are and I'll come and get you.'

If only life was that simple.

Holly wiped her face, cleared her throat. 'I'm at a police station actually and I have to stay here for a little while longer to help them with their enquiries.'

'Oh God, you're not in trouble, are you?'

Holly sighed. 'I don't know what's going to happen, but I've not been arrested if that's what you mean. It's a long story and I'll tell you all about it when I see you again. I just wanted to apologise for dashing off and leaving you in the lurch like that.'

'We honestly thought, when you and Greg disappeared at the same time, and there was blood all over the chopping board. Well... it didn't look good. I thought maybe one of you might have had a kitchen accident and the other had taken them to the hospital, but we checked and neither of you were there. And anyway, I knew you would have called me. I knew something else had happened, so I went to the police and they did come and have a look, but they didn't seem very interested in following it up. Said there was no real evidence of a crime. I mean, we cut ourselves all the time, don't we?'

Holly frowned, puzzled. *Greg disappeared at the same time?* That was a surprise. And good news too, because it meant he hadn't reported her for assaulting him with a knife, like she'd feared. Obviously, it had been self-defence on her part, but she hadn't imagined anyone would accept her version of events.

She realised Sofia was still speaking. 'I'm so sorry about Greg. I know I should have done something about his behaviour earlier, but I'll admit I was being selfish because he was head chef and he was good and they're hard to come by. He filled up the dining room, which was great for business, but it wasn't right.' She sighed. 'I should have thrown him out as soon as you told me he was pestering you. And once he'd gone, it turned out he'd been bothering a couple of the waitresses too.' There was an angry edge to her voice. 'Sexual assaults that he should have been sacked for. But he'd told them he'd deny everything and get them thrown out for causing trouble. They didn't dare say anything because they needed the work.'

Holly's brain went into overdrive, recalibrating everything she thought she knew, adjusting all the narratives that had been going on in her head. Greg had disappeared. He hadn't gone to the police. She wasn't going to be arrested for stabbing him with a kitchen knife. There had been no need to run away in the first place, no need to get wrapped up with Finn and then Mark.

This whole horrifying series of events could have been avoided if she'd stood her ground and believed in herself. If she'd gone to Sofia with the truth when the last incident with Greg had happened, she would still be in Buxton with a job and career prospects. But there was no point berating herself; what was done was done. It was time to think about the future.

'Can I come back?' Holly asked. 'Would that be okay?'

She had nowhere else to go and she'd liked living and working at the hotel until Greg had arrived. It was a friendly community of staff and the most welcome she'd felt anywhere in her life. The right place to start again... unless the police decided there was a problem with anything she was about to tell them.

There were a few things she had to admit to first. All of her lies. All of them. Starting with her identity. Perhaps she'd end up in prison for a while, but if she knew there was a place for her in Buxton when she got out, it would give her hope. Something to hold on to and help her keep her nerve.

Whatever the consequences, she was going to cleanse herself of the past and start her new life being true to who she really was. She would be brave, tell all her secrets, and maybe the consequences wouldn't be as bad as she'd thought.

'There's just something I need to tell you...' If she was going to turn over a new leaf, she might as well start here. 'Holly Rhodes isn't my real name. It's a stolen identity. I did it to protect myself when I was sixteen.' She sighed. 'That's another story I need to tell you about.'

'Oh, Holly, I don't care what your name is. I knew there were things you weren't telling me. I knew you had a backstory. I mean, don't we all? But actions speak louder than words and you're a good person. I know that, I've seen it.'

Sofia's kindness was too much for Holly to cope with and she completely broke down, unable to say another word while she sobbed down the phone.

'It's okay,' Sofia said. 'Don't you worry about that now. You just get through whatever you have to do with the police, give me a ring when you've finished and we'll see about getting you home to the hotel.'

Home. Sofia was right. The hotel in Buxton was her home, and now she knew she was welcome back she felt calmer inside, not so worried about the police interviews to come.

* * *

Later, when she'd spoken to her solicitor, an efficient-looking woman who appeared to be nearing retirement age, she watched her flick back through her notes. Her lips pursed, pen tapping against the desk as she considered Holly's list of wrongdoings.

'Okay, let's start at the beginning, shall we? Using your dead friend's identity... You were sixteen, so a child at the time, and an adult, a youth worker, then helped you use that stolen identity to get a bank account so you could get benefits and get off the streets. They were your mentor, someone you trusted to guide you through a course of action, so I don't think you can be held culpable.'

Holly hardly dared breathe as the solicitor took her through the list.

'In terms of the drug deliveries, you were coerced into it and were frightened the gang supplying the drugs would find you, so you ran away. I think we can argue there were mitigating circumstances, but identifying the people involved would definitely help your case.' She looked up from her notepad and gave Holly a reassuring smile. 'Even all these years later, some people never move on with their lives.'

Holly let out a sigh of relief. All those years, holding that fear tight, dragging it round with her. It felt so good to throw off the shackles.

'But will I be charged? Will I have to go to court?'

The solicitor shrugged. 'It's up to the police and the Crown Prosecution Service. I can't give you a definite answer. But even if they did prosecute, you wouldn't go to trial if you pleaded guilty and that would reduce any sentence. I would imagine a suspended sentence at the worst. Probably a fine.'

'I want to help the police with everything,' Holly said, determination ringing in her voice. 'I want to put it right.'

The solicitor nodded. 'It's going to take some time, but they won't hold you on remand.'

'You mean I'll be able to go?' In her mind she'd thought she would be marched off to prison, and she'd been mentally preparing herself. Now she could think about going back to Buxton and Sofia.

'That's right, as long as they have a contact address and phone number for you, where you promise to stay.'

Holly felt like her head had detached itself from her body and was about to float away. She wanted to jump up and scream, but instead, she just laughed, tears streaming down her face.

'Remember, you were a child. You were vulnerable. And your friend's death was not your fault. Everything else has stemmed from that situation. And you were definitely the victim of both Finn and Mark and you have bruises to prove it. You also have Mark's confession that he killed Finn, and hopefully the Scottish police can find some hard evidence to link him to the murder.'

She leant across the table and gave Holly's arm a squeeze. 'You've committed no significant crimes here. Crimes were committed against you and the worst that is going to happen is you'll need to testify in court, but we'll cross that bridge when we come to it. We're talking months away.'

At that point, Holly wasn't really listening. She was sitting in a bubble of joy, thankful that at last she'd found the courage to tell her story. All of it. And she had someone to support her in sorting out the repercussions.

It paid to be brave, she decided as she left the police station. *I'm going home,* she thought. *And this time, I can be Erin, the real me.*

She started humming the Lenny Kravitz song, knowing that she was going to get away, and once she'd got her passport sorted, and all her legal duties were over and done with, then she could fly away anywhere she wanted to.

71

TEN MONTHS LATER

Mark sat at the piano in St Pancras Station, London, and played a little warm up. It was a lovely instrument, donated by Elton John, no less, and as he played, he imagined he was the very man himself, playing his song – 'Candle in the Wind'. It had the words 'Goodbye Norma Jean', which were a nod to his mother, and that made him smile. Good riddance. It was strange how things had worked out in the end. He'd no idea what had happened to her and he found he didn't care. Life was lovely without her going on at him all the time, trying to stop him from being himself. He hoped she was lonely and had a horrible end to her life. No less than she deserved.

Now that he was on his own, he was free to express himself exactly how he wished. He had a whole new look and the women seemed to like it. He had a sculpted beard, which changed the shape of his face. And he'd dyed his hair dark brown, along with his eyebrows and beard. It was a bit of a pain to keep on top of, but worth it to have his freedom. He kept his hair longer now, and wore a pair of stylish, thick-framed glasses. He looked so different he hardly recognised himself in the mirror, so he was confident the police wouldn't find him. It had been fun reinventing himself, and he thought it was something he'd keep doing, just to stay ahead of the law and give him the freedom to do the thing he loved – playing piano to an audience.

He didn't put posts on Insta any more because that was way too risky, but he did browse on there and had seen posts of himself playing, put up by members of his audience. It gave him such a thrill, it was hard to describe.

It was a shame things hadn't worked out with Holly. She'd seemed a lovely girl on the surface, but there was a darkness in her that wasn't attractive at all. Imagine leaving him locked in that cage? How cruel was that? But no matter, he would carry on looking for his princess. Someone who was pure and wholesome and trusting. Holly, he realised now, was cynical and manipulative and—

He sighed, not wanting to sour the day, and anyway, things had worked out quite well in the end. He thought back to his escape, something he often did, because he was rather proud of how he'd got away.

Once Holly had gone, and he'd been on his own in the cage, he would admit he'd had a bit of a cry for a minute or two. A necessary cleansing of his frustration and anger. But he was distracted by a movement outside, and there was Archie sitting on the roof of the outbuilding. His heart had filled with joy. His best friend hadn't flown away after all. And that fact, the knowledge that Archie didn't want to leave him, completely recharged his mental batteries.

He'd constructed the cage he was now locked in and he knew how it was put together. It was designed to keep a parrot enclosed, not a man. His mother and Holly wouldn't have thought about that. And neither had he in his initial panic. But once he was thinking straight, he realised all he had to do was unhook the structure from the wall. It was secured in four places and once he'd lifted the hooks out of their rings, the cage was free-standing. All he'd had to do then was shuffle it round a bit, and he was free.

There was no time to waste though, because he didn't know how quickly Holly and his mother would be able to call the police. The nearest neighbour was at least a mile away, but in a car, it wouldn't take long to get there. He had one chance to get away and he mustn't mess it up.

He rushed upstairs and threw some essentials into a bag, then hurried downstairs again, grabbing some food for Archie and his leash, before dashing out of the back door. He called for Archie, but he'd gone again. Frantically, he scanned a whole 360 degrees but he was nowhere to be seen. With a frustrated grunt, he made his way across the garden to the woods, where he could easily stay hidden.

After stashing his bag, he crept back towards the house, desperate to get Archie secured on his leash. He watched the police come, startled to see Holly in the back seat of the car. And wouldn't you know, that's when Archie decided to reappear, landing on a branch just above his head. Thankfully, he was hungry and Mark managed to lure him down with a handful of food, happy to have him secured to his wrist again.

At that point, although he wanted to stay and watch what the police were doing, he knew he had to leave and find himself a safe place. He was familiar with the woods, having spent many an afternoon exploring when they'd first moved in, so he had a hiding place in mind. It involved a bit of scrambling up to a little cave in an escarpment above the house. Nobody would find him there.

And they didn't, despite their best efforts.

From his hidey hole, he watched a helicopter circling and could hear calls from the woods below. He made sure to stay back, so the rock protected him from any heat-seeking technology. They got close, but they didn't think to climb up the crag. Much later, he watched the helicopter disappear and as the woods went quiet, he settled himself in his temporary home.

He didn't sleep too well though, because he remembered something. The poisoned food he'd made for his mother. He'd left it on the tray in her bedroom. If they took her accusations seriously, they'd test the food and then... well, he wasn't sure. If they weren't testing for hemlock, would they know it was in there? He puzzled over that all night, tossing and turning until he had to tell himself the police were idiots and there was no way they'd be looking for hemlock as a poison. Why would they?

Hopefully, with no evidence that he'd actually been poisoning his mother, they'd probably just think she was nuts. No charges for him to answer there.

The thing with Finn could be an issue though, and ever since it had happened, he'd been getting flashbacks to the night he'd died. Poor Finn. Things hadn't worked out well for him and that was a shame, but mistakes are made and unfortunately Finn had been one of them. Collateral damage. In a way, it served him right for abusing Holly, but Mark would admit that he'd probably been a bit hasty in terms of getting rid of him in such a permanent manner. In truth, he'd been caught up in the moment, his perceptions of Holly and her situation, plus a few drams of whiskey, colouring his actions. He'd been in love. Was that a defence?

He'd gone back to the gamekeeper's cottage, late at night, thinking he would spec out the place a bit more. Not long after he arrived, he was hiding in the trees when Finn's truck pulled into the drive, followed by a car. He watched Finn and another man go into the outbuilding. The butchery. He snuck round the side of the building and peered in the window. Finn had a knife in his hand and was cutting up a joint of meat, wrapping it in bags before handing it to the other guy, who had his back to him. Money changed hands and Mark slid round the side of the building while the other man left.

When he got back to the window, he watched Finn count the money and stuff it in a pocket before getting out a plastic wallet and rolling a cigarette. The door opened and Mark pressed himself into the shadow of the hedge when Finn came outside, watching him wander off towards his truck while he smoked.

Finn's phone rang, and while he answered it, Mark crept into the butchery and saw two knives on top of the workbench. He picked up the biggest one. It was long and sharp and blood-stained. He'd watched him using it, saw how easily it had sliced through muscle and sinews. His fingers tightened round the handle, liking the feel of it in his hand. He felt this surge of energy, and he knew what he had in mind was right. Justice was on his side.

He heard Finn's voice getting louder, knew he was heading back Mark's way, and he pressed himself against the wall at the side of the door, his body blurred by the shadows. Finn was whistling as he came back in and Mark struck without hesitation, the knife sliding into Finn's chest with little resistance. He didn't fight, didn't try and defend himself, the shock on his face almost comical.

While Finn was still standing, his hands clutching at his chest, Mark pulled the knife out and pushed him out of the door, towards the river. Finn was helpless to resist, the life quickly draining out of him as he staggered around, not knowing where he was or how dangerously close to the edge of the bank he was standing. The helpless man had little idea what was going on, which had been a mercy, and Mark had no regrets, no feelings of remorse as he gave him one final push and watched him tumble down into the river. The water level was high after all the earlier rain and Finn's body slid down through the rapids and disappeared over the waterfall. He'd taken the knife and hidden it in a bin in Dumfries. Nobody would be looking for it there and he was thankful, the following day, when he heard the bin lorry coming round.

Mark had never imagined Finn would remain in the pool at the bottom of the falls, hadn't understood there was a whirlpool created by the weathering of the rock and the strength of the currents. What a shock it had been to see him floating there the following day.

Obviously, it had been scary being interviewed by the police, but he knew they had nothing on him, he'd just been in the wrong place at the wrong time. *Honest, Officer.* By the end of the questioning, he'd started to believe his own lies and was happy to repeat his story as many times as they wanted. Nobody was going to catch him out.

Now, sitting at the piano, he smiled to himself as he played and sang, losing himself in the music and the words of the song, until another voice joined him. A lovely sweet vocal that made his heart skip. He beamed at the young woman who stood beside him. She looked a bit scruffy, her clothes well-worn and her hair twisted into dreadlocks, but her voice was pure and beautiful. She had a Cinderella-type vulnerability to her that he found very attractive. Could she be his princess?

His current living accommodation was an abandoned holiday home. You could tell nobody had been near the place for years and North Wales had a number of these hidden gems.

Nobody knew he was living there except the water board and electricity company. He'd used his mum's name to get connected. Who would notice?

The song ended and he smiled at the young woman. He flicked his hair out of his eyes, a mannerism he'd become quite fond of. Admittedly, he looked sloppier than he'd like, but women seemed to go for his new look. And what did it matter if it worked?

'That was lovely,' he said to the woman. 'Your voice has a gorgeous tone.' She blushed and his heart started to hum. He grinned at her, fingers tinkling along the keys. 'Shall we do another? What shall I play?'

'Do you know "Rocket Man"?'

He played the first few bars. 'Sure do. Let's give it a try.'

They did a couple more songs before he asked her, 'Do you want to grab a coffee?'

She shrugged. 'Okay. It's not like I've got anything else to do. Or anywhere else to go for that matter.' Her eyes dropped. 'I just got kicked out of my house share.'

Oh, my word. This is meant to be. His heart was literally going to burst out of his chest with excitement.

He stood. 'Well, let me buy you lunch, then.'

She chattered away to him as he led her to a nearby café. This time it was going to be different. This time he wouldn't have to hide his woman from his mother. There would be no locking in rooms, no chasing after escapees, no digging vegetable beds when it all went wrong and the woman ended up dead. This would be fourth time lucky. He could feel it in his bones.

72

DS Jones picked up his phone and listened to the caller for a moment, his eyes widening.

'Hold on, Bev, I need my boss to hear this, just a sec.'

He jumped up from his desk and looked around the open-plan office, spotting DI Pritchard talking to another member of the team at their desk. He hurried over.

'I've got a call from an off-duty officer who's on a little break in London. You gotta listen to this. Honestly, it's gold.'

DI Pritchard followed him back to his desk and he put his phone on speaker. 'Okay, Bev, tell us again what you've just seen.'

'I'm at St Pancras Station in London, just walking through with my boyfriend and we hear the piano playing and stop to listen. And there's this guy, and the way he was singing just hit a chord with me, if you'll pardon the pun. I think it's him. I think it's Mark Richards. The guy we've been after for abduction, and murdering those two Jehovah's Witnesses and the guy in Scotland. And the rest.' She sounded breathless, excited. 'I'm sending a video. He's not playing now, but he's in a café. I'm standing outside, so he's not going anywhere without me following him because I'm dead sure. He's changed his appearance but after watching all those videos of him playing, his mannerisms are the same. And his voice. I swear it's him.'

DS Jones opened his emails and played the video, his heart doing an excited flip as he watched the man play and listened to him sing. He'd also watched a lot of videos of this man playing over the ten months of the investigation. Hours of them. He knew how he sat, he knew how he played and he knew what he sounded like.

'It is!' He punched the air. 'It bloody is.'

'Gotcha,' said DI Pritchard, a satisfied grin on his face. 'Good work, Bev. Stay where you are, we'll get back-up organised now.'

Phone calls were made and a while later, Bev sent another video of Mark Richards being escorted out of the café by two uniformed police officers.

DI Pritchard went home a happy man that evening. They had the evidence to charge Mark Richards, after building the case for ten months; they'd just been missing the man. He was going away for a very long time.

EPILOGUE
SIX MONTHS LATER

Mark heard the judge say 'whole life sentence' and he blanched. Had he heard that wrong? He wasn't sure and he couldn't ask him to repeat himself. Whole life sentence; did that mean no parole? He thought his bowels might betray him and empty their contents on the floor. The whole trial had been a disaster, his defence barrister useless, and it didn't matter that he hadn't admitted guilt; the evidence was pretty damning.

It was his stupid mother's fault. If she'd stayed quiet when the Jehovah's Witnesses had been there, he wouldn't have had to get rid of them. And her shouting had spooked Holly so she'd escaped. And then Holly had misunderstood the dynamic between him and his mother and... Well, it had been impossible to give his story the coherence in court. The way he'd been questioned made everything disjointed, took things out of context. But he knew his mother was to blame.

He'd made mistakes, but that was because he was a human, not a machine. He hadn't washed out the teapot with the hemlock tea in it. How careless was that? But it was because he'd been flustered, distracted by Holly climbing out of the bloody window. It was easy to make mistakes when you were flustered.

And then he hadn't cleared up the meals he'd made for him and his mother because he'd been rushing to get out of the house before the police arrived. And what do you know – the police tests did find hemlock in one of them because he'd poked bits into the stupid couple's mouths. That meant they were specifically looking for it. He never imagined there would be any connection. Not for one minute. But that's what happened when you were forced to change plans, forced to improvise and have several plates spinning at the same time.

Quite how the police had arrived so quickly had been a mystery until he'd come to court and heard the police evidence. He hadn't found a phone in the Jehovah's Witnesses car but that was because the woman's body was lying on top of it. She'd made an emergency call. They played it in court. And in that call, she'd told them not only that she was concerned about his mother, who'd accused him of poisoning her and looked to be unwell. But she'd also claimed that he'd poisoned the tea he'd given them. So that was a slam dunk he hadn't seen coming.

Holly also appeared as a witness. There was a hardness about her he really didn't like and it was a mystery to him now that he'd ever found her attractive. She told them he'd kidnapped her and held her against her will, which was a lie but at that point nobody believed a word he said, and how could he prove he didn't do it? Especially with the bolt being on the outside of the door. She also said he'd admitted to murdering Finn. And of course, they had his phone, so they'd checked everything on there and now they were investigating the deaths of two other women. Sometimes life just hurled a whole stream of lemons and there was absolutely no lemonade you could make.

It didn't help that his bloody mother had been sat there watching the whole time, looking all glowing and healthy, with a new bloke on her arm. How the hell had that happened? And the lies she'd told when she was giving evidence, it made a mockery of the whole thing.

The only positive was Archie had been adopted by a lovely old lady, who sent him letters, supposedly from the bird, which was a little weird but it brightened up his day. Archie still loved him and he would cling to that.

He sat in the van on his way back to prison, his solicitor having just told him that he was to be tried for Finn's murder in Scotland the following week. Something to look forward to, he supposed, because being in court was a lot more interesting than being in prison. They didn't have any forensic evidence, he knew that; it was all circumstantial and the Scottish system was a bit different, so he had high hopes of getting off that one. Not that it mattered. If he was in for a whole life term, what difference would another life sentence make?

He just had to make the most of what prison had to offer.

Going forwards, he had joined the music group on his wing, and the best news was the leader of the group was a young lady called Evelyn – such a pretty name – who came in once a week for an hour. He thought she might have the hots for him because she always suggested they sing something together. And last time, she'd actually sat next to him on the piano stool while they'd played a duet, which had been pretty amazing. They'd high-fived at the end and the joy in her face lit a touchpaper in his heart. He smiled to himself, remembering. Who knew what could happen in the future? Could she be the one? His soulmate?

ACKNOWLEDGEMENTS

The writing and publishing of any book is a real team effort and I would like to thank all of 'Team Rona' for their help getting this book into the world.

First up is my fantastic editor, Isobel Akenhead. This is the twelfth book we have done together and her enthusiasm for my writing never wanes. I have wanted to write a storyline like this for a while now, so I'm delighted that Isobel has championed it and I can finally get these twisted people out of my head and on to the page. It was a fun one to write!

Huge thanks to all the editorial support team at Boldwood Books, including my copyeditor, Jennifer Davies, and proofreader, David Boxell, for your care and attention to detail. Also, Hayley Russell, Jenna Houston and Wendy Neale for getting the book out into the world and then shouting about it.

As always, my little team of beta readers have been a great help with their input to early drafts – thank you Kerry-Ann, Sandra, Mark, Dee, Chloe and Wendy.

And huge thanks to my children John, Amy and Oscar and my step-daughter Kate for just being there for me and lighting up my life when the writing gets a little tough.

Huge thanks also to my lovely readers for all your kind words and support.

Finally, a mention to my dogs, Maid and Evie, for making me get away from my desk and take them out for adventures whatever the weather. It gives me space to think and come up with the sneaky plot twists, and anyway... we like a bit of rain, don't we?!

ABOUT THE AUTHOR

Rona Halsall is a #1 bestselling author of psychological thrillers including, most recently, *The Bigamist* and *Bride & Groom*. She lives in Wales with her mad little Border Collie, Maid and Romanian rescue dog, Evie.

Sign up to Rona Halsall's mailing list for news, competitions and updates on future books.

Visit Rona Halsall's website: www.ronahalsall.com

Follow Rona on social media here:

facebook.com/RonaHalsallAuthor

x.com/RonaHalsallAuth

instagram.com/ronahalsall

bookbub.com/authors/ronahalsall

ALSO BY RONA HALSALL

Keep You Safe

Love You Gone

The Honeymoon

Her Mother's Lies

One Mistake

The Ex Boyfriend

The Liar's Daughter

The Guest Room

The Wife Next Door

The Bigamist

Bride and Groom

The Fiancé

The Soulmate

THE

Murder

LIST

THE MURDER LIST IS A NEWSLETTER DEDICATED TO SPINE-CHILLING FICTION AND GRIPPING PAGE-TURNERS!

SIGN UP TO MAKE SURE YOU'RE ON OUR HIT LIST FOR EXCLUSIVE DEALS, AUTHOR CONTENT, AND COMPETITIONS.

SIGN UP TO OUR
NEWSLETTER

BIT.LY/THEMURDERLISTNEWS

Boldwood

Boldwood Books is an award-winning fiction publishing company seeking out the best stories from around the world.

Find out more at www.boldwoodbooks.com

Join our reader community for brilliant books, competitions and offers!

Follow us
@BoldwoodBooks
@TheBoldBookClub

Sign up to our weekly deals newsletter

https://bit.ly/BoldwoodBNewsletter

Made in the USA
Middletown, DE
14 February 2025

71352247R00177